"Who are you—really?"

Jason demanded. "Why have you had to move so often? What past are you running away from? Maggie, talk to me," he said, taking a step toward her.

"I...can't," she said, the words so quiet he could barely hear them.

Frustration churned inside him. Refusing to back down, he closed the gap between them until they were mere inches apart. "Why not, Maggie? What could be so bad that you can't talk to me about it?"

She shook her head, unable to say a word. *Unwilling* to say a word.

"Don't you see, Maggie? I care about you. I want to help you." *I want you,* Jason added to himself, reaching out a hand to stroke the velvety smooth skin at the hollow of her cheek.

Maggie flinched at his touch. At the touch of a man she wanted more than anything.

And could never have...

Dear Reader,

Spring always seems like a good time to start something new, so this month it's Marilyn Pappano's wonderful new Western miniseries, HEARTBREAK CANYON. *Cattleman's Promise* is a terrific introduction to the men of Heartbreak, Oklahoma—not to mention the women who change their lives. So settle in for the story of this rugged loner and the single mom who teaches him the joys of family life.

Unfortunately, all good things must end someday, and this month we bid farewell to Justine Davis's TRINITY STREET WEST. But what a finale! Clay Yeager has been an unseen presence in all the books in this miniseries, and at last here he is in the flesh, hero of his own story in *Clay Yeager's Redemption*. And, as befits the conclusion to such a fabulous group of novels, you'll get one last look at the lives and loves of all your favorite characters before the book is through. And in more miniseries news, Doreen Roberts continues RODEO MEN with *A Forever Kind of Cowboy*, a runaway bride story you'll fall in love with. *The Tough Guy and the Toddler* is the newest from Diane Pershing, and it's our MEN IN BLUE title, with a great cop hero. Christine Scott makes the move to Intimate Moments with *Her Second Chance Family*, an emotional and memorable FAMILIES ARE FOREVER title. Finally, welcome new writer Claire King, whose *Knight in a White Stetson* is both our WAY OUT WEST title and a fun and unforgettable debut.

As always, we hope you enjoy all our books—and that you'll come back next month, when Silhouette Intimate Moments brings you six more examples of the most exciting romance reading around.

Yours,

Leslie J. Wainger
Executive Senior Editor

Please address questions and book requests to:
Silhouette Reader Service
U.S.: 3010 Walden Ave., P.O. Box 1325, Buffalo, NY 14269
Canadian: P.O. Box 609, Fort Erie, Ont. L2A 5X3

HER SECOND CHANCE FAMILY

CHRISTINE SCOTT

Published by Silhouette Books

America's Publisher of Contemporary Romance

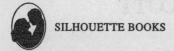

SILHOUETTE BOOKS

ISBN 0-373-07929-X

HER SECOND CHANCE FAMILY

Books by Christine Scott

Silhouette Intimate Moments | Silhouette Romance

Her Second Chance Family #929

Hazardous Husband #1077
Imitation Bride #1099
Cinderella Bride #1134
I Do? I Don't? #1176
Groom on the Loose #1203
Her Best Man #1321
A Cowboy Comes a Courting #1364

CHRISTINE SCOTT

grew up in Illinois but currently lives in St. Louis, Missouri. A former teacher, she now writes full-time. When she isn't writing romances, she spends her time caring for her husband and three children. In between car pools, baseball games and dance lessons, Christine always finds time to pick up a good book and read about…love. She loves to hear from readers. Write to her at P.O. Box 283, Grover, MO 63040-0283.

To Pat McCandless, a good friend and fellow writer

Prologue

The dirt road was narrow, rutted. Maggie Stuart drove the BMW slowly, avoiding the worst of the potholes. The beams of her headlights struggled to cut through the darkness, illuminating her surroundings only a few feet ahead. Not that there was much to see. The road looked to be deserted, the area sparsely populated.

Six months ago, she'd have been too afraid to come out this far into the country alone at night. Six months ago, she'd been afraid of many things.

A farmhouse came into view. The building looked abandoned. Windows were broken, the front porch listed precariously on its foundation, and not a light could be seen. Nearby were two outbuildings: a large, weathered barn and a smaller, utility-size garage.

It was by the garage that she spotted the car.

As Maggie pulled her sleek BMW alongside the rusty old Ford, two people emerged from it. Both were women. Both were strangers. Maggie shifted her car into Park, but left the engine running. Just in case she felt the need for a quick getaway.... She sighed. Would she ever feel safe again? Would she ever completely trust someone again?

Glancing at the sleeping figure of her five-and-a-half-year-old son on the seat beside her, Maggie said a silent prayer for courage, then stepped out of the car.

"Maggie?" the tall, dark-haired woman asked. Her companion, a short, round-figured redhead, remained silent as she stepped out of the glare of the headlights and into the shadowy darkness. She scanned the area like a burglar casing the property.

Unnerved, Maggie nodded. "Yes, and you are?"

The dark-haired woman shook her head. "No names. Where's your son?"

Maggie swallowed hard. "He's in the car, sleeping."

The dark-haired woman nodded. "Let's take care of business first. We'll wake him soon enough." Out of her coat pocket, she withdrew an envelope. "There's everything you'll need in here—birth certificates, social-security numbers, driver's license... After tonight, you and your son will have a whole new identity."

Maggie hesitated before taking the envelope.

The dark-haired woman frowned, her eyes searching Maggie's face. "Are you sure you want to go through with this? It's not too late to change your mind."

Maggie drew in a deep breath, then released the air with a whoosh, along with it letting go some of the tension building inside her. "I don't have a choice. It was fortunate that I knew of someone your group had assisted. I had nowhere else to turn. The courts refused to listen when I asked for their help. They want me to turn my son over to my ex-husband. But I can't—he's dangerous. I have to protect my son."

The other woman's face remained impassive. "You're

not alone, Maggie, you know that. We've all been through this in one way or another. That's why the underground was established. If no one else will help, we have to take care of ourselves.''

With more determination than she actually felt, Maggie reached for the envelope, stuffing it into the pocket of her coat.

The dark-haired woman continued. ''Just remember, use cash until you can establish accounts in your new name. It would be best if you didn't stay in California. Most women feel more comfortable putting as much distance as they can between themselves and their abuser.''

''I understand,'' Maggie said, fighting an unexpected churning in her stomach.

''And Maggie—'' the other woman's voice was gentle ''—once you're settled, join a support group, get some counseling. You're going to need some emotional help to get you through this.''

''I'll be fine,'' Maggie insisted, her voice harsher than she'd intended. Embarrassed, she averted her eyes, refusing to meet the dark-haired woman's gaze.

''It's okay,'' the woman said softly. She glanced questioningly at her friend.

The redhead shook her head. ''She wasn't followed.''

The dark-haired woman nodded. ''We're ready, then. Let's get your things out of the car.''

As instructed, Maggie had packed light. One suitcase each for her and Kevin. Feeling like the fugitive she'd soon become, using the cover of the night, she'd left behind a beautiful home and a closet full of designer dresses. Maggie had no regrets. The clothes, the house, the expensive car, they all represented a life that was beautiful only on the outside. Inside it was ugly at its core.

With quiet efficiency, the bags were transferred from the

BMW to the Ford. Her son was next. Gently Maggie lifted Kevin from the BMW and buckled him into the front seat of the Ford. His head slumped to one side, setting his glasses slightly askew. Exhausted from this midnight rendezvous, he never awoke.

The dark-haired woman handed her the keys to the Ford. "We'll drive your car back to the city and leave it at the airport. They'll find it eventually. But by the time they do, you'll be long gone. If we're lucky, they'll think you left the country."

Without another word to Maggie, she strode to the BMW, preparing to leave. The redhead was already in the front seat, taking Kevin's place. Things were happening too quickly. Maggie felt a surge of panic fill her chest.

"W-wait," she stammered. The woman turned, glancing at her sharply. Maggie felt heat flush her cheeks. "I—I don't know how I'll ever repay you."

Frowning, the woman said, "We got your money. You've already reimbursed us for the car and the IDs."

"No, I mean…I don't know how to thank you."

The other woman smiled for the first time. "Have a good life, Maggie. Take care of your son." With that she climbed into the BMW. The door slammed, echoing in the stillness of the night. Gravel crunched beneath the tires as the car drove away.

Maggie stared after the fading taillights. A part of her wanted to run after the pair, to stop them, to tell them she'd changed her mind. But she knew that was impossible.

There was no turning back. In the eyes of the law, she was now a fugitive, a mother who'd kidnapped her own son. Not a mother who was trying her best to protect him.

Disappearing, becoming a whole new person, was her only chance to survive. It was her son's only chance at a normal life.

A distant howl of a coyote broke into her thoughts. The darkness pressed in around her. The air felt suddenly cold, chilling her to the bone. Maggie wrapped her coat snug against her slender frame and hurried to the car.

Compared to the luxury of the BMW, the Ford seemed sadly lacking. She inserted the key and turned on the ignition. The car chugged to life. Maggie released a grateful sigh of relief. The car worked, which was all that mattered, she told herself.

With one final glance at her son, she popped the car into gear and headed out into the night and into a new life.

Chapter 1

Eighteen months later

"**K**evin, settle down or you're going to be late for school."

Maggie glanced at the excited face of her seven-year-old son with a mixture of disbelief and amusement. It had been a long time, if ever, that she'd seen her son quite so enthusiastic about anything.

Kevin poked his glasses higher onto the bridge of his nose with one finger and blessed her with a gap-toothed grin. "Aw, Mom. I'm not going to be late. I've got plenty of time. Did I tell ya'? We're going to have costumes. Tommy Marshall's mom is making them."

"You told me," Maggie said, setting a glass of orange juice in front of her son. She ruffled his blond hair, making the stubborn cowlick at his crown stick up even farther than usual. "Eat your cereal."

Obediently he scooped a spoonful of raisin bran into his mouth. Chewing thoughtfully, a frown playing on his young face, Kevin swallowed hard, then said, ''Our teacher told us it's going to be the best second-grade play ever.''

''I'm sure it will be,'' Maggie said, glancing at her wrist-watch.

She had thirty minutes to get her son off to school and herself off to work at the diner. Weather permitting, most days they walked together to their respective destinations. Just one of the many advantages of living in a small town, Maggie mused. She enjoyed the time spent with her son and felt immense relief knowing he was safely in school. At three o'clock, when her shift at the diner was over and school let out, the procedure was reversed.

Unlike most boys his age, Kevin hadn't rebelled against this show of maternal protectiveness. But then again, so far, Kevin's childhood hadn't been like most other boys. A lump of regret settled in her throat. She reached for her coffee cup and took a sip.

''You're going to come, aren't you?'' Kevin demanded.

Swallowing her coffee and washing down the lingering remnants of unease, she shot him a mock look of indig-nation. ''Of course, I'll be there. I wouldn't think of miss-ing my own son's performance of Father Time welcoming spring.''

''Sarah Moore's going to be Mother Earth,'' he said, scowling. ''I have to sit next to her during the whole play.''

''Well, I'm sure there're worse things.''

''Yeah, I could be a wood nymph and have to run around in tights, tossing spring flowers like Tommy has to do,'' he said, giggling.

Giggling? She stared at him for a moment, too surprised to move. Spontaneous laughter from her son? It had been weeks since she'd witnessed such an event, perhaps even months. Not for the first time, she thanked the day she'd decided to move to Wyndchester.

Since that fateful night when she'd disappeared to find a new life, they'd moved several times, never staying long in one place. The constant change had been hard on Kevin, eroding his sense of stability. He'd become quiet, withdrawn. But all that changed when they'd moved to Wyndchester.

Wyndchester was a small town tucked into the rambling hills of the Missouri Ozarks. It was far enough away from the congestion of Branson, yet close enough to share in some of the tourist trade. Visitors on their way to the Las Vegas of the Midwest often stopped in for lunch or a walk through the town's older historic homes and its collection of quaint antique shops.

The diner where Maggie worked as a waitress, known for its good food and reasonable prices, was a favorite among the locals. With wages and tips, she made an honest—though not extravagant by any means—living for her and her son. Not quite the income she could have expected from the nursing career she'd abandoned in California. But more important than money, the town afforded her an even more precious gift. Since their arrival, she'd watched in amazement as her son blossomed under the lull of the small town's peaceful ambiance.

Even she had begun to relax and feel at home.

Home. Maggie shot a wistful glance around the small kitchen, taking in its yellowed linoleum floor, faded wallpaper and sagging cabinets. Compared to the oceanfront house with its million-dollar view she'd left behind eighteen months earlier, this little place wasn't much of a prize. But it served its purpose. It was a roof over their heads and a haven of safety for their travel-weary souls.

The clock above the sink caught her eye. She tsked.

"Kevin, look at the time. Go upstairs and brush your teeth. Scoot, or we'll be late."

Kevin shoveled one last spoonful of cereal into his mouth, then ran for the kitchen door, nearly tripping over shoelaces that never seemed to stay tied. Quickly Maggie packed a sandwich, an apple, chips and juice carton into his lunch bag. She glanced around the small kitchen, searching for his backpack.

Not finding it, she headed into the hall and called, "Kevin, is your school bag upstairs?"

The doorbell rang before he could answer.

Maggie frowned, glancing anxiously at her watch. Now wasn't the best time for visitors.

"It's up here, Mom," Kevin called down the stairs as he stood on the landing, hopping on one foot as he tried to tie his shoe on the other.

"Kevin, you're going to fall down the steps," she said, moving toward the door. "Sit down and tie that shoe."

A thump on the landing told her he'd taken her advice. Maggie smiled and shook her head, still having a hard time believing it was true. For the first time in months, Kevin was behaving like a normal boy.

The heavy oak door creaked in protest as she opened it, setting her nerves on edge. She blew out a breath, releasing the tension, and pasted a smile on her face to greet her visitor.

And the world dropped out beneath her feet.

Her worst nightmare came true.

On her doorstep, in full uniform, stood a police officer.

The woman answering the door stared at him, her smile wilting, the light in her green eyes fading. She wore a robin's-egg blue waitress uniform with a white apron. Her strawberry blond hair was pulled back with a blue ribbon.

The dusting of freckles on her pale face gave her a very youthful appearance, although he guessed her to be in her late twenties. With a trembling hand, she clutched the door frame, swaying slightly as she leaned against it for support.

She looked as though she'd seen a ghost.

As a veteran police officer, Jason Gallagher had seen many different reactions to his appearance at a person's door, some friendly, some not. He never knew when people might take it into their heads to run. Or if they might reach behind them and grab a gun to welcome him properly. His training kept him attuned to the slightest action that seemed out of place, suspicious.

And the woman at the door was acting mighty suspicious. She had all the signs of a woman about to faint dead away with shock.

"Maggie Conrad?" he asked, taking off his hat, trying his best to appear nonthreatening.

"Y-yes," she stammered.

Behind her a young boy, probably seven or eight, sidled up beside her. A skinny kid, he peered at Jason through thick, owlish glasses. His hair was blond like his mother's, but short and tousled. In size and coloring he was so similar to Scott—Jason's own son—that for a moment Jason forgot to breathe.

The boy watched him closely. He seemed to sense his distress, absorbing it and intensifying it in his small frame. His eyes wide, he stepped back, positioning himself slightly behind his mother.

Jason realized that he was staring, probably scaring the boy, so he brushed away the unsettling memories and returned his attention to the mother. "My name's Jason Gallagher. I moved in last night into the house next door." He gave a tentative smile. "Looks as though we're neighbors."

"N-neighbors?" Maggie blinked, looking confused.

Slowly the boy reached for her hand, weaving his fingers through hers, tugging gently.

She turned to her son and, for a moment, seemed to stare at him unseeingly. Then, with a shake of her head, she looked up again and gave a slight smile. "It's good to meet you, um...Officer Gallagher?"

His smile deepened. "Well, actually, I'm the new chief of police in town. But why don't you just call me Jason?"

"The chief of police," she repeated, a mere whisper of a sound that sent a shiver down his spine.

He took a closer look at the woman who'd caused such an unexpected reaction. She was tall, at least five foot eight, and slender. The waitress uniform hung loosely, seeming out of place on her fine bone structure. With those model-like, high cheekbones, refined features and creamy complexion, he pictured her in something soft, silky and expensive.

She fidgeted beneath his scrutiny, biting down on her full lower lip. "Is there something you wanted?"

Flushing, Jason wondered if she could read his thoughts. He searched his mind, trying to remember the reason for his visit. "Mail," he said suddenly, startling her. "I've got some of your mail."

"Oh," she said, nodding, looking relieved.

"It was in my box, mixed in with the junk mail." He reached for the envelopes he'd tucked into his back pocket. "I almost threw these out by mistake. I hope the delay hasn't caused you or your husband any inconvenience, Mrs.—"

"My husband is dead," she said quickly, dropping her gaze. "I'm a widow."

Jason tried not to think about the relief the words brought him. "I'm sorry to hear that, ma'am."

Hesitantly she accepted the letters. Her fingers, long and slender, grazed his palm. Her skin felt warm, although not completely soft. They looked like the hands of an artist, but were work-roughened like those of a laborer. The touch sparked a tingling of awareness. A sensual heat radiated up his arm.

She gave a tiny gasp, telling him she, too, had been affected by the contact.

He looked at her in surprise.

She snatched her hand away, refusing to meet his gaze. "Th-thank you...for the mail."

Perhaps it was just his imagination or his cop instinct overreacting, but the longer their conversation lasted, the more uncomfortable she seemed. As though it was a strain to be near him, talk to him.

"It's no trouble," he said. Trying his best to ease the situation, he focused his attention on the boy. "What's your name, son?"

Instead of answering, the boy just looked at his mother.

Jason shifted uncomfortably, one foot to the other. What was going on here? Granted, some people were intimidated by a man in a uniform. But these two, hell, they looked scared to death.

Maggie nodded, giving her son a slight smile of encouragement.

Lifting his small chin, his glasses glittering in the morning sunlight, the boy frowned in concentration and said, "My name is Kevin Conrad. I'm seven years old."

"You don't say?"

The frown deepened. "Yes, I do."

Jason bit back the urge to smile. "It's nice to meet you, Kevin."

"It's nice to meet you, too," the boy replied politely.

Maggie cleared her throat. "I hate to sound rude, but we're running late. We really must be going."

"Of course," Jason said quickly. "I'm sorry to keep you."

"Yes, well...I hope you'll enjoy living in Wyndchester." She reached for the door, closing it as she spoke. "It's a nice little town."

"That's what I hear," he said.

"Well—" she gave what appeared to be a strained smile "—goodbye."

The door closed with a firm click.

So much for building a rapport with the neighbors, Jason told himself. Heaving a sigh, he tugged his hat back in place, then moved away from the door. His feet thudded against the wooden porch, sounding too loud in the sudden quietness.

A nice little town with friendly people. That was what the mayor had told him when he'd been interviewed for the job. That was what the head of the town council had said when he'd approved his position. That was what the landlord had told him last night when he'd picked up the key to his newly rented house.

He glanced back at his neighbor's place and saw a curtain move in a window. If Maggie Conrad was an example of the friendly folks of Wyndchester, he was in for some very lonely days and nights.

Maggie leaned against the door, breathing deeply, letting her jackhammering heart slow to a dull thump. "Kevin, get away from the window," she said sharply.

Startled, he dropped the curtain, letting it flutter back into place. He stared at her, his hands in his pockets, looking as scared as she felt.

"Sorry," she mumbled. "I didn't mean to snap."

Her legs felt like jelly. She stumbled to the stairway and dropped onto the bottom step. Elbows on her knees, she buried her face in her hands and tried to think about what she should do.

A policeman. Living next door. She couldn't have asked for worse luck.

Without a word, Kevin sat down beside her. She felt the brush of his jeans against her thigh, the warmth of his skin as he pressed his cheek against her arm. He smelled of toothpaste and soap. Moments ago, he'd been happy, excited, full of childish energy. Now he'd reverted back to his former self.

A boy who, in times of crisis, was used to making himself invisible.

Dropping her hands from her face, she straightened and enfolded him in a hug. "It'll be okay. Mommy just needs to think."

He clung to her.

She felt the erratic beat of his heart, the tension thrumming through his small body. Her protective instincts surged inside her. And she knew she would do anything to keep him safe.

Sighing, she disentangled herself from his embrace. She stood, looking down at him with all the regret she felt in her heart. "We have to leave."

Kevin seemed to shrink before her eyes. He stared at her, not saying a word. She knew he understood that she was not talking about going to school or to work.

Once again, as had been the case so often in the past eighteen months, they were being forced to pack up and leave town at a moment's notice.

Maggie brushed past him, making her way up the stairs. There wasn't much time. Their new neighbor was no doubt wondering about their strained conversation. A policeman would be suspicious. She couldn't afford to wait until he figured out that something was wrong.

She started with Kevin's room first. Pulling a suitcase from his closet, she began to systematically pack his clothes. Socks, underwear, T-shirts, they all had their place. Everything had to be packed into a minimum of space. Nothing large, nothing bulky. Nothing that couldn't be fitted into the trunk of the Ford. The house was rented, already furnished. She'd lose her deposit check, but it couldn't be helped.

Her hands trembled slightly as she packed, but she felt stronger now. She had purpose. She'd made a decision.

Even if that decision was to run. Again.

"Mom."

Kevin's voice startled her. Holding a T-shirt in her hand, she whirled to face him.

He stood in the doorway. Tears shimmered in his eyes. He was blinking hard, trying to stave the flow. "What about the play?"

The play. For the first time in his brief history in school, he'd been asked to be the lead in a class play. It may not seem like much to the average child, but it meant the world to him.

Maggie sank onto the bed, the box spring sighing beneath her weight. "Oh, Kevin, I'm sorry."

"Why do we have to go, Mom?" he asked, moving into the room. "The policeman didn't look mean. He seemed nice, friendly."

"I know, honey. But—"

"He doesn't know us, Mom."

"But he might find out and—"

"I won't tell him. I won't tell anybody."

Maggie's heart clenched. Her eyes blurred with tears of shame, of regret. "I know you wouldn't, Kevin. But sometimes people have a way of finding out no matter how hard we try to keep it from happening."

For a long moment Kevin stared down at his feet, not wanting her to see the tears welling up in his own eyes. He'd been so brave for so long. All she'd ever wanted for her son was the one thing she couldn't possibly give him. A normal life.

Finally, his voice so low she had to strain to hear him, he said, "Maybe if he knew about Daddy, he'd help us."

Slowly she shook her head. "No, honey. He couldn't, even if he wanted to."

She glanced out the bedroom window, taking in the trees wearing their bright green colors of new spring growth, the squirrel making its kamikaze dive to a lower branch and the bird building its nest in the cover of the leaves. Life in Wyndchester seemed so simple, so peaceful, so safe. She understood Kevin's reluctance to leave. Here, she, too, almost felt insulated from the past.

"Just for a little while, Mom," Kevin pleaded. "School's almost over. The play's in just a couple of weeks."

Two weeks. Surely that wasn't so much to ask.

Maggie considered the possibility. If they left now, whatever suspicions her conversation with their new neighbor had aroused would be confirmed. Of course, they'd be long gone and on to a new town, a new life, before he had time to act on those suspicions.

But if they stayed, if they were careful, he need not know exactly what it was they were hiding from him.

Kevin stood watching her, barely breathing, waiting anxiously for her decision.

Jason Gallagher wasn't a threat. Not yet, anyway. He barely knew them. If they kept it that way, then surely they'd be safe.

What was the saying? The best place to hide is the place they'd least expect. Right beneath their noses.

Maggie sighed. "All right, Kevin. We'll stay for a couple of weeks. That's all I can promise for now."

A smile broke out on his face. A twin set of dimples appeared, deepened. He flung himself into her arms and held on tight. "Thank you, Mom."

More tears threatened. She blinked hard and rubbed a hand briskly against his back. "We really are going to be late for school now."

"I'm ready."

She took his tear-splotched face in her hands, kissing his forehead lightly. "Go wash your face. Then we can leave."

With a nod, he sped out of the room.

Maggie's smile dissolved. She drew in a choppy breath, allowing her fears to resurface. Eighteen months ago she'd made an irrevocable, life-altering decision. She'd lost faith in the justice of a court system that would award custody of a child to a man who beat his wife and was a threat to his own son. That was why she had decided to take the law into her own hands.

She had packed her bags, had taken Kevin and had run.

It had been a matter of life and death, she told herself. For if she had stayed and followed the letter of the law, surely she never would have survived. It would only have been a matter of time before her ex-husband would have killed her.

Unfortunately, by protecting herself and Kevin, in the eyes of the law, she was a criminal.

Kevin's life may not be stable now. But at least he had the security of a mother who loved him. And he was away from a father who would hurt him. If the people who'd sworn to uphold the law of the land could not help them, then she would have do it herself.

No one, not even Jason Gallagher, was going to take her son away from her.

Chapter 2

"Mrs. McKinney's pretty much a regular caller. Not a week goes by without something bothering her," Officer Stan Wilson said, turning left at the corner, steering the patrol car toward the outskirts of town. "Her husband died last year of cancer. They'd been married fifty years. Sometimes I think she's just lonely."

Jason did not comment. He knew only too well the pain suffered at the loss of someone you love. The pain of his son's unexpected death still left a hollow place in his heart.

Pain? Jason frowned. An unwanted image of his new neighbor, Maggie Conrad, and her son, Kevin, flashed in his mind. Something about their brief encounter had struck a chord of unease, one that had been nagging him most of the morning. Was it because he'd seen a haunted look of pain in her eyes, as well?

He pushed the unsettling thought from his mind and concentrated on the task at hand. Three hours earlier, after a brief assembly of both day and night shifts, Jason had shocked his staff by opting to spend his first morning on patrol. He couldn't think of a better or quicker way to get to know the town of Wyndchester than to see it firsthand. Stan Wilson had had the dubious honor of drawing him for a partner.

Stan was in his early twenties. He stood well over six feet, with the lean, lanky build of the young. He had pale blond hair, a healthy dose of freckles and a quick smile. Despite his youthfulness, he had a sharp wit and a psychologist's mind for analyzing a person's personality quirks.

"What's the call about this morning?" Jason asked.

"Malicious mischief, vandalism. She says somebody got into her yard last night and tore it up."

Jason raised a brow. "Doesn't sound like something she could have imagined."

Stan shrugged. "Most times the complaints just don't pan out."

"Well, let's go check it out."

Stan picked up the mike and let the dispatcher know they'd be making the call. A few minutes later, the patrol car coasted to a stop in front of a white clapboard house. The house and its yard had the stamp of meticulous attention from someone who obviously cared a great deal. From the sparkling clean glass windows to the painted concrete doorstep, the house had that freshly scrubbed appearance. In the yard, the grass was neatly trimmed. The sidewalks were lined with ruler-straight borders of spring flowers.

Jason stepped out of the car, glancing around for any sign of vandalism. And found nothing. Not a flower trampled, not a window broken, not a mailbox dinged or dented. It appeared Stan was right about this caller.

"Looks okay to me," Stan said, echoing his thoughts.

Jason sighed. "No harm in ringing the doorbell."

The woman answering the door looked like an advertiser's dream of the perfect grandma. She had fluffy white hair, a round face and a well-cushioned body. She peered at them from behind a pair of spectacles perched at the end of her nose. "It's about time you got here, Officer Wilson. I've been waiting all morning."

Stan squirmed uncomfortably, blushing slightly at the reprimand.

"Sorry, ma'am," Jason said, stepping in. "We had other calls to make first."

Her faded blue eyes narrowed. "I don't think I've seen you before. What's your name, young man?"

Jason almost smiled. At thirty-five years of age, it wasn't often that he was called young anything. "Jason Gallagher, ma'am. I'm the new chief of police."

She stared at him for a moment, her jaw working as she digested the news, then gave a brisk nod. "No use wasting our time chatting on the doorstep. The mess is out back."

Jason and his officer stepped aside, allowing the woman to lead the way to the backyard.

"I noticed it first thing this morning," she called over her shoulder. "I was making my morning pot of coffee when I looked out my kitchen window and nearly had a heart attack. Don't know why anybody would want to cause so much damage." Her voice trembled slightly. "Looks to me like kids did it. Just plain mischief-makers."

For once Jason had to agree. His step faltered as he got his first glance at the carnage in the backyard. Pots of flowers in all shapes and colors had been overturned, smashed and strewn haphazardly across the yard. Delicate bars of wooden lattice, supporting fledgling shoots of bluebells and roses, were knocked over and broken in places; the buds were trampled, lying limply on the ground. Daffodils, dug up from their roots, were tossed onto the sidewalk.

Stan released a whistling breath, shaking his head in disbelief. "You didn't hear any of this going on at all last night?"

Mrs. McKinney tapped both ears. "Got hearing aids. I turn them off at night."

Jason squatted, studying the scratch marks in the dirt beside the daffodils. "Do any of your neighbors own a dog, Mrs. McKinney?"

"A dog?" She frowned, considering the question. "Not that I know—"

Before she could finish, however, a muscular, black-and-brown rottweiler ambled into the yard. The dog stared at them for a moment as if sizing them up. Obviously finding them no threat, he lifted a leg to one of the few remaining daffodils, marking his territory.

Mrs. McKinney's mouth tightened into a grimace. She gave Stan a hard look. "Well, don't just stand there, Officer Wilson. Arrest him."

"Arrest him?" Stan's nervous glance traveled to Jason, then back to Mrs. McKinney. "But ma'am…he's a dog."

As though understanding that he was the topic of conversation, the dog marched through a bed of low-growing, purple flowers and plopped himself down on the delicate blooms, casting his observers a look that could only be called challenging.

"I don't care if he is a dog," Mrs. McKinney growled. "He's trespassing. I want that mutt out of here."

"But, ma'am, we can't arrest a dog for trespassing—"

"No, but the town does have a leash law, doesn't it, Officer Wilson?" Jason asked, walking slowly to the rottweiler. He held out a hand, allowing the dog a sniff. Finding no resistance, he rubbed the back of its neck, turning the collar to get a better view of the tags. "Says here he belongs to a Henry Turnball."

"Henry?" Mrs. McKinney repeated in disbelief. "Oh, for goodness' sake, he lives in the brick house down the street. He was a good friend of my husband's."

A slight huffing and wheezing sounded behind them. They turned to spot an older man half-walking, half-jogging up the sidewalk with a dog leash in hand. "Luther," he gasped.

The dog's ears perked to attention and he stood to greet his master.

The man glanced around the yard, moaning slightly. "Oh, Luther, what have you done now?"

"This your dog, sir?" Jason asked.

"Yes...well, actually, he's my son's, Henry, Jr.'s." He struggled for breath as he snapped the leash on Luther's collar. "I'm taking care of him for a few weeks while he's away on business. Don't tell me the dog's caused all this trouble?"

"Yes, sir," Jason said. "I'm afraid he did."

"Mildred, I am sorry," Henry said, looking sheepishly at his old friend. "I had no idea he'd found a way to sneak out of the house. Not until I caught him nudging open the screen door with his nose. I promise you, it won't happen again."

Mrs. McKinney sighed. "Well, the harm's already done."

"I'll take Luther home," Henry said. "Then I'll come back and help you clean up this mess."

"Just tie him up to the clothesline," Mrs. McKinney said, motioning away his concern with a wave of her hand. "Let's get a cup of coffee before we start."

"I'd like that." Henry smiled. "I've been meaning to come over for a visit. I'm just sorry it took this to get me over here."

Jason cleared his throat noisily. Startled, Mrs. McKinney

glanced at Jason and Stan, as though just realizing that they were still there. "Chief Gallagher, Officer Wilson, could I interest you in a cup of coffee?"

"No, thank you, ma'am," Jason said. "We need to be moving on. If there isn't anything else…"

"No," Mrs. McKinney said, shaking her head. She gave Henry a shy smile. "This is between friends. We'll take care of it ourselves."

Jason exchanged a silent glance with Stan. Both men struggled to remain sober. With a nod, Jason turned to leave.

Stan followed close on his heels. Once out of earshot, he whispered, "This is the first time I've seen Mrs. McKinney smile in almost a year."

"It's spring, Officer Wilson. There's a lot to smile about."

Stan grinned. "It sure doesn't hurt that Mr. Turnball's a widower, now does it?"

Jason raised a brow. "Thinking of taking up matchmaking, instead of police work?"

"No, sir. I like my job just fine."

Jason glanced at his watch. "It's almost noon. What do you say we break for lunch?"

"Sounds good to me," Stan said. "I know just the place. Mel's diner."

"The food good?"

Stan paused at the door of the patrol car and shrugged. "It's all right. But that isn't the diner's biggest draw. Mel's has the prettiest waitresses in town." Grinning, his junior officer slung himself into the front seat.

With a shake of his head, Jason joined him. Belatedly he remembered his nervous new neighbor and the waitress uniform she'd worn. He felt a stirring of unease tighten his chest. The last thing he wanted was for Maggie Conrad to think he was checking up on her.

Wyndchester was a tourist town. There had to be at least four or five restaurants off the main street alone, he assured himself. Although his new neighbor certainly qualified as pretty, what were the chances of her working at Mel's?

"Everything all right, Maggie?" Bob Williams, one of the regular customers at Mel's diner, asked.

Maggie blinked, surprised by the question. "Sure, Bob. Why do you ask?"

He sat back in his seat at the counter and studied her. "Well, because, as much as I like my coffee, I'm still only able to drink one cup at a time."

Her gaze dropped to the counter, where she'd just finished pouring Bob a second cup—as in, two cups and two saucers—of coffee. Embarrassed heat flushed her skin. She whisked the extra cup away. "I'm sorry, Bob. I don't know what's wrong with me today."

"That's okay, Maggie," he assured her, his gentle face wrinkling into a smile.

Bob was in his midsixties. He had a head of salt-and-pepper hair and a smile that never failed to warm her heart. Maggie hadn't known her own father. Although as a child, she'd often fantasized how different her life would have been if she had. Bob would have fit her idea of the perfect father to a T.

"It's a lovely spring day," Bob added. "No wonder you'd have other things on your mind."

"We're a little busy today," she murmured as though that explained her error. She didn't want to admit to anyone, not even herself, that thoughts of the town's new police chief had been the cause of her absentmindedness.

She followed Bob's glance around the diner. As usual

almost every table was filled. Even the front counter was packed. The room swelled with the buzz of friendly conversation and the clatter of dishes and silverware. It smelled of coffee and the Blue Plate Special: meat loaf, mashed potatoes and green beans. Unlike the other restaurants in town, Mel's was frequented by locals. Patrons that came again and again. Those who remembered if the service at their last visit had been good or not.

Bob sipped his coffee. "You're a little short-staffed today, aren't you?"

Maggie nodded, trying not to let her concern show. "Jenny hasn't come in yet."

Jenny Lewis was young, barely twenty. Maggie was unable to remember the last time the girl had been late. She sighed. At least worrying about Jenny kept her mind off her own problems.

"Anybody seen the new chief of police yet?" One of the regulars at the front counter asked.

Maggie flinched at the question. She drew in a steadying breath, hoping no one had noticed her reaction. So much for avoiding her problems.

Heads up and down the counter shook a negative response.

"I hear he's moved in next door to you, Maggie," the man persisted.

Eyes focused on her.

Since leaving her home in California, she'd tried her best to blend into the communities where she'd stayed. She'd worked and lived her life quietly, without drawing attention to herself or to Kevin. But not here in Wyndchester. The citizens of this little town wouldn't allow anyone to go unnoticed. Maggie forced a smile. "That's right. I saw him just for a moment before I left for work."

"What does he look like?" Bob asked.

Maggie shrugged, trying to blot out the image of the tall, handsome policeman with the almost black hair. She refused to remember the dimples that deepened on his cheeks when he smiled. Or the twinkle in his pale blue eyes when he spoke to her son. Aloud she said, "I didn't really get a good look."

"I hear he's from Chicago," another man piped in.

"A homicide detective," someone else added.

"What's a man with his experience doing in a town like Wyndchester?" Bob asked, frowning thoughtfully.

His friend chuckled. "The question is, how long will a man with his experience *stay* in a town like Wyndchester? I'll give him a couple of months, four tops, before he's driven out of town by boredom."

"I'll give him six months," a nearby patron quipped.

"Put me down for a year," another customer said.

A flurry of bets were placed.

"What do you think, Maggie?" someone asked.

Maggie didn't answer, not wanting to lay odds on the new chief of police or his adjustment to the job. She refused to get her hopes up and pray for his speedy departure. Besides, she wouldn't be around long enough to know whether or not Jason Gallagher stayed. She intended to be long gone before the summer even started.

Not that she wouldn't miss this little town. Maggie glanced around the diner and felt a pang of regret. In the short time she'd been here, she'd grown fond of Wyndchester. Not only were the people friendly, but the town felt safe, comfortable, fitting her like a favorite pair of shoes, reminding her of a time when life wasn't so uncertain.

No wonder Kevin didn't want to leave.

A fellow waitress, a buxom woman with brassy blond hair, interrupted her thoughts. "Maggie doesn't care how long the new chief's staying," Dot said, giving Maggie a sassy wink. "It's whether or not he's married that matters, right, Maggie?"

Laughter erupted in the diner.

Maggie blushed.

Bob came to her rescue. "Now, Dot, if anybody's going to marry Maggie, it's going to be me. I've already asked her four times. She just isn't ready to be tied down yet. Isn't that right, Maggie?"

Her blush deepened.

"She's newly widowed, Dot," another man admonished. "Give her time before you start pushing her toward the altar."

Maggie shifted uncomfortably. She'd never been a good liar. Using a new last name was difficult enough. When she'd moved into town, telling everyone she was a widow seemed an expedient way to handle unwanted questions. No one would ask where Kevin's father was. Nor would they wonder why she avoided even the most persistent of suitors. Although deceiving people who were so nice did go against her conscience.

"Her husband might be dead, but that doesn't mean she is," Dot insisted, draping an arm around Maggie's shoulders. "Mel's got Maggie working too hard. It's time she enjoyed herself some."

"We don't even know what the new chief looks like, Dot," a woman at a nearby table said. She waved a hand at the boys at the counter. "We don't want to fix Maggie up with somebody fat and bald, like these old coots."

Protests arose from the counter.

The bell above the door rang, heralding the arrival of another customer.

A hush fell on the dining room.

Maggie's gaze flew to the door, curious as to who might

have caused such a startled reaction. When she did so, her heart stuttered. She forgot to breathe.

Standing at door, looking tall, intimidating and much too handsome was the topic of the diner patrons' conversation. It was Jason Gallagher. Her new neighbor. The town's chief of police.

Jason spotted her the moment he entered the diner. He ignored the uneven thump of his heart and gave her a nod of recognition.

Maggie neither returned the gesture, nor moved to acknowledge his presence. Instead, she stared at him, the color draining from her face.

He wasn't blind to the fact that he'd become the center of attention. People were looking at him, watching him watch Maggie. He forced himself to turn away, to follow Stan Wilson to a table at the far side of the diner, all the while wishing he could go to her and explain.

Explain what?

That Mel's hadn't been his choice of restaurants? That it was a coincidence that he was here at all? That he wasn't curious about her? That, while he'd only met her this morning, he didn't feel a little jolt of attraction each time he saw her?

The whole explanation would be a bald-faced lie. Maggie Conrad aroused a sensual interest in him that he'd never experienced quite this way before. An awareness that was as ill-advised as it was unwanted.

He hadn't come to Wyndchester looking for an involvement with a woman, he reminded himself sternly. If there was anything to be learned from his past, it was that he was unlucky at love. Whether it be with his ex-wife, or even his son, bad luck seemed to dog him whenever he got too close to another person. Opening himself up to the uncertainty of a new relationship was not part of his plans.

Habit caused him to seat himself at a booth with his back to the wall and a full view of the diner before him. Blame it on cop instinct, but he never turned his back on the unknown. Not seeing what was behind him could destroy him. Although he doubted he was in much danger here in Wyndchester.

Stan drummed his fingers on the tabletop and grinned. "Looks like you're the talk of the town, Chief."

"Who, me?" He tapped a finger to his chest, then glanced around the restaurant. Heads were still turned in their direction. He caught the curious gazes of nearby patrons before they were discreetly averted.

"Yes, sir." Stan chuckled. "They certainly aren't interested in me. I'm old news, boss. I've been on the force for three years."

At the counter Maggie and a buxom waitress were having a heated conversation, casting an occasional glance his way. The other waitress was grinning. Maggie was not. Obviously she wasn't pleased by her new neighbor's appearance.

At a nudge from the other waitress, Maggie armed herself with a couple of menus and a pot of coffee and headed his way.

Jason's pulse quickened as he watched her approach. Her legs were long, shapely. Despite the white, crepe-soled shoes, her stride was graceful, like a dancer's. Her slim hips swung gently side to side, keeping time with her even steps. Jason felt a tug of longing in the pit of his stomach. Maggie provoked a different sort of hunger in him. One that had nothing to do with food.

"Good afternoon, Officer Wilson," she said, placing the

coffeepot on the table, handing each of them a menu. She gave him a nod. "Chief Gallagher."

Noting the formal greeting, he answered in kind. "Hello, again…Mrs. Conrad."

Stan's brows raised. "You two know each other?"

They paused, neither speaking for a moment.

Jason found his voice first. He cleared his throat. "We're neighbors. I'm renting the house next door to, um, Mrs. Conrad's."

Another uncomfortable silence.

"Next door, eh? Well, that's real nice," Stan said, filling the void. He looked from one to the other, seeming amused by their discomfort. "Hey, I'm starved. What's good today, Maggie?"

Looking grateful for the change in topic, she fished her order pad from her apron pocket. Once again Jason found himself studying her long, tapering fingers, struck by an almost uncontrollable urge to reach out and catch them in his. He gripped the menu tightly, struggling to keep his hormones in line.

"The Blue Plate Special's always a good bet," Maggie said. With a quick, impersonal tone, she recited, "Today it's meat loaf, mashed potatoes and green beans, and apple pie for dessert."

The bell over the door jangled.

Reflexively Jason looked up to see the newest customer. Only it wasn't a customer. It was another waitress. A petite, dark-haired girl, who looked so young Jason would have guessed she was playing hooky from school.

Greetings rose from the crowd at her entrance.

A tall, bald man dressed all in white—T-shirt, pants and apron—stuck his head out the kitchen door, a sour expression on his face. His hands on his hips, he barked a few questions at the latecomer.

Smiling shyly, the girl gave a timid shrug, then raised her left hand in explanation. She wore a diamond ring the size of a small rock.

Oohs and aahs and a shower of congratulations from the lunch crowd greeted the silent announcement.

Jason heard Maggie's gasp of surprise. He saw the smile of delight soften her face. Excitement sparkled in her eyes. And he changed his original opinion of his new neighbor.

Maggie Conrad wasn't pretty.

She was beautiful.

A subdued Stan Wilson snapped his menu closed. "I'll have the special, Maggie."

Maggie jumped, startled out of her thoughts by his abrupt request. Then with a nod, she wrote down the order.

"Make mine the same," Jason said slowly, frowning at his officer's sudden change in mood.

Without asking, Maggie poured each of the men a cup of coffee. She took a step away. Now that she'd taken their orders, it seemed to Jason she was in a hurry to be gone. "Your orders will be up in a jiff."

"Maggie," Jason blurted, stopping her hasty departure.

She looked at him in surprise, the sparkle fading from her eyes.

Jason searched his mind for something, anything to say to prolong her stay. But couldn't think of a single excuse to delay the inevitable. Scowling slightly, he said, "Never mind. It wasn't important."

She frowned. "Right. Well, then, I'll be back with your orders."

He watched helplessly as she hurried to the young waitress's side, put an arm around her shoulders and led her into the kitchen. The doors swung shut behind them, obstructing his view of the pair. Feeling inexplicably miffed by Maggie's abandonment, Jason picked up his cup and sipped the hot brew, burning his mouth in the process.

Swearing softly, he pushed the coffee away. He was acting like a lovesick puppy, panting after a forbidden treat. And for what? A woman who'd just as soon spit on him than look at him. The sooner he accepted it the better. The lady wasn't interested.

A fist slammed on the tabletop, rattling the coffee cups. Jason, startled, took a good look at his junior officer. "Something wrong, Officer Wilson?"

"No, sir," Stan said, his expression a reflection of Jason's own glum frustration. There was only one explanation for such an emotion—woman trouble.

Jason nodded his head in the direction of the kitchen. "You know that girl?"

An explanation of whom Jason was referring to was unnecessary. Obviously the young woman sporting the diamond was on Stan's mind. He studied his clenched fists, his usual high spirits gone. "Her name's Jenny Lewis. She was a couple of years behind me in school."

"It appears she's getting married," Jason said, watching the other man closely.

Stan's face drew into a scowl. "Looks that way, doesn't it?"

"Something wrong with that?"

Stan didn't answer.

"She does seem to be on the young side," Jason mused, leaning back in his seat. "Hell, she looks like a baby. I bet she isn't old enough to have graduated from high school, let alone get married—"

"She's old enough," Stan interjected, his eyes flashing with anger. Then, flushing deeply, he averted his gaze, staring down at his hands once again. "Old enough to be stupid, that's for sure."

An uncomfortable silence fell across the table.

Jason reached for his coffee cup, deciding it better to take his chances with the hot brew than to face his officer's fiery temperament.

"What the hell is she thinking?" Stan hissed.

Jason flinched, nearly dropping his cup. The coffee splattered his hands, burning his fingers.

"I mean, the guy's a jerk. He's a real son of a—" He stopped. Glancing around the diner, looking embarrassed by his outburst, Stan's jaw closed with a snap.

A response was required, Jason realized, as he dabbed at the spilled coffee with a handful of paper napkins. His stomach churned with unease at the prospect. When he'd taken this job, he hadn't realized that giving advice to the lovelorn would be one of his duties.

If only he'd had better luck in the love department himself, he'd feel more equipped to handle the situation. Remembering Maggie's prohibitive gaze whenever he was near, he sighed. It would seem he was better at scaring a woman off than attracting her.

Jason cleared his throat. "Officer Wilson...Stan, obviously this girl's engagement is bothering you. I wish I could give you some advice, but I'm just not sure what—"

"That's okay, Chief," Stan said, looking miserable. "This is something I have to take care of myself."

Jason tried not to let his relief show. "Well, if there's anything I can do..."

He let the obligatory words fade away. Without thinking, he picked up his cup and took another sip. And felt the heat of the coffee scald his tongue. Swearing softly, he dropped the cup back into its saucer with a clatter.

This was turning out to be one hell of a day, he thought, heaving another sigh. One hell of a day.

Chapter 3

"Our little Jenny's caught the richest man in town," Dot said, clucking her tongue in approval. "Doesn't that beat all?"

"His *daddy's* the richest man in town, Dot," Jenny said, rolling her eyes. "Joe's broke. He just graduated from law school. He won't even start working in his daddy's law firm until June."

Dot persisted. "Yeah, but someday—"

"Yeah, someday after he passes his bar exam, builds up his clientele, pays off his college loans," Jenny said, ticking off the list on her fingers. "Believe me, Dot, it'll be a long time before Joe'll ever be considered wealthy."

"You have to admit, though, the boy definitely has potential," Dot said, a smile twitching at the corner of her crimson-colored mouth.

Maggie watched the exchange with an amused eye. Minutes earlier she and Dot had whisked Jenny out of the dining room and found refuge from the prying eyes of the customers in the storage room off the kitchen. They'd been pressing the poor girl for details of her engagement ever since.

"Dot," Maggie said, her tone chiding, "give Jenny a break. Money isn't everything."

"Only when you've grown up without it, honey," Dot countered. "There's nothing romantic about scrimpin' and savin' all your life." She pointed a manicured fingernail at Jenny. "You tell that to your Officer Wilson."

"Stan isn't *my* Officer Wilson," Jenny protested.

Maggie frowned. "Am I missing something? I thought you said you were engaged to Joe Bosworth."

"I am," Jenny said, her cheeks flushing. "Stan's just a friend."

Dot snorted her disbelief.

"An old friend of the family," Jenny insisted, raising her chin in stubborn defiance. "I can't help it if he feels differently."

"Hmm," Maggie murmured.

"Hmm is right," Dot said.

The owner of the diner, Mel—a big man who unsuccessfully hid his baldness beneath a chef's hat—thumped open the door to the kitchen and poked his head into the storage room. Despite his size and trademark gruffness, everyone knew he was a softie at heart. "Orders are stacking up. Let's finish this break after the rush."

Giving a mock bow of subservience, Dot muttered, "Whatever you say, oh great and mighty slave driver." Then with a wink of her eye and a swing of her hips, she disappeared through the doorway and into the dining room.

Maggie started to follow.

Jenny stopped her. "Maggie, wait. I've got something to ask you."

"What is it, honey?"

"It's about the wedding," Jenny said. She licked her lips, looking nervous. "I'd like you to be my matron of honor."

"Me?" Maggie pressed a hand to her breast.

"Of course, you," Jenny said, smiling shyly. "You've always been so good to me. I feel like you're the big sister I never had."

Maggie stared at her, uncertain what to say. Just this morning, she'd decided to leave town as soon as Kevin was finished with school. How could she explain to her young friend it was doubtful she'd even be in Wyndchester when the wedding took place?

"I don't know, Jenny. Kevin and I, we've been talking about going on a vacation later this summer...."

"That's okay. The wedding's in June."

"So soon?" Maggie asked, surprised.

Jenny sighed, nodding toward the door of the dining room. "I know what everybody's going to say. That it's a rush wedding. That we *had* to get married. But that just isn't so. Joe and I...we haven't...well, you know." She gave an embarrassed shrug. "I told Joe I wouldn't make love to him until we were married. I think that's why he's in such a hurry."

Maggie smiled. "I think it's wonderful, Jenny. It takes a lot of willpower to say no to someone you love."

"Yeah, well..." Jenny's troubled gaze flitted away.

Maggie couldn't help but think Jenny wasn't acting like a woman in love with her future husband. She remembered Dot's mentioning Officer Stan Wilson's interest in Jenny, warning the girl to keep him at arm's length. At first, she'd chalked the warning up to just another example of Dot's endless teasing. Now she wondered if it was true.

Maggie placed a hand on the girl's shoulder. She felt the

delicateness of her bone structure, the slight trembling beneath her fingers. "Is there something wrong, Jenny?"

"No, of course not." Jenny gave a nervous laugh. "It's just…Joe's family, they're different from mine. They're the town's high society. Sometimes Mrs. Bosworth makes me feel uncomfortable, like I'm unworthy of her son." Jenny looked into Maggie's eyes, her gaze pleading. "I really could use a friend to stand up for me at the wedding."

Maggie hadn't made many friends in her life, and she had no brothers or sisters. As a child she'd been quiet, introverted, more comfortable with her nose in a book than playing with other children. As an adult she'd been discouraged by her husband from establishing friendships with others. He'd wanted to be the center of her world. There hadn't been room for anyone else.

Now this young woman, this child, was reaching out to her, asking her to be a friend. Maggie didn't want to say no. Her vision blurred as tears threatened. "I'd be honored, Jenny."

Jenny smiled, her own eyes misting. "Thank you, Maggie."

"Order up, Maggie," Mel called through the kitchen door.

Maggie blotted her eyes with the hem of her apron, giving a self-deprecating laugh at her show of emotion. "Time to get to work before we start blubbering like babies."

Together they left the storage room. Jenny took her place at the counter. Maggie hurried to collect her order: two Blue Plate Specials, one for the chief of police and one for his officer.

After the stillness of the storage room, the noise of the diner was a blow to her senses. Sunlight streamed in through the windows, nearly blinding her. Heart hammering, she felt the weight of Jason's gaze as she returned to his booth. For a moment she felt disoriented, almost dizzy with sensory overload.

"Enjoy your meal, gentlemen," she said, placing the plates on the table, not quite meeting the police chief's eyes. She turned to leave.

Jason's deep voice stopped her. "Is everything all right, Ma...Mrs. Conrad?"

She looked at him, wide-eyed and startled.

His gaze traveled from her teary eyes to her fluttering hands. "You seem a little upset."

"I'm fine," Maggie said quickly.

He continued as though she hadn't spoken. "If there's anything I can do—"

"No, Chief Gallagher, there's nothing you can do," she said, her tone sharper than she'd intended, his concern unnerving her. Once and for all she had to set the boundaries of their nonexistent relationship. She could not allow him to become a part of her life. Gathering her courage, she straightened her shoulders and sent him a determined glance. "I'm twenty-eight years old, not a child by any means. Though I may not have a man in my life to take care of me, that doesn't mean I'm not capable of taking care of myself."

He shifted in his seat. "I didn't say that you—"

She didn't let him finish. "Just because we're neighbors, Chief Gallagher, doesn't mean you're privy to my personal life. I'd appreciate it if you'd mind your own business."

With the biting reprimand still hanging in the air, she turned on her heel and strode from the booth.

Jason stared after her, blinking in surprise.

Officer Wilson picked up his fork and gave his boss a commiserative glance. Sighing, he said, "Maybe coming to Mel's wasn't such a good idea, after all, eh, Chief?"

Jason did not answer.

* * *

Later that day, as dusk was beginning to fall, Jason was busy taking boxes of unpacked items to his garage for storage. The soft breeze felt cool, just a nip of a chill against his bare arms. From somewhere nearby, the scent of hamburgers grilling on a charcoal fire wafted in the air, teasing his nostrils, reminding him he hadn't eaten since lunchtime. Even then, he'd barely touched his food. He'd been too angry with his new neighbor to do his appetite justice.

That afternoon Maggie Conrad had looked him in the eye and had brushed away his concern as though he were nothing more than a pesky fly. In no uncertain terms, she'd told him to butt out of her life.

Not that what Maggie thought of him mattered, he told himself. The lie struck a discordant note. He nearly dropped the box he cradled in his arms. Using his knee to keep it from slipping from his grasp, he silently cursed the fates that had brought such an obstinate woman into his life.

Unable to help himself, his gaze darted across the yard to the light that shone like a beacon in Maggie's window. Swearing softly, he muttered, "Keep movin', Gallagher. There's nothing over there that concerns you."

The lady of the house had made that much perfectly clear. Not once, but twice in one day. Even a mule knew when to give up a fight.

He continued across the yard to the unattached garage in the back of the property. His car was parked in the driveway, so the garage stood empty, gathering dust and thick layers of shadows. Using his elbow to maneuver, Jason switched on the light. A bare lightbulb came to life, scarcely making a dent in the darkness.

Sighing, he stepped into the small building. Last night, he'd arrived too late to do much more than open a suitcase and fall into bed. This afternoon the movers had arrived, dropping off the meager supply of boxes his life comprised. Now he was left with the task of sorting through the mess.

He'd tackled the job with the enthusiasm he bestowed on most unpleasant chores, like doing the laundry or going to the dentist. The sooner he got it over with the better.

First he'd unpacked boxes of essentials, things he used on a daily basis, like clothes, dishes and towels. Next on his list were the items delegated as occasional essentials. These included his fishing rod and reel, his collection of Jimmy Buffet tapes and suspense books by his favorite author.

Last to be taken care of were the nonessentials, which was what he was doing now, storing them in a safe, out-of-the-way place. The box he carried now held memories that were too precious to throw away, yet too painful to have to face on a daily basis—if at all.

He scanned the garage. There were shelves in the back, wide enough and deep enough to store a large box. He waded through the dust and debris littering the floor, promising himself to give the building a thorough cleaning whenever he got a chance. Cursing, he ducked to avoid the cobwebs hanging from the ceiling.

Although it embarrassed him to admit it, he had one irrational fear in life—the common house spider. He could look a man carrying a gun or a knife in the eye without so much as a flinch. But force him to face an eight-legged creature and his knees turned to jelly.

It had amused his ex-wife no end when she'd discovered his Achilles' heel. During their divorce proceedings, she'd threatened to use it as leverage when he'd dragged his feet in signing the final papers.

"Blackmail, pure and simple," he groused.

Not that he hadn't accepted that their marriage was over. They'd been too young and too different for it to have ever worked. The birth of their son was the only thread that had held their marriage together. It didn't take long for both of them to realize that even their love for Scott wasn't strong enough to make it last. But Jason was a creature of habit. He'd held on to the marriage like a lifeline. To him, enduring a bad marriage seemed less forbidding than facing a future rife with uncertainty.

Which probably explained why the death of his son had sent him into such a tailspin. For the life of him, he didn't know how any man could cope with the fact that one minute he was sending his son off to school and the next hearing a fellow police officer tell him his son had been badly hurt in an accident on the way to the school. He doubted he'd ever recover from the shock.

A scraping sound startled him.

With cop-quick reflexes, Jason dropped the box and spun around on his heel. His years on the force had taught him to be wary, even in his own home. Unfortunately his reaction scared the willies out of the young boy who stood in the doorway of his garage.

Eyes wide, mouth hanging open, his new neighbor stared at him from behind the thick lenses of his glasses.

"Kevin?" Jason asked, taking a cautious step toward him.

The boy began to back away, looking ready to sprint for safety.

"I didn't mean to startle you," Jason said, keeping his voice low, his tone soothing. "I wasn't expecting anyone behind me." He grinned sheepishly. "I thought you might be a spider."

"A spider?" The boy's gaze darted around the garage, as though in search of the little critter in question. He swallowed hard, his pulse beating visibly in his throat.

"Yeah, I hate spiders," Jason admitted. "I've been unpacking most of the evening. The house has been too quiet. Just me and the sound of my own voice cussin' whenever I can't find something I need. It's got me spooked.''

He was rambling, talking too much, not making any sense. At least, not to a seven-year-old. But his words were having the desired effect. The tension in Kevin's face eased some. He closed his mouth and chewed on his lower lip. His eyes now shone with curiosity, rather than fear.

"My mom's good at packing and unpacking," Kevin said finally. "She's real fast."

"That's great. Maybe she'd like to come over and give me a hand with all my boxes of junk."

Kevin shook his head. "I don't think she'd want to do that."

The boy knew his mother well, Jason mused.

Kevin peered around him, eyeing the box Jason had dropped. "What's that?"

Jason turned, noticing for the first time that, in the commotion, the lid had fallen open. The sight of the child's baseball glove resting on top of the box hit him like a sledgehammer to the gut. Slowly he reached for the glove. It had belonged to his son. He ran a hand over the worn leather. It felt dry, stiff from lack of care.

"It's a baseball glove," he said needlessly. He wasn't sure what bothered him most, seeing the glove again and along with it the painful memories of his son, or knowing that an item that had once given such a great deal of pleasure was now being stored in a box and wasted. He raised his eyes to look at Kevin. "Would you like to have it?"

Kevin blinked, obviously surprised by the offer. "I—I don't know…"

Jason tucked the glove under his arm and picked up the box. Closing the flaps, he placed it on the shelf, then turned his attention once again to the boy. "Why don't we discuss it over a soda?"

Kevin cast a nervous glance across the yard to his house, then looked at the glove. A decision was made in that single exchange. "Okay, just for a little bit."

"I've got root beer," Jason said, leading the way.

"Sounds good," Kevin said, his voice as somber as a judge.

Once they reached the back-porch steps, Kevin stopped, refusing to go any farther.

Jason handed him the glove. "Why don't you hold on to this while I get the drinks?"

Kevin nodded, not answering. He took a seat on the bottom step and waited.

In the kitchen as he poured the sodas, Jason watched the boy turn the glove over and over in his hands and tried to figure him out. The care with which he handled the glove spoke of admiration, respect. His awkwardness told him the boy probably had never held a baseball glove before in his life.

Jason stepped out onto the porch, handing Kevin a mug of root beer. "The glove belonged to my son."

Kevin looked at him, frowning slightly. "Won't he need it?"

Jason sucked in a deep breath. The question was innocent enough. Yet, the thought of answering it rocked him. "No," he said finally. "He won't need it."

Thankfully Kevin did not pursue the issue further. After taking a sip of his root beer, he set his mug down on the step beside him. He slipped the glove onto his hand, looking at it admiringly.

"It hasn't been used for a couple of years," Jason told him. "It probably needs to be oiled."

Kevin smacked a fist into the palm of the glove.

"Have you played much baseball?" Jason asked, feeling uncomfortable with the silence.

The boy shook his head. "Nah, I've never been on a team."

"Why not?"

He shrugged. "We move too much."

The explanation piqued his interest. But before Jason could ask the boy about the moves, they were interrupted.

"Kevin?" Despite the alarmed tone, he recognized Maggie's voice. In a moment she was standing right in front of him, her hair windblown, her breathing ragged, as though she'd just sprinted across the yard in a blind panic. "What are you doing over here?"

In his haste to get to his feet, Kevin dropped the glove and nearly knocked over his mug of root beer. While he didn't look scared, he did look chastened. He hurried to her side. "I'm sorry, Mom."

Myriad emotions flickered in Maggie's eyes, none of which Jason understood. She'd changed out of her work clothes. Now she wore a pair of faded blue jeans that emphasized her long legs and a yellow T-shirt that hugged her slender curves. Her feet were bare, as though she'd been in too great a hurry to bother slipping on a pair of shoes. Despite her casual appearance, she looked no more approachable than she had this afternoon in the diner. "I'm sorry," she said to Jason. "Kevin won't bother you anymore."

"He's no bother. In fact, I've enjoyed his visit." He shot Kevin a grin. "You're welcome to stop by anytime, Kevin."

Kevin didn't answer. And Jason knew his offer would probably be ignored.

Maggie placed a hand on her son's shoulder. "We need

to go inside now." Then she added, by way of explanation, "It's getting late."

They turned to leave.

Jason stood. He scooped up the glove and stopped them. "Don't forget this, Kevin."

The boy hesitated. Uncertainty danced in his eyes as he looked longingly at the glove. Then he looked to his mother for permission.

Maggie hurried to answer. "Oh, no—that isn't necessary. We couldn't—"

"I insist," Jason said, holding the glove out to the boy. "Kevin told me he hasn't had much chance to play baseball. The glove's old, but it's comfortable and broken in. Just needs a little oiling."

Maggie glanced at her son. The silent plea in the boy's eyes was obvious even to Jason. She relented with a defeated smile. "All right." She raised her eyes to Jason's and said stiffly, "Thank you, Mr. Gallagher."

Jason smiled. "Jason, please."

Color flooded her skin. And Jason wondered why she seemed so discomfited by the informality.

"Thank you, Mr. Gallagher," Kevin said, echoing his mother. He reached for the glove, his response a little more exuberant than Maggie's. His face lit up in a grin, the first Jason had seen on the boy.

"Let's go, Kevin," Maggie said, putting a hand on her son's shoulder.

Still smiling, Kevin said, "Good night, Mr. Gallagher."

"Good night, Kevin."

Maggie licked her lips, looking nervous and anxious to leave. "G-good night, Mr. Gallagher."

Lord, but the woman was stubborn. He felt an obstinate streak of his own surfacing.

"Good night, Maggie," he said, drawing out her name slowly, tenderly, the way a lover might.

Jason regretted his attempt to tease her the minute he heard her sharp gasp of surprise. Surprise that turned quickly to anger. With her pert nose tipped skyward in indignation, she closed ranks and herded her son to the safety of her own house.

He watched her departure with a sinking heart. Shaking his head, giving a wry chuckle, he muttered, "Glad to see you haven't lost your touch with the ladies, Gallagher."

The butterflies in Maggie's stomach still fluttered as she tucked her son into bed that night. She didn't know what upset her most—her son cavorting with the enemy or the enemy's attempt to cavort with her.

Jason Gallagher was becoming more dangerous by the moment.

Whether she wanted to admit it or not, he was having a profound effect on her life. Not only was he influencing her son, but he'd had an influence on her. A disturbing one at that.

For the first time in years, she'd been tempted by a man.

When he'd said her name, she'd felt as though she'd been caressed by a lover. The sensations tripping through her body had been electric, shocking her. The words had fallen from his lips with such sweet tenderness that she'd wanted to reach out, run her fingers through his hair and sample his mouth for herself.

It had been years since she'd felt anything but fear around a man.

"There's an autograph on the glove," Kevin said, interrupting her thoughts. He opened the palm of the glove to show her. "Look, it says, Andy Van..."

"Slyke," she said, finishing the name for him. "It was nice of Mr. Gallagher to give you his glove."

"It's not his. It belonged to his son."

"His son?" She felt a prickling of curiosity. Jason wore no wedding ring. Other than the baseball glove, she saw no sign of a child's presence in his home. She couldn't help but wonder about his family life.

"He said his son wouldn't need it anymore," Kevin explained. "That's why I can have it."

She frowned at the glove, resenting not so much its presence as what it represented. "Kevin, why didn't you tell me you wanted a baseball glove? I could have gotten you one."

He fingered the lettering of the autograph, not answering right away. Finally he said, "I didn't want to bother you."

"Kevin, it wouldn't have been a bother," she admonished gently. Hesitantly she asked, "Do you want to play baseball?"

He shrugged, looking embarrassed. "You have to live in a town a long time before you can be on a baseball team."

The simple explanation was a sharp reminder that her son was being robbed of his childhood. Maggie drew in a shaky breath. "Not necessarily. Lots of boys join teams in the middle of a season. I bet there are some boys in your class who might be playing ball right now."

Kevin's eyes widened. "Tommy Marshall's dad coaches a team."

"Do you want me to ask him if you could play?"

"You mean it?"

She tried to laugh, making light of the situation, but the attempt fell flat. "Of course I mean it. There's no reason you can't play ball while we're staying in Wyndchester."

Her son sat up in his bed and enveloped her in a hug.

His gratefulness was like rubbing salt into an already sting-ing wound of regret. "Thanks, Mom."

Tears threatened. Before she ruined the moment by be-coming maudlin, Maggie brushed away his gratitude. "It's time for bed."

She plucked his glasses from the bridge of his nose and kissed his cheek.

He grinned at her. In his hand, he still held Jason's glove.

"Get some sleep," she said, reaching for the light.

Darkness settled over the room when she turned off the lamp. Kevin sat up in bed. "The night-light, Mom," he said, his voice bordering on shrillness. "The night-light."

"I'll get it," she said quickly, hurrying to soothe his fears. The darkness...the unknown...still frightened her son. Silently she berated herself for allowing the years of turmoil her son had had to endure. She snapped on the night-light.

Releasing a pent-up breath, Kevin settled back in bed, clinging to the baseball glove like a lifeline.

"Good night, Kevin."

"Good night, Mom," he said, his voice back to normal. With a yawn, he rolled over on his side and closed his eyes.

Maggie lingered at the doorway for a moment, then qui-etly shut the door. It was late, but she felt too restless to sleep. Instead, she headed downstairs. The floorboards creaked beneath her feet as she descended the stairway. It felt hot in the kitchen, stuffy and airless. Feeling too on edge to sit still, she opened the back door and stepped out onto the porch.

The cool night air soothed her. Inhaling deeply, she walked to the edge of the porch and sat down on the wooden swing that hung from the porch ceiling. Allowing the swing to sway on its own, she let the inky shadows encompass her.

Unlike her son, in Wyndchester she didn't fear the darkness. Nor did she feel the need to lock her doors and hide. Here, she felt safe.

In time, so would her son.

A door opened in the house next door. Jason stepped outside onto his porch.

Maggie reacted instinctively. She tucked her feet beneath her and curled into a tight ball of invisibility, watching him from a safe distance.

He was still dressed in jeans and a worn polo shirt. His weary sigh drifted across the yard, setting off an odd tingling sensation in the pit of Maggie's stomach. Leaning a shoulder against the porch rail, he looked as tired and as unsettled as she felt.

She wondered what demons kept him awake at night.

She wondered about the son whose baseball glove he'd been willing to part with.

She wondered why her new neighbor intrigued her so.

Jason ran his fingers through his thick dark hair, tousling the curls, making him look disheveled and dangerous. He raised both hands above his head, touching the ceiling of the porch, stretching like a cat as if to unkink his tightly coiled body. The movement caused the fabric of his knit shirt to stretch tautly across his chest, emphasizing his well-developed muscles.

In most men, such a show of strength and power would have intimidated her, frightened her. But she'd seen the gentleness with which he'd treated her son. In her heart, she knew she had nothing to fear from Jason Gallagher.

Except the balance of her life, and that of her son's.

Jason was still an officer of the law, she reminded herself. A law she'd willfully and knowingly broken. If he were to find out the truth, he would have no choice but to destroy her hard-sought equilibrium.

A shudder of regret traveled down her spine. Because of Jason, she would soon be forced to leave this haven. It was only a matter of time.

Until that day arrived, however, her biggest challenge would be to keep a discreet distance between her family and her new neighbor. Already her son was showing signs of rebelling. Kevin's allegiances were being influenced by an easy smile and a gentle manner.

Maggie's temptation had a more primal root. She glanced across the yard at the man next door. Even in the dim light of the porch, she could see his rugged good looks. The quiet strength and determination in his stance. He was a man who exuded confidence.

Jason Gallagher might be different from most men she'd known in her life, but she'd never allow him to get close enough to find out.

Chapter 4

"Looks as though our police chief's headed this way," a white-haired customer at the counter in Mel's said. He nudged his buddy next to him, nodding toward the street window.

"A-yup," his friend agreed. The older man lifted the cuff of his plaid shirt to glance at his watch. "Ten o'clock on the dot. Time for a coffee break."

At this hour of the morning, the breakfast rush had thinned to a trickle. Still holding court at the counter were a group of diehard customers. Retired and with extra time on their hands, these older men wiled away the hours as they discussed local events and sipped their morning coffee. Most days, Maggie enjoyed their company, entertained by their teasing banter. When the subject turned to Wyndchester's newest resident, however, she couldn't help but wish she were miles away.

Unable to help herself, Maggie glanced outside where Jason was crossing the street. In deference to the warm day, he'd left his cap and jacket at the police department. A soft wind lifted his dark hair, sending it tumbling across his forehead. Sunlight glistened against his bare forearms. His long, determined stride spoke of a self-assuredness Maggie envied.

"He's getting to be a regular, ain't he?" another man observed.

"A-yup," the white-haired customer agreed.

His friend lifted a curious brow. "Must not like the coffee at the police department."

"Oh, the coffee's okay. I think he's just comin' here for the company." The white-haired man glanced at Maggie, a twinkle of amusement in his gray eyes. "Isn't that right, Maggie?"

Heat suffused her face. Not trusting herself to answer, she picked up a sponge and busied herself with an unnecessary cleanup of the spotless counter. At her obvious discomfort, a round of chuckles sounded across the diner.

Only one man remained sober. Bob Williams—her favorite of all the geriatric gossips—reached out and patted her arm, stilling her frenetic cleaning. "Ignore them, Maggie. The ol' coots don't mean any harm."

"I know. It's just—" Maggie gave a quick, self-deprecating grimace "—I never was good at taking a little teasing."

"Not many of us are," he assured her with a weak smile.

For the first time, Maggie noticed the older man's flushed face. "Are you feeling okay, Bob?"

He waved away her concern, although his blue eyes were clouded with unmistakable pain. He tapped his chest with a fisted hand. "Just a little heartburn. I knew sooner or later too many of Mel's breakfasts would catch up with me."

"I could scrounge up an antacid if you'd like."

"No, I'll be fine." He scowled, although a hint of a smile lingered behind the stern expression. "Now how did the conversation turn to me? I was trying to help you, Maggie."

Her grin returned. "I don't need help, Bob. I'm just fine."

Her good humor and bravado melted with the sound of the bell over the door. An instant quiet descended upon the restaurant as Jason entered. The men at the counter shifted in their seats, angling for a better view, chorusing a round of hellos for the new arrival.

Maggie froze as Jason scanned the diner, taking in the nearly empty tables and booths. A shiver traveled down her spine as his blue-eyed gaze came to rest on her. With a nod of acknowledgment, he headed for the counter.

Ignoring the chuckles and the whispered *I told you so*'s from the crew at the counter, Maggie picked up a pot of coffee. Her pulse fluttered as she made her way to her newest customer.

"Mornin', Maggie," Jason said, his deep voice echoing in her ear, sending a shiver of awareness through her body. His easy grin seemed much too friendly, enticing her to respond in kind.

"Good morning, Chief Gallagher," she said stiffly, fighting temptation.

His grin deepened. Undeterred, he leaned close, elbows on the counter, his tone confiding, and said, "One of these days, Maggie, I'm going to come in here and you're going to call me Jason. And I don't know who'll be more shocked, you or me."

Heat flooded her. No matter how hard she tried, she couldn't seem to shake her neighbor's persistent attempts at winning her friendship. Even worse, he was coming awfully close to accomplishing the deed. She couldn't remember the last time she'd felt quite so tempted by a man.

Flustered, she grabbed a cup and saucer from the shelf beneath the counter. Slamming them down with more force than she'd intended, the rattle of china on china resonated throughout the room. Embarrassed, she felt her hand shake as she poured the coffee. Refusing to meet Jason's gaze, she asked, "Is there anything else I can get you?"

"A smile would be nice."

She did not answer. Her blush deepening, she glanced down the counter at the gray-haired men valiantly trying to eavesdrop on their conversation. Lowering her voice, she said, "Look, I don't want to seem rude, but Wyndchester's a small town. Everybody knows everybody else here. People talk. Word gets around pretty quick. I've got a little boy at home. I don't want to give anyone the wrong impression about you...and me."

A discomfiting silence gaped between them.

Maggie hazarded another glance at her neighbor.

There wasn't a trace of amusement in his blue eyes. His expression somber, his gaze unwavering, he said, "Giving anyone the wrong impression is the last thing I want. I wouldn't dream of hurting you or Kevin. All I'm looking for is a friend, Maggie."

The sincerity of his tone caught in Maggie's chest. Her resolve to keep Jason at arm's length slipped a notch. For just a moment, she considered surrendering in this battle of wills. He seemed so honest, so open. What harm could possibly come from letting him into her life?

What harm?

Unwanted memories collided in her mind. All too vividly she remembered her encounters with the police in California. On the occasions she'd called for their assistance in stopping her ex-husband's rampages, once it was known who her powerful and influential husband was, the police had looked the other way.

She'd suffered unforgivably because she'd been foolish enough to put her trust in those officers who were supposed to uphold the law.

How could she believe Jason was any different?

"What's wrong with just being good neighbors?" he persisted, startling her out of her unwanted memories.

"Oh, I don't know," she said, with a flat-sounding chuckle. Pushing away the bitterness, she strove for a light tone. "I've always heard good fences make for the best of neighbors."

Jason did not smile. He looked disappointed. Disappointed at her answer. Disappointed with her.

Her heart thumped unevenly in her chest. She felt hollow, empty inside, as though she'd lost a chance at something very special. Anxious to escape his reproachful gaze, she said, "If there's nothing else, I'm busy right now—"

A crash of plates hitting the floor interrupted her bald-faced lie.

Cries of alarm sounded in the diner.

Startled, Maggie whirled around and watched in horror as Bob Williams stood at the other end of the counter, clutching his chest in pain. Then, as though in slow motion, he stepped forward, teetering drunkenly on his feet. Before she could will her frozen limbs to move, her special friend slumped like a rag doll onto the floor.

Despite her shocked expression, Maggie reacted with a cat-quick response. She slammed the coffeepot onto the counter, sending a spray of the hot liquid into the air. Ignoring the mess, she scrambled around the counter and hurried to the fallen man's side.

Jason's cop reflexes kicked into gear a second later, more

in response to the urgency he saw reflected on Maggie's face than for professional reasons. Pushing himself away from the counter, he hurried to join her, forgetting that only moments ago she'd done her best to discourage his efforts to get closer.

The man lying on the floor was a regular at Mel's. At the moment, his name eluded Jason. He looked to be in his late sixties, and Jason remembered him as a pleasant, quiet man, ready with a quick smile and a friendly conversation. Right now, however, this normally robust man lay very still. His face was deathly pale, with a bluish tint around his lips.

"Bob…" There was a tremor in Maggie's voice. Kneeling beside him, she repeated his name, her tone stronger this time, more insistent. "Bob, can you hear me?"

When he did not answer, Maggie touched two fingers to the man's neck, just below the hollow of his chin. "There's no pulse." She slipped a hand beneath his neck, lifting until his head fell backward. Placing her face close to his, she yelled, "He's not breathing. He's having a heart attack."

Not sure why he trusted Maggie's quick diagnosis, Jason glanced sharply at the men nearby, who were only now rising numbly to their feet. "Get on the phone. Call for an ambulance." As they stared at him without moving, Jason said, "Do it *now*."

One of the men nodded and hurried to do as he was bid.

Maggie wasted no time. She pinched the bridge of Bob's nose and blew four quick breaths into his mouth. Then, with more strength than Jason realized she possessed, she began chest compressions, counting aloud as she pushed down with her arms straight and the palms of both hands flat on Bob's sternum.

On the count of five, Jason took over the breathing. The man's chest rose as his lungs filled with air.

In a whoosh, the breath escaped as Maggie continued the compressions.

They worked side by side for what seemed like an eternity, although in reality, it couldn't have been more than a few minutes. During that time, the diner remained eerily quiet. All that could be heard was the sound of Maggie's steady voice, counting off the compressions. When Jason heard the distant wail of a siren, it sounded heaven-sent.

Although she was drenched in perspiration and her arms were trembling from the exertion, Maggie didn't stop the lifesaving compressions. Not until the paramedics burst into the diner. Pushing her aside, the man-and-woman team went to work, taking over where she'd left off.

Jason rose to his feet and stepped back to give them room.

Maggie stayed on the ground, kneeling close by in case she was needed. She wrapped her arms around herself, looking cold and pale as shock settled in. It wasn't until one of the paramedics announced, "We've got a heartbeat," that she closed her eyes and drew in a shaky breath.

Her distress was almost palpable. It took all of Jason's willpower not to reach out, enfold her in his arms and comfort her.

Metal locks clicked into place as Bob was lifted onto a gurney. The noise snapped Jason to attention. Knowing his job wasn't over yet, he pushed himself away from Maggie, away from temptation.

He approached the customers hovering nearby. "Does Bob have a wife?"

A white-haired man, the one who'd called for the ambulance, shook his head. "Bob's a widower. His wife's been gone almost five years."

"Any other family?" Jason asked.

"He's got a daughter," another man answered. "She lives in St. Louis."

"Does anyone know how I could get a hold of her?"

The white-haired man nodded. "Yeah, I've got her address and phone number at home. Bob gave it to me in case of an emergency..." The words faded. The man gave a sharp humorless laugh, before shaking off his sense of irony. Softly he said, "I'll call Bob's daughter. It's better she heard the news from someone she knows."

"Thank you, I'd appreciate that," Jason said with a quick nod. Knowing he needed to get to the hospital to finish his report, he turned, searching the crowd of onlookers for the one person who concerned him most. He found Maggie alone behind the counter, cleaning the long-forgotten spilled coffee.

His approach went unnoticed until he placed a hesitant hand on her shoulder. Her reaction was quick and unexpected. She jumped and spun around, her eyes wide and startled.

"I'm sorry," Jason murmured, not sure why his best intentions always turned out so badly where Maggie was concerned. He searched her face, trying to understand the reason behind her skittish reaction. "Are you okay?"

"A little shaky, that's all," she admitted. She inhaled deeply, pushing a wayward strand of strawberry blond hair from her eyes. Releasing the breath on a sigh, she said, "I just hope Bob's going to be all right."

"He's got a fightin' chance. Thanks to you."

"No, not me. I didn't... It was nothing," she stammered. She rubbed her hands up and down her slender arms, looking chilled despite the heat of the diner. "I just happened to be in the right place at the wrong time."

He wasn't sure why her dismissive manner bothered him, but it did. Even though he'd known her only for a short time—less than two weeks—he'd come to realize that calling attention to herself was the last thing Maggie wanted. He'd never met a woman so bent on blending into the background. This time, however, he wasn't going to allow her to do that. She was going to get the credit she deserved.

His expression stern, his tone stubborn, he said, "No, you saved his life. You knew it was his heart and started CPR before any of us had a chance to even think twice. You were amazing, Maggie. A trained medical professional couldn't have reacted any quicker."

The color drained from her face. Her hand shook as it fluttered to her throat. "Anyone could have done just as much. I—I've taken a class in first aid. CPR was just one of the lessons they taught us."

Jason frowned, puzzled by her seeming so flustered at his compliment. "No matter, you should be proud of yourself."

"Look, I appreciate the compliment, but..." She waved a hand at the crowded diner. Bad news traveled fast in a small town. Curious townspeople were filling the place to catch up on the latest happening. "I've really got to get back to work."

Sighing, Jason pushed himself away from the counter. "And I need to get to the hospital to check on Bob." He hesitated, glancing at her uncertainly. "If you want, I'll give you a call later, let you know how he's doing."

"I'd like that," she said, her voice so soft he could barely hear her.

He studied her before leaving. The experience had left its mark on Maggie. She looked so worn, so drained of her normal energy. He wished she'd allow him to do more to alleviate her shock. "Take care of yourself, Maggie."

The smile was faint but unmistakable. "Don't worry, Jason. I will."

He hesitated again, then forced himself to move before he did something really stupid. Despite the grim circumstances that had dampened the day, there was a decided bounce in his step as he strode from the diner and out into the brilliant sunshine.

It wasn't much, he told himself, but it was a start.

After nearly two weeks of coaxing, Maggie had finally called him Jason.

It was her least-favorite task. A chore she'd dreaded more than anything else during this past year and a half of hiding.

Later that evening, after finishing her shift at the diner and sharing a light dinner with Kevin, Maggie set her mug of hot tea on the kitchen table and pulled out a map of the United States. Laying it flat on the tabletop, she smoothed a hand across the wrinkles of the well-worn document.

Red circles dotted the miles between Wyndchester and California, marking the cities where she and Kevin had already spent time. Places to which she could never return.

Her vision blurred with unwanted tears. She lifted her mug and sipped the hot tea, delaying the inevitable. After what had happened at the diner this morning, it was time to choose a new place to live.

Maggie sighed at the fateful path her life seemed destined to travel. While thankful for the years of medical training that had saved her friend's life, she knew she had revealed too much of herself today. In helping Bob Williams, she had put Kevin and herself in danger.

The glint of curious admiration in Jason's eyes had been unmistakable. She was such a terrible liar. And the police chief was no fool. It wouldn't be long before he would question her fib concerning a first-aid class.

It was only a matter of time before he knew the truth. That she wasn't who she said she was.

A noise startled her. The muted thump of something hitting the house drew her out of her pensive thoughts. She stood, squinting out the kitchen window where the sound had originated. There, in the backyard, she spotted her son scuffing his heels against the grass as he crossed the yard toward the house.

With a frustrated expression on his face, Kevin stooped and picked up a fallen baseball. Knuckling his glasses back into place, he tossed the ball as high as he could into the air. It didn't get far. But no matter, he managed to miss the easy toss. Once again, the ball arced away from the catcher, thunking loudly as it hit the house.

Maggie sighed. Leaving the map on the table, putting off her decision for later, she joined her son outside. "Hey, Kevin. How's it going?"

"I'm busy, Mom," he said, frowning in concentration, not sparing her a single glance.

"I can see that." She bit her lower lip to stop a smile. "Looks like you're getting ready for baseball."

Embarrassment flickered across his young face. "Tommy's dad says I need work on my catching."

Feeling totally out of her depth, Maggie hesitated. Then, clearing her throat, she asked, "Would you like some help? I could try throwing you a couple of balls."

Kevin shot her a doubtful glance. "You know how to play baseball?"

"Well, no. Not exactly," she admitted.

The truth was, sports were not her forte. As a girl, she'd been an academic, a bookworm. The only child of an overly protective single mother, she'd always felt more comfortable with schoolwork than social activities.

Unwilling to let the memories of her past interfere with

helping her son now, she pushed the doubts from her mind. "I may not be a pro baseball player. But I could try."

Kevin heaved a long-suffering sigh. "Okay, Mom. Let's see what you can do."

Fifteen minutes later, Maggie had to admit the truth. She wasn't sure who was more awkward at playing baseball, Kevin or herself. Between the two of them, they got more exercise chasing all their misses than they did from actually catching and throwing the ball. They were so bad, in fact, she couldn't decide whether to laugh out loud or to cry in frustration.

She did neither. She was too afraid of upsetting the balance of Kevin's precarious mood. It was times like these that she longed for a positive male influence in her son's life.

Emphasis on the positive.

Experience had taught her that any man could be a father. A good father, however, was not so easy to find. As she knew only too well.

An unwanted rush of guilt tightened Maggie's throat. She swallowed hard, determined not to let Kevin see the doubts that haunted her. Not for the first time, she regretted the choices she'd made in her life.

When her ex-husband had aggressively pursued her, she'd been terribly naive. He was smooth and polished, a charmer when he wanted to be. No wonder she'd been an easy target for him.

Unfortunately the charm had been only a facade. Once they were married, his need to dominate emerged. So had the tirades, the abuse and the whittling away of her self-esteem. It had taken her a long time to find the strength to escape his control.

Now she was left to pick up the pieces of her life and Kevin's. A job that, in most ways, she felt confident to handle—until now. While she hated to admit it, no matter how determined she might be, there were some parental duties that proved to be impossible.

The screen door opened at the house next door.

Maggie glanced across the yard and saw Jason stepping out onto his porch. With an amused smile, he leaned a shoulder against the porch railing as he watched their attempt at baseball.

"Wonderful," Maggie muttered to herself. "My humiliation is now complete."

Momentarily distracted, she gasped as the ball whizzed past mere inches from her nose.

"Mom, you've gotta pay attention."

Maggie gulped. "Thanks for the warning, Kevin."

The ball tumbled into the neighboring yard.

Jason sauntered out onto the thick, green grass, and picked up the wayward ball. Then he tossed it into the air with an ease Maggie could only dream of possessing. Slowly, without asking, he crossed the yard and joined them.

He went directly to Kevin, handing him the ball. Taking Kevin's hand in his gently, he showed him the proper way to hold the ball. "Put your first two fingers here, on top, along the seams. That's it. Now, put your thumb right underneath, right there on the bottom seam. Good."

Bringing his throwing arm back, Jason turned Kevin's small body so his front shoulder was pointed toward her. "Keep your weight on your back foot, your arm behind you, the elbow bent. That's it. Now, keep your eye on your target." He flashed another grin, giving Kevin a conspiratorial wink. "That's your mother. Take a step forward, putting your weight on your front foot now. And let go of the ball."

Maggie ducked as the ball sailed past her with a speed

and accuracy she'd thought her son would never attain. There was no way she could have caught that hand-burning throw.

The chuckle of amusement coming from across the yard was unmistakably adult male.

Hands on her hips, she glared at their uninvited guest. "If you haven't noticed, I don't have a glove. I'm at a disadvantage. I'd like to see you catch that thing without suffering bodily harm."

Undaunted by her show of ill temper, Jason slowly strode toward her. She saw the flash of even white teeth as his smile deepened. Maggie's breath caught as he neared, stopping mere inches from touching her. Gooseflesh prickled her skin as he gave her body an appreciative scan. "It would be a shame if you were to get hurt."

Warning bells sounded in her mind, telling her to run, not walk, across the yard and escape his unnerving presence. But she didn't. She couldn't. She was frozen to the spot, waiting for his next move.

A confusing mix of relief and disappointment churned inside her as he stepped around her and headed for the forgotten baseball.

Ignoring the irrational grumblings of neglect stirring deep within her, Maggie scooted out of harm's way. She took a seat on the top step of her back porch and she watched in amazement as Jason turned her clumsy little boy into a halfway decent baseball player. For the first time ever, their backyard was filled with hoots of laughter, words of encouragement and a healthy amount of teasing from all three parties involved.

Maggie marveled at the change. Moments ago the situation seemed hopeless. Neither she nor Kevin knew the first thing about baseball. But all that ended with Jason's arrival. He'd turned a dismal scene into one filled with promise and hope. Her son was given a chance to fit in, to be normal. For that, she would be eternally grateful.

Time passed too quickly. Thickening clouds scudded past in the evening sky. An early twilight settled across the yard.

Maggie stood, swiping a hand across the backside of her jeans. "Time to go in, Kevin."

"Not yet, Mom," Kevin pleaded.

Jason smiled and gave a helpless shrug.

Maggie shook her head, moving toward the pair. "It's getting dark, Kevin. I think it's going to rain. Soon there won't be enough light to see the ball."

"Aw, Mom," Kevin whined.

"I'll tell you what, Kevin," Jason said, heading off an argument. "As long as I don't have to work, how about if we set aside a little time each night to practice?"

Kevin's face lit up. "Really?"

"Yeah, really." Jason glanced at Maggie. "That is, if it's okay with your mom."

The smile on Kevin's face faltered. As though bracing himself for disappointment, he raised an anxious brow and looked to Maggie for approval.

Maggie bit her lip, stopping the refusal that lay on the tip of her tongue. Her protective instincts were telling her that she shouldn't allow Jason to get any more involved in their lives. But the hopeful look in her son's eyes swayed her better judgment.

How could she say no? Not when he'd had so many disappointments in his young life already.

"Kevin, why don't you let me talk to Mr. Gallagher for a minute? You go inside and get ready for your bath."

"Aw, Mom."

"Scoot," she said, her tone brooking no argument.

Kevin dragged his heels as he headed for the house. The

screen door banged shut behind him, making his displeasure clear.

As soon as Kevin was out of earshot, Jason said, "I'm sorry. I didn't mean to put you on the spot."

"You haven't," she lied, averting her gaze. "It's just I—I don't want Kevin to cause you any trouble."

"Kevin? Trouble? Far from it." He shook his head, a ghost of a smile touching his lips. "The truth is, it's been a long time since I've had a chance to play pitch and catch. I didn't realize how much I missed it."

There was something in his tone, a wistfulness that hadn't been there before. Once again, Maggie was reminded of something Kevin had mentioned when they'd first met—his son, Jason's missing child. She fought the urge to ask him about the boy who wouldn't be needing to use his abandoned baseball glove.

"I guess it'll be okay," she said, unable to believe the words slipping from her mouth. For some reason, she felt she could trust Jason. Or was it merely her heart telling her it was time she needed to trust someone, anyone, again? "As long as you don't mind…"

"I don't mind," Jason said, his gaze steady on her.

She couldn't find the words to end their conversation, to bid him good-night. Nor did she have the strength to look away. Silence lengthened between them. The breeze picked up, carrying with it the promise of an approaching storm. Maggie shivered, blaming the cooling effects of the changing weather for her reaction, not the discomfiting presence of the man before her.

Jason was the first to break the spell of silence. He shifted his stance, one foot to another, as though searching for safer ground. "Bob Williams is out of danger. I checked with the hospital before my shift was up."

"I know," she said, smiling despite herself. "I called earlier, too."

He returned her smile. "Saving a man's life leaves a lasting impression. I guess neither of us will be able to forget the experience for a while."

"No, I guess not." Maggie searched his face. There was no glint of curiosity. No hidden messages. Just an honest statement of fact.

Relief poured through her. Less than an hour ago, she'd been on pins and needles, waiting for Jason to accuse her of being a liar, to have guessed the truth. That she was a trained medical professional. That he knew she was a woman running from the law, running from her past.

But now all that seemed to have changed.

In Jason's pale blue eyes, she saw a loneliness that was reflected in her own heart. Perhaps they weren't so different, after all. For the first time she believed him when he said he was only looking for a good neighbor, a friend.

The slamming of a door in her house reminded her that her son was still waiting for an answer. She glanced at the light glowing in the kitchen and knew it was time for her to go. "I think I'd better check on Kevin."

"I suppose that might be best," he said with a smile. "That is, if you still want your house to be standing in the morning."

Despite the casual reply, she heard a hint of disappointment in his tone. He didn't want her to leave.

Heat lightning flickered in the distance, warning her to tread carefully.

Unnerved, she took a cautious step back, heading for her house, her haven of safety. Feeling awkward and clumsy, she said abruptly, "Good night, Jason."

"Good night, Maggie," he returned, his expression unreadable in the thickening darkness.

Turning on her heel, she fled across the yard, not stopping until she was safely inside. Only then did she allow herself a second glance.

By then he was gone. He'd disappeared into the night with a swiftness that surprised her. She refused to acknowledge the disappointment thrumming through her veins.

Calling herself a fool, she turned away from the door and stared at the map on the kitchen table.

Maggie's heart caught in her throat. She'd forgotten about the map and her decision to find a new home. Somehow, leaving Wyndchester didn't seem quite as urgent as it had earlier.

Walking to the table, she picked up the map and slowly folded it along its well-worn creases, putting it away for another day.

Chapter 5

The storm outside broke soon after Maggie went into the house. The storm inside was averted, once Kevin was given an assurance that she would allow him baseball-practice sessions with Jason. A short time later, Kevin went peacefully to sleep for the night. Now, except for the steady drumming of rain on the roof, the house was finally quiet.

With the windows closed against the weather, the rooms were hot and airless. Maggie felt as though the walls were closing in on her. Second thoughts were the real cause of her disquietude, she reluctantly admitted to herself. She had allowed Jason a foothold in her life.

Short of disappointing her son, she didn't know how she could have acted differently. Lifting her hair from the back of her neck, she gave a weary sigh. Perhaps a soak in the tub would soothe her nerves.

Before she had time to act on the impulse, the doorbell rang. Maggie froze. A bolt of panic traveled through her, riveting her to the spot. No matter how much distance she might put between herself and her ex-husband, there would always be the fear that somehow he would find her.

She forced herself to move and walked slowly to the living-room window, flipping on the porch light as she went. Pulling back the lace curtain slightly, she peered outside. To her surprise, Jenny Lewis, the young waitress from the diner, stood on the stoop.

Fears forgotten, she hurried to the front door, slid off the safety chain and unlocked the dead bolt. Then she threw open the door and greeted her friend. "Jenny, this is a surprise. I…"

Her voice faltered, the words fading at the sight of the young woman. Despite the damp heat of the night, Jenny was shivering. Rain had splattered her clothes, leaving dark blotches on her blouse and denim skirt. Her dark hair was slicked back from her face as though she'd just run her fingers carelessly through it. She was pale, her face tear-stained.

Jenny attempted a smile and failed. "I hope you don't mind my calling so late. But I really needed to talk to someone."

"Don't be silly," Maggie said, taking her friend by the arm and pulling her inside. "My door's open to you at any hour."

"Thank you, Maggie." Jenny's tiny frame seemed even more fragile beneath the weight of whatever was troubling her.

Maggie's nurturing instincts kicked in. "Can I get you a hot drink? Something to eat?"

"No." Jenny pressed a hand to her stomach. "I don't think I could keep anything down even if I tried."

Maggie motioned toward the living-room couch. "Why don't you sit down?"

Nodding, Jenny stumbled across the room and sank onto

the worn couch. She looked so miserable Maggie's heart caught.

"Aw, honey. What's wrong?" she asked, sitting down next to her, draping an arm about her shoulders.

"It's Joe."

"Your fiancé?"

Jenny nodded.

When she didn't continue, Maggie prompted her. "Did you two have a fight?"

"No, Joe's out of town studying for the bar exam." Her voice trembled. Her eyes sparkled with unshed tears. "I haven't talked to him in almost a week."

"Then…what is it?" Maggie shook her head, feeling confused.

"If Joe were here, I wouldn't have been with Stan tonight," she whispered, averting her gaze, unable to look Maggie in the eye.

"Stan?" Slowly understanding dawned. "You mean *Officer* Stan Wilson?"

Jenny nodded miserably. She kept her eyes focused on the faded cabbage roses in the rug at her feet as a single tear trickled down her cheek. "He wanted to talk to me about the wedding. I thought…what harm could there be in talking? We've known each other for a long time."

Fear constricted Maggie's chest, making it hard to breathe. "Jenny, look at me," she said, turning her friend to face her. "Did Stan hurt you?"

"No, of course not. Stan would never…" She shook her head, embarrassment clouding her expression. "That wasn't the problem."

Maggie frowned. "I don't understand."

"I kissed him," Jenny said, the words so soft Maggie could barely hear them.

Relief coursed through her. She bit her lip to stop from

smiling. "Jenny, I don't think you need to worry about one little kiss."

"It was more than a kiss," Jenny blurted in a rush. "Stan and I...we almost..." Twin spots of color stained her pale cheeks. Her voice quivering, she said, "We almost made love."

Maggie cleared her throat, searching for the appropriate response. "Jenny, sometimes in the heat of the moment we do things we might not normally consider."

"You don't understand. I *wanted* to make love to him. If it wasn't for Joe's engagement ring getting caught on Stan's shirt, I *would* have made love to him."

"I see," Maggie said, careful to keep her tone neutral. It wasn't her place to judge anyone else's actions, especially not when it came to matters of the heart.

Jenny buried her face in her hands. Tears choking her voice, she moaned, "What's the matter with me, Maggie?"

"There's nothing wrong with you, honey." Maggie rubbed a soothing hand against her friend's back, feeling the quivering sobs that shook her slender frame. "You're just having second thoughts, that's all."

"Second thoughts?" Jenny sat up, laughing bitterly, as she wiped at the tears dampening her face. "Not thinking, that's my problem. Joe's everything I've ever wanted in a man. He comes from a good family. He's got a college education. And once he passes his bar exam, he'll be making such a good living I'll never have to worry about money again."

"But does he make you happy?"

Jenny didn't answer.

Maggie drew in a considering breath before plunging on. "Jenny, I know I've told you this before, but money isn't everything."

"I'm not so sure about that," Jenny said, turning a flat,

emotionless gaze on Maggie. "You've never seen where I live, have you?"

Maggie shook her head.

"My home is in a trailer park outside of town. I live there with my mother because we can't afford anything better. My daddy ran off when I was just a little girl. My momma's been drowning her sorrows in booze ever since."

Maggie didn't comment. Instinctively she knew Jenny wasn't looking for pity. What she needed was a sounding board, a person with whom to share her problems. Quietly she waited for Jenny to continue.

Jenny pressed her lips into a thin, hard line. For a long moment, she stared blankly across the room, as though focusing on a distant memory. Abruptly she broke the silence. "When I was five, I used to believe in fairy tales. Every night, I'd dream about a white knight who'd come and rescue me from my fate. When I was thirteen, I knew that fairy tales didn't come true. That the only way I was going to move out of the trailer park was by being smart."

Emotion filled Maggie's heart. She and Jenny had more in common than she'd first realized. Both had been raised by single mothers. Both had had less-than-happy childhoods. While Maggie's mother never drank, she'd been bitter about her husband's abandonment, hating all men with equal zeal. Her rancor had permanently tainted Maggie's life.

Maggie had rushed into marriage, determined to prove her mother's warped view of men wrong. When her marriage failed, her confidence was rocked. She still wondered if her mother had been right. If any man could ever be trusted.

Sternly she pushed the unpleasant memories from her mind, concentrating, instead, on her friend's problem. "Jenny, I don't know what to tell you. My heart says you shouldn't agree to a marriage for the sake of financial security alone.''

"I do care about Joe," she said quietly.

"But do you love him?"

New tears threatened. "I thought I did."

"Aw, honey." Maggie enfolded her in a hug, ignoring her wet clothes, circling her in the comforting warmth of her friendship. "You just need some time to think things out so you won't do anything you'll regret later."

"Time is the one thing I don't have. The wedding's only a few weeks away." Releasing a harsh breath, Jenny rose to her feet. "I've got to go. I've bothered you long enough for one night."

Maggie shook her head. "Don't ever think that. Promise me, Jenny. If you ever need someone to talk to, come to me. Anytime."

"I promise," Jenny said, her smile weak. She moved toward the door. "Thanks for listening, Maggie."

"I don't know how much help I've been. You should really be listening to your heart," Maggie said, opening the door. "It'll tell you more than I could."

"That's not so easy to do," Jenny said. She stepped outside, staring at the ribbons of falling rain. "Not when common sense is telling me to do something else."

Maggie sighed. "Take care of yourself, Jenny."

Jenny didn't answer. With a wave of her hand, she hurried off the porch, disappearing into the rain-shrouded night.

Slowly Maggie closed the door behind her. Physically drained, she collapsed against the solid wood frame. She closed her eyes and shook her head. Of all the people from whom Jenny could have sought emotional advice, why did she have to choose her?

Maggie would have thought it was painfully obvious that she didn't have a clue when it came to loving a man.

Unbidden, her mind's eye conjured up an image of her mother's face, narrowed with bitterness, as she railed against men, Maggie's father in particular. The image flashed forward, giving her a disturbing picture of her ex-husband's face contorted in anger.

Unwanted tears stung her eyes. Blinking hard, not allowing herself such weakness, she pushed herself away from the door. The air in the house felt hotter, more stifling, than before. She couldn't breathe. She couldn't think straight, not without memories of the past getting in her way.

Making up her mind quickly, she strode barefoot through the living room into the kitchen, not stopping until she stepped outside onto the cold, wet grass of her backyard. She shivered as the rain pelted her overheated skin. Letting the droplets rain down upon her, she lifted her hands, then her face to the cloud-ladened sky.

Under the cover of darkness, slowly, quietly, she spun around in a mind-clearing circle, willing the bath of steady rainwater to cleanse all the doubts and bitterness of her past away.

Jason froze in his tracks. He felt like an intruder, a peeping Tom, watching a scene that was never meant to be viewed. One minute he was dashing through the rain, taking the trash out to the garbage can in the garage, the next he was privy to a moment so erotic he could never have imagined it, not even in his wildest dreams.

Maggie was standing in the middle of her backyard, circling and swaying. Her arms were upraised, as though in welcome to the rain that soaked her skin. Her clothes clung to her slender curves, leaving little to the imagination. She looked like a sea nymph out of place on solid land.

Seconds ticked by like hours. Guilt and awareness stirred deep inside him as he stood helplessly watching the scene. If he left the cover of the garage, Maggie would see him. Embarrassment on both their parts would be the only result.

But if he stayed, hidden beneath the darkness of the garage's eaves, he would feel every bit the voyeur he'd unwittingly become.

His decision was made for him.

Unexpectedly, with a cry of pain that ripped his heart in two, Maggie came to an abrupt stop. As though the strength had left her, her knees buckled and she slumped to the ground. Despite the drumming of the rain on the roof above his head and the pounding of his pulse in his ears, he heard her soft sobs of despair.

Not giving himself a chance to reconsider, he acted on impulse. Crossing his backyard to hers, he ignored the rain that peppered his skin. Puddles of water pooled in the grass, soaking his shoes, chilling his feet as he stepped unseeingly through them. Raindrops fell into his eyes, blurring his vision, blurring his reasoning.

He blinked hard, steeling himself for Maggie's reaction to his presence. He doubted if his intrusion would be met with open arms. A slap on the face would be more likely.

But the thought of rejection didn't stop him. He'd seen the toll the day's events had taken on her. This morning she'd saved a man's life. This evening she'd struggled to deal with the problems of raising a son on her own. It wasn't any wonder she'd broken beneath the weight of such pressure. Whether she wanted to admit it or not, Maggie needed a friend to lean on, someone to comfort her after a long and horrendous day.

He intended to be that friend.

As Jason neared, his step slowed. Kneeling on the soggy ground, her face buried in her hands, Maggie's slender body shook with each sobbing breath she drew. His determination faltered. Perhaps he was wrong. Perhaps one's anguish, especially so deep and so painful as Maggie's, shouldn't be witnessed by another soul.

Before he could change his mind, however, as though sensing his presence, Maggie jerked her head to attention. Through the sheets of pouring rain, she stared up at him. Her mouth opened, but no sound emitted. Then, her eyes wild and unseeing, she scrambled backward, slipping and sliding on the wet grass as she struggled to her feet.

"Maggie," he said, keeping his voice soft, his approach slow, trying to soothe her panic.

She did not answer. All he heard was a whimper of terror, not unlike that of a cornered animal. Maggie was scared to death. Of him? But why? Granted, he'd surprised her, caught her off guard by joining her in the rain. But he'd done nothing to harm her, nothing to warrant such a primal reaction.

"Maggie, wait," he said, louder this time, his voice firm, trying to penetrate her paralyzing shell of fear. He reached out a hand, but did not touch her, then lowered himself to her eye level. Down on one knee, his hand still extended, he wondered how to help her. "Maggie, look at me. It's Jason. I promise, I'm not going to hurt you."

The words had the desired effect. Maggie stopped her struggle. Sitting on the rain-soaked grass, she stared at him. Thick, wet strands of hair clung to her face. Her T-shirt and jeans were molded to her slender curves. Her breasts rose and fell with each shuddering breath she drew.

Encouraged, he kept his voice slow and easy, soothing her with words while his hands itched to reach out and touch her. "I was outside in the garage. I heard you...crying. I thought maybe I could help." His heart pounding, he added, "You've got to believe me, Maggie. I didn't mean to scare you."

She didn't answer. Although the look in her eyes wasn't quite so wild or as terrified.

An uneasy silence fell between them. The only sound was their strained breathing and the rain as it pounded down, relentless in its assault.

He saw her trembling in the meager light spilling from the kitchen window of her house—from the chill of the rain, or from a lingering fear, he wasn't sure which. Needlessly he said, "You're shivering."

"I'm fine," she said at last. Her unsteady voice brought him a rush of sweet relief.

"You're soaked. You need to go inside," he persisted, standing slowly.

Glancing away, looking too weak to argue, she nodded an agreement. Her bare feet slid out from beneath her on the wet grass as she tried to stand.

Without thinking, Jason reached out a hand and slipped it under her arm to steady her.

She flinched at his touch. But he didn't let go.

"I'm not going to hurt you," he said, looking into her wide-eyed gaze. He felt the tremors that shook her body and, once again, wondered at the cause of such fear. "It'll be quicker if you let me help you."

With obvious reluctance, she yielded to his assistance.

Holding her as close as he dared, he lifted her to her feet. Together they crossed the yard to her house. The lights shimmered in the windows, looking so much more inviting than the dark and wet skies. The soles of his tennis shoes thudded against the wooden porch. Her bare feet padded softly next to his.

Maggie hesitated at the door, uncertain what to do next.

Jason took the initiative. Without asking, he opened the

screen door. The hinges squeaked a protest, warning him to move carefully. The door banged shut behind them, startling him, as they stepped into the kitchen.

It was the first time he'd been inside her house. Despite the circumstances, he liked what he saw. The wooden cabinets were old, but they had recently been painted a creamy white. Blue-and-white-checked curtains brightened the windows. Colorful rag rugs covered the worn linoleum floor. Maggie's little kitchen felt like a home.

Jason helped her to the table, seating her on one of the chrome-and-vinyl chairs. Reluctantly he released the grip he had on her arm, immediately missing the reassuring feel of her body. He lingered close, taking a moment to study her pale face. The fact that she didn't seem to object to his proximity spoke of the depth of the shock she was still in.

Brushing away his concern, ignoring his own discomfort caused by wet shoes and damp clothes, he looked around for something constructive to do. He spotted the cobalt blue teapot on the stovetop. Crouching down to her level, searching her green eyes for a spark of life, he said, "I'm going to make you a hot drink."

She blinked, looking at him as though through a mist of confusion. Then her response, soft and weak though it was, gave him hope for her recovery. "There are teabags...on the shelf... in the flowered canister."

He smiled his relief. "Okay. It'll just be a minute."

Clumsily, he splattered water as he filled the teapot, belying his show of confidence. Maggie didn't move, not even when he banged open the cabinets, searching for a cup. Instead, she stared blankly at the floor, watching the water drip from her clothes and puddle at her feet.

"You need a towel, Maggie. Where can I find one?" he asked, his tone firm, allowing no argument.

There was a touch of resignation in her voice as she said, "Upstairs, in the hallway closet."

Nodding, he strode through the kitchen, making his way as quickly and quietly as possible up the stairs. Kevin was asleep. The last thing he wanted was to wake the boy and let him see his mother in such distress. Grabbing a couple of thick towels from the closet shelf, he hurried back to Maggie.

She was at the stove when he reentered the kitchen. Her back to him, he couldn't see the expression on her face. But she appeared stronger, the trembling not quite so noticeable. She wouldn't be needing his help much longer. Gripping the towels in his hands, he ignored the tug of disappointment in his chest and waited for her to ask him to leave.

There were two mugs of tea in her hands when she turned around. Embarrassed color bloomed on her face as she glanced at him. "I thought we could both use a hot drink."

"Thanks," he said, trying to hide his surprised relief. "I'd like that."

She placed the mugs on the table, pulling one of them toward her as she took her place, once again, on the vinyl-and-chrome chair. Looking up at him, holding his gaze with hers, she asked, "Won't you sit down?"

It was his turn to feel the heat of embarrassment. Handing her the towels, he pulled out a chair and slid into the seat, his wet clothes making a squishy noise.

She returned one of the towels to him, the trace of a smile lifting the corner of her mouth. "I think *you* might need one of these."

"Thanks," he mumbled, burying his hot face in the cool, clean-scented towel. He'd tried to be the hero, rescuing the damsel in distress. Somehow the tables got turned. *Just who was saving whom now?*

He felt the weight of her gaze. Like a butterfly, her gaze flitted away when he looked up and caught her studying him. Holding the towel on her lap, she picked up her tea and blew the steam off the top. Unable to help himself, Jason studied the delicate shape of her pursed lips.

Slowly, as though aware of his interest, she lowered the mug without drinking. Biting down nervously on that beautiful lower lip, keeping her gaze focused on the table, she said, "I'm sorry about before. I don't know why I acted so jumpy."

"There's no reason to apologize."

"You caught me off guard. I wasn't expecting anyone..."

"Like I said, there's no need for an apology. If anyone should be sorry, it's me. I'm the one who invaded your privacy."

She looked at him, her green eyes searching his face. "Why did you?"

"Invade your privacy?"

She nodded, her gaze uncertain.

Jason shifted uncomfortably in his seat. What could he say? The truth? That since the day he'd met her, she intrigued him? That no matter how hard he tried, he couldn't keep his mind off her?

He didn't think she was ready for that much honesty.

Instead, he released a long breath and embellished the truth. "A hazard of my job, I guess. I can't sit back and watch someone in trouble. It seems I have to stick my nose into other people's business, even when it doesn't belong."

She turned her cup in a half circle on the table. Watching the clouds of cooling tea, she appeared lost in thought, considering his answer. "I'm not in trouble. Not now, anyway.

Before he died, my husband..." Her voice broke. She swallowed hard.

Jason waited. His nerves felt taut as he forced himself to be patient, letting her struggle for the right words. Experience had taught him that anything this hard to say must be important.

Finally she blurted, "My husband...he had a bad temper."

"He hit you." Miraculously he kept his tone even, despite the hot fist of anger that gripped his heart. Drawing in a steadying breath, he asked, "Kevin, too?"

She nodded, unable to look at him.

A weight lifted from his shoulders. Answers to questions that had nagged him fell into place. Maggie's skittishness, her reluctance to be neighborly, the fear he saw in her eyes every time he drew near, now he understood all of those things.

How could he have been so blind? In his line of work, he'd dealt with domestic abuse many times. Maggie had that haunted, hollow-eyed look about her, the one he'd seen so often in the eyes of abused wives. If it hadn't been for his pride getting in the way, surely he would have noticed before.

"Pardon me for saying so, but I'm not sorry that your husband is dead. In my book, any man who hits a woman and a child doesn't deserve to live."

She looked at him, startled by his vehemence.

Not too smart, Gallagher, he chastized himself. Once again he'd let his emotions control his judgment.

"He can't hurt me anymore," she said, shaking her head, a trace of that familiar stubborn determination returning to her voice.

Jason wondered who she was trying to convince. Him? Or herself? Choosing his words carefully, he said, "Maybe not physically. But mentally he's still got you in the palm of his hand.''

"I'm dealing with it," she said, her tone sharp, final, inviting no further discussion.

Frustrated, Jason stared at her. He'd seen how she'd dealt with her past. By crying outside in the pouring rain, so her son wouldn't hear her sobs. As though sensing his disapproval, she hugged her arms tightly around her waist and shivered. Sighing, he pushed himself to his feet. "You need to get out of those wet things. It's time for me to leave."

Maggie didn't protest.

He paused, taking one last moment to study her. Her complexion was pale, making the freckles on her face stand out even more. Wet strands of strawberry blond hair curled about her shoulders. Her damp and muddied clothes clung to her body. Yet despite her disheveled appearance, Jason knew he'd never seen a more beautiful woman.

"Thank you, Maggie." The words sounded strained, his throat thick with unspoken emotion.

Confusion shadowed her eyes as she looked up at him, her brow furrowing in a frown.

Quietly he said, "For trusting me enough to share your past. You didn't have to do it, but I appreciate that you did."

A flicker of unreadable emotion crossed her face. She averted her eyes and turned her head away.

Knowing he'd overstayed his welcome, although wishing he could do more to help, Jason strode from the room, leaving Maggie to deal with the demons of her past on her own.

Chapter 6

"Mom, we're going to be late," Kevin complained, squirming impatiently at the door of the bathroom as he watched her apply her makeup.

"Kevin, the Spring Carnival doesn't have a set opening time," Maggie said calmly. "We can come and go whenever we please."

"I want to go *now.*"

Maggie chuckled. "I know you do. And we will—if you'd just let me finish getting ready."

He tried a new tack. His expression sober, his tone sincere, he said, "You don't need makeup, Mom. You look pretty just the way you are."

"Why thank you, sir," she said, smoothing a hand along the skirt of her mint-colored print sundress. Then, matching the sincerity of his tone, she added, "But when you're as old as I am, you really don't want everyone to see all your freckles."

Kevin sighed and leaned against the frame of the door.

Watching him out of the corner of her eye, Maggie dusted her cheeks with powder. "Did I tell you how proud I was of you today? You did such a great job playing Father Time in the class play."

"Only about a million times."

She smiled, then reached for a tube of peach-colored lipstick. "You didn't forget any of your lines."

"No, but my beard kept falling off."

"Hardly noticeable," she said, brushing away his concern. "The point is, you weren't afraid. You got up there in front of all those parents and did what you had to do. That took a lot of courage."

He shrugged, looking half embarrassed, half pleased with the compliment. Changing the subject, he said, "Sarah Moore forgot one of her lines. I had to tell her the beginning of it to get her started."

"That was nice of you."

"Yeah, well, she's okay. For a girl, anyway."

Maggie bit back a smile and applied her lipstick, hoping that nothing would ever change her son's simplistic view of the male/female relationship. Glad that his father's erratic behavior in the name of love and marriage hadn't jaundiced his innocence.

"I guess I'm finished," she said with one last glance in the mirror.

"Finally." Kevin heaved a sigh. He turned and headed for the staircase.

Maggie followed at a slower pace, the heels of her sandals clicking on the wooden steps. Her heart fluttered with trepidation. If it wasn't for Kevin, she wouldn't be going to the school's Spring Carnival. If it was up to her, she'd stay in her own house where it was safe and familiar.

Meeting new people, socializing with the locals outside the diner—it was all a new experience for her. One she wasn't sure she was ready to handle. One she wasn't sure was wise.

Since running away from California, it had always been her policy to stay on the fringes of a town's social circle. For a year and a half, she'd been a spectator, not a participant. But as Kevin grew older, his needs had changed. He craved friendship, the camaraderie that came with being part of a group, the security of being accepted by others.

How could she deny him such a normal part of childhood?

And, to be honest, was she so different? Since coming to Wyndchester, she realized how isolated her life had become...how lonely she was.

"Come on, Mom," Kevin said, forcing her out of her troubled thoughts. He stood impatiently at the front door, frowning as he watched her hesitant pace down the stairs. "You're moving too slow."

"I'm wearing sandals and a sundress. It wouldn't look right if I ran in a dress," she said, grabbing her sweater from the coatrack. She handed Kevin a jacket. "Take this along for later. In case it gets cold."

"Why didn't you wear tennis shoes and jeans like me?" he grumbled, opening the door.

She shrugged. "Because it's fun to dress up."

Rolling his eyes, he gave a silent opinion of an adult's view of a good time. He stepped outside and bolted across the porch. His tennis shoes thumped on the wooden floor. Maggie shook her head and double-locked the door behind her.

A light breeze caressed the bare skin of her arms. The sun was just beginning to set, turning the sky into a pastel palette of pinks and blues. It promised to be a beautiful evening for a street party. Maggie's spirits lifted, her qualms forgotten in the serenity of the moment.

Until they passed the house next door.

No lights shone inside. It looked quiet, deserted. Kevin paused, glancing at the white house with the dark blue shutters. "Do you think Mr. Gallagher will be at the carnival?"

Butterflies danced in her stomach. Maggie felt her face warm with embarrassment. The last time she saw Jason, she hadn't been at her best. "I don't know, Kevin. He's been awfully busy lately."

So busy, in fact, that in the three days since their encounter in the rain she hadn't seen hide nor hair of him. Not at the diner. Not in their adjoining backyards. His absence had become so obvious Maggie couldn't help but wonder if he was avoiding her.

Not that she blamed him. He'd witnessed her at her worst. She'd been an emotional wreck, haunted by the past, on the brink of losing total control. Jason had seen her distress and had tried to help.

And how had she reacted?

With fear.

In the darkness of the stormy night, she'd lost all perspective. In her mind it hadn't been Jason reaching out to her, it had been her ex-husband. Expecting a blow, her protective instincts had kicked into gear. Blindly she had fought to flee his threatening presence.

But she'd been wrong. Jason wasn't a threat. He'd been gentle and strong, keeping his distance, yet at the same time soothing her fears.

And when she'd confided a small portion of her past, he'd thanked her for her honesty.

Distracted, Maggie caught a heel on a bump in the sidewalk. Her heart lurched as she kept herself from falling. Her cheeks flushed at the painful memory rather than the near fall.

Honesty. She'd never felt so dishonest before in her life.

Jason believed she was a widow. He didn't know she was a fugitive from justice, running away from an abusive ex-husband. With her lie, she'd betrayed one of the few men who'd shown her nothing but kindness and sincerity.

Kevin grabbed her hand, tugging hard, demanding her attention. "Look, Mom. There's the party."

Ahead, Maggie saw strings of lights crisscrossing the playground and the streets that bordered the school. Beneath the lights, the grounds were teaming with people of all ages. Carnival rides and game booths were scattered about. Sounds of conversation and laughter and a band tuning up in the distance drifted on the soft breeze. The scent of popcorn and cotton candy filled the air, making her mouth water.

It had been so long since she'd been to a party. A buzz of excitement raced through her veins. Kevin didn't bother to conceal his emotions. He hopped eagerly from one foot to another, obviously impressed by the scene. To Maggie, the awed expression on her son's face was priceless.

"There's a Ferris wheel, Mom!" he said, pointing.

"I see it. And look, there's a carousel, too."

Kevin pulled on her arm. "Come on, Mom. Let's go ride 'em."

"Me?" Maggie laughed, dragging her heels. "I don't know, Kevin. I don't remember the last time I ever—"

Tommy Marshall, Kevin's best friend, came to her rescue. He skidded to a stop before them, mere inches from a collision. "Come on, Kevin. The rides just opened. Let's get in line."

Kevin looked to her for permission, a silent plea in his eyes.

Maggie hesitated. Letting go, putting her son's safety in the hands of others, was something she'd never felt comfortable doing. She swallowed her fears and forced a smile.

"Of course you can. Go ahead. I won't be far behind—in case you need anything."

Kevin grinned, then sped off without her.

For the next hour Maggie kept a discreet eye on her son's activities. His young face was lit up with an excitement equal to that of any of the other children running about the schoolyard. Occasionally his eyes searched the grounds. When he found her, he smiled and waved. Then, reassured, he went back to his friends.

Maggie swallowed the lump in her throat. It wouldn't be long before he wouldn't need her. Pushing the thought from her mind, she turned before Kevin could see the tears misting her eyes.

And collided with the solid form of a male body.

Startled, Maggie blinked in surprise, an apology on the tip of her tongue. The words died as she looked up into a pair of familiar blue eyes.

For the first time in years, the closeness of a man did not scare her. Instead, her discomfort was of a much more confusing nature. Awareness buffeted her senses as she stared at Jason Gallagher's amused face.

"Sorry..." they chorused.

Maggie's cheeks flushed.

They tried again.

"I didn't see..."

"I wasn't looking..."

They stopped, studied each other warily. One second passed, then two...and they burst into a tension-easing round of laughter.

Jason wasn't in uniform this evening. He wore a pair of blue jeans that molded his long, muscular legs and a navy blue polo shirt that emphasized the breadth of his shoulders. He looked relaxed and far too handsome.

Maggie drew in a steadying breath and inhaled the spicy

scent of his cologne. She felt light-headed, and her stomach churned with another shot of awareness.

"Where's Kevin?" Jason asked.

Maggie pointed to the ferris wheel. "With friends, going on the rides."

Jason nodded. "I'm sure he's having a good time."

A silence fell between them. Maggie struggled to fill the gap. "You're not working tonight?"

"Not officially," he said with a smile, his even white teeth flashing against his tanned skin. "I'm just keeping an eye on the party goers. Making sure everything stays peaceful."

"I'm glad you've got the night off," she said without thinking. When he turned a questioning gaze on her, she felt the heat rise on her face. She stammered an excuse. "You've been so busy lately. I mean, I haven't seen you…" She cleared her throat. "Kevin was wondering when he'd play ball with you."

Maggie averted her gaze as the heat of embarrassment swept her body. Although she'd wondered about his absence these past few days, the last thing she wanted was for Jason to think she was keeping tabs on his comings and goings.

"I've been out of town, Maggie," he said quietly, as though he'd read her mind. "There was a district meeting in St. Louis I had to attend."

Unwanted relief poured through her. He hadn't been avoiding her. She hazarded a glance at him and saw the somber set of his face. "It's okay. You don't have to explain."

"I know I don't have to explain, but I wanted to. After all, I did promise Kevin I'd help him with baseball. I don't want to give him—" he paused, searching her face "—or anyone else the wrong idea."

Maggie didn't answer. She couldn't. A blanket of confusing awareness had settled over her. A silence, thick with the promise of friendship—and, perhaps, something more—lengthened between them. Strains of music from the band playing a slow, country tune filled the air. Loud voices of party goers sounded close. A roulette wheel clackety-clacked nearby. Yet Maggie barely heard the noise. All she could hear was the pounding of her heart.

To her relief, Officer Stan Wilson, dressed in uniform blues, approached them. With a smile of recognition for Maggie, he said, "Sorry to bother you, Chief. But I thought I'd better let you know we've got a group of teenagers over there—" he motioned toward the far side of the playground "—we caught sneaking in bottles of long-neck beer."

Jason sighed, nodded. He shot Maggie an apologetic glance. "I'd better go."

The moment had become too intimate. She'd been given a reprieve. Maggie tried not to let her relief show. "Of course. You've got a job to do."

He raised a brow, his expression hopeful. "Maybe I'll see you later."

"Maybe." Maggie shrugged, trying her best to appear indifferent.

Jason's expression shifted, his disappointment obvious. With a silent nod goodbye, he turned and weaved his way through the crowd. Maggie had no problem following his progress; he stood a head taller than most of the crowd. He moved with a grace and ease that was unusual for a man his size. Even with a distance between them, she could still feel the powerful effect of his presence.

Slowly Maggie released a breath she hadn't realized she'd been holding. Then she willed her racing heart to slow. She wasn't sure what troubled her most—the fact that there was something different about their relationship, that more than a friendship was growing between them.

Or that she welcomed the change.

The boys were sixteen and seventeen, still wet behind the ears. But they had the swaggering bravado of men much older. They seemed amused by their predicament, cracking jokes about being caught with the beer. Not seeming to understand they'd just broken the law.

Jason shook his head. He really didn't need this trouble tonight. His patience with the group of rowdies growing thin, he turned to Stan Wilson and said, "Load 'em up and take 'em to the jail."

"To the jail?" Stan raised a brow in surprise.

"They broke the law, didn't they, Officer Wilson?"

"Well, yeah, but…" Stan leaned close, his tone confiding. He pointed at a dark-haired boy wearing a pair of tight blue jeans and sporting several rings in his right ear. The boy looked city slick, street smart. He seemed out of place in a small town like Wyndchester. "That's Sammy Bosworth over there. His daddy's a big-shot lawyer. His momma practically runs every social function in town. They'll be raising a real stink if we arrest their son."

"I don't care whose son it is. Those kids think this is a joke. I think it's time we sobered them up. Don't you agree?"

A glint of admiration flickered in Stan's eyes. "Yes, sir, I certainly do." He stood taller, adjusting his gun belt around his slim hips. With a pleased smile, he nodded at the group of officers waiting nearby. "We'll take care of it right now, Chief."

Jason watched his officer's departure with a frowning gaze. Bosworth. The familiar name played in his mind. Brokenhearted Stan Wilson was in love with Joe Bosworth's fiancé. What were the chances that Joe and Sammy Bosworth were related?

Jason clenched his jaw in frustration. In a town this size? The chances were too good.

The boys—not without shouts of protest and a sprinkling of macho obscenities at the arresting officers—were placed in nearby patrol cars. Leaving the boys in the capable hands of his officers, Jason returned to the carnival.

He felt drawn to the ferris wheel. A burr of disappointment latched onto him when he didn't see Maggie in the spot where he'd left her. Perhaps it was for the best, he told himself, as he searched the grounds. No matter how hard he tried, he couldn't seem to find a way around her skittishness.

He'd seen the relief in her eyes when Officer Wilson had joined them. He wasn't blind to the fact that she was uncomfortable being alone with him. But knowing what he did now, that her late husband had been abusive, he wondered if it was only him or all men who scared her.

He hoped for the latter.

Because if it was true, and if he was patient enough, someday he just might have a chance at breaking through Maggie's protective shell.

He spotted her on the makeshift dance floor.

Jason stopped and watched as Kevin and Maggie attempted a dance on the blacktop playground. Not surprisingly Kevin was as awkward at dancing as he was at throwing a baseball. He was all thumbs and left feet. Attempting a two-step, he stomped on his mother's toes more times than not.

But Maggie didn't seem to mind. The melodic sound of her laughter carried across the night air. He'd never seen her look more relaxed or more beautiful. For her son, she smiled without reserve. Her green eyes twinkled with excitement. Her face shone with an inner light, one only love could bring. Jason felt a pang of envy and wondered what it would be like to be on the receiving end of such a look.

Then, in the middle of the dance, as though she'd felt the heat of his gaze, her smile melted. She glanced up, her troubled eyes searching the crowd.

And she found him.

Across the dance floor, their gazes met and held. Jason felt spellbound. He couldn't look away. Unreasonably he feared that if he did, she'd disappear into the night and he'd never see her again.

Maggie was the first to avert her gaze, returning her attention to her son.

When the dance ended, Jason hurriedly made his way to the pair, determined not to let her slip away. Maggie looked startled, her eyes widening when she spotted him. Kevin's back was to him when he approached. With the exaggerated politeness of a suitor, he tapped Kevin on the shoulder.

Kevin spun around. His face lit up with a bright smile when he recognized him. "Mr. Gallagher, you came!"

Jason smiled. "Evening, Kevin. Are you having a good time?"

"Yes, sir."

"That's great," he said, glancing at Maggie. She'd edged a step away, poised on the brink of fleeing. Before she could escape, he cleared his throat, feeling as tongue-tied and awkward as a schoolboy. "Kevin, if you don't mind, I'd like to steal your dance partner for a whirl around the dance floor."

Jason heard the sharp inhalation of Maggie's breath. She shook her head, opening her mouth to give what clearly would be a refusal.

But not before Kevin, his unwitting conspirator, gave his

instant approval. "Sure, Mr. Gallagher. You can dance with my mom all you want."

"Why, thank you, Kevin." He turned his attention to the boy's mother. Smiling encouragingly, he sought her consent. "Maggie?"

Looking as though she'd like to say no, Maggie bit her lower lip and shrugged in answer.

Not proud of himself, Jason took that as a yes.

His eyes dancing with excitement, Kevin raced across the blacktop, joining a group of boys who were watching from the bales of straw that surrounded the dance floor. A round of giggles and the fingers pointed in their direction told Jason that he and Maggie were the fodder for the young gossips. Kevin didn't seem to mind. His smile only seemed to grow wider in response.

Grinning with amusement, Jason looked at Maggie. She wasn't smiling. Her cool expression and frosty gaze said it all. She was not pleased with the situation.

The band began to play. Music swelled softly into the spring night air. The dance was to be a slow one.

Not giving Maggie a chance to change her mind, Jason pulled her into his arms. Keeping a respectful distance, yet holding her close enough to feel the heat of her body, Jason twirled her onto the dance floor.

Her reaction was immediate. She stiffened in the circle of his arms.

Swearing under his breath, Jason wondered if he'd made a mistake. Maybe he'd pushed her too hard, too fast. He never did know the meaning of doing anything slow.

Believing he could take on the responsibility of solving the world's problems had always been a fault of his. Fool that he was, he thought he could charm Maggie's fears away with a simple dance. He should have realized that it would take more time to heal her wounds.

"A lot of people here tonight," he said, searching for a way to break the ice.

She nodded, averting her gaze, looking anywhere but into his eyes.

Jason suppressed the urged to sigh. Doggedly he tried again. "I guess you know quite of few of the townspeople through the diner."

"I suppose," she said, her voice quiet, almost grudging in tone.

Encouraged, he gave a sheepish grin. "I've been in town more than three weeks and I'm still having trouble learning everybody's names, let alone their backgrounds."

"It takes time," she said, still not smiling.

Another awkward silence.

Jason was going through his own personal hell. Dancing with Maggie, holding her close, was a dream come true. Each time he inhaled, her sweet scent of powder and spring flowers filled his nostrils. Her skin felt smooth and warm. In his arms, she felt so delicate. When their bodies touched, she felt so soft where he was hard. Slowly, but surely, awareness heated the blood in his veins. Jason gritted his teeth. It took all his willpower to keep his body from having an ill-timed reaction.

"Chief Gallagher, this is a surprise." An older woman's voice sounded nearby, startling him out of his lustful thoughts.

Mildred McKinney and Henry Turnball smiled as they sidled up next to him and Maggie on the dance floor. The trashing of Mrs. McKinney's backyard had been one of the first calls he'd made here in Wyndchester. Henry Turnball's dog had been the culprit. Once on opposing ends of a complaint, the pair now appeared as though they'd made their peace with each other.

Jason smiled. "Mrs. McKinney, how are you this evening?"

"Oh, I'm just fine. I don't know when I've had such a good time," she said, glancing at her partner and smiling girlishly. "It's been years since I had a chance to kick my heels on a dance floor."

"Dancing keeps a body young," Henry said, giving her a mischievous wink.

"Stop that now, Henry. Or the chief here will have to lock you up for indecent behavior."

The couple giggled, looking much younger than their seventy-some years. Picking up the step, Henry directed his partner in a new direction. They waved their goodbyes as they waltzed away.

Maggie watched their departure with bemused interest. "They seem like such a nice couple. So happy. Even after all these years."

"Um...well, the truth is, I think they just started dating. You see, Mrs. McKinney's a widow. Mr. Turnball is her neighbor." Jason chuckled. "Officer Wilson and I, we sort of had a hand in playing matchmaker for the two."

She lifted a brow in surprise. "You did?"

"It's a long story."

"I like long stories," she said, the first encouraging words she'd said all night. An unexpected smile touched her lips. "Especially when they have a happy ending."

"Then I think you'll like this one," he said.

His gaze never left her face as he told her the details of the rottweiler caper. Their bodies drifted closer. Her laughter echoed in his ears, stirring awareness deep inside him. Little by little Maggie relaxed in his arms.

Jason, on the other hand, felt as though he were about to spontaneously combust from the combined heat of their bodies. His heart hammered in his chest. His muscles tightened in a vain effort for self-control. And contrary to his best intentions, his body reacted to Maggie's closeness in a most indiscreet manner, sending blood and heat to points southward. He gave a silent moan, feeling anything but relaxed.

Adding to his discomfort, one song turned to two, then a set of three…and Jason felt the sensual tension build inside him.

Maggie was a beautiful, desirable woman. He wanted her more than he'd wanted any other woman. He wasn't afraid to admit these feelings. For the first time he indulged himself. He pulled her closer, letting her know the strength of his attraction.

And Maggie did not seem afraid.

Instead, she gave a contented sigh, settling her soft, warm body against his. In a show of complete trust, she placed her head on his shoulder and let her eyes drift shut.

Jason drew in a deep breath, raising his eyes to the heavens. *Maggie, Maggie, Maggie, if only you knew what sweet misery you're putting me through.*

Too soon the music ended.

In the corner of the dance floor, where shadows lengthened and the crowd wasn't so thick, they remained tangled in each other's arms. Reluctantly Maggie lifted her head and looked up at him.

Jason couldn't find the strength to let her go.

They stared at each, the seconds passing slowly.

She drew in a deep breath. And he felt the warm fullness of her breasts press against his chest.

"Maggie…" he said, the word a mere whisper.

Her lips parted, but she did not answer.

He leaned closer, his mouth just a hairbreadth away from hers. Until he saw the look in her eyes, the uncertainty mixed with the want. And he knew he'd gone far enough for one night. Gathering all his strength, he forced himself to pull away.

Myriad emotions clouded Maggie's eyes. She took an unsteady step backward, looking lost and confused.

He wanted to reach out and reassure her, to tell her just how much he needed her. Instead, he smiled and said, "Thank you for the dance, Maggie."

She smiled back. It looked forced. "You're welcome, Jason."

Slowly he became aware of their surroundings. The band was tuning up for another song. Couples were beginning to crowd the floor for another round of dancing. Excited voices and laughter sounded much too close, reminding him they weren't alone.

With one last reluctant glance, Jason nodded his goodbye and turned away to continue his unofficial patrol of the festivities, allowing himself a modicum of hope in the disappointment he saw reflected in Maggie's eyes.

Chapter 7

Jason wasn't normally a paranoid man.

On the Monday morning after the Spring Carnival, however, he walked into the offices of the police department to a flurry of curious stares, whispered conversations and snickers of amusement from his staff. A hush fell on the group when he stopped to look around the room. Eyes were averted. Guilty expressions and a sudden interest in work told him his imagination hadn't been working overtime.

He had been the topic of the department's conversation.

Unlike his fellow lawmen, Officer Ray Schmitz felt no need for discretion. He acted as the office spokesman. "Say, Chief, where'd you learn how to dance so good?"

Jason narrowed a glance at the officer who'd asked the question. He was a big man, with blond hair cut in a crew-cut. Jason knew him to be competent policeman and a hard worker, who could be counted on to handle an emergency call with a levelheaded efficiency. At the moment, however, he had his feet propped lazily on his desk and a goofy smile pasted on his square, lantern-jawed face.

Behind him stood the officers from the evening shift, ready to pass on the reins of duty. Nearby, the morning crew awaited their daily briefing. At Officer Schmitz's question, there was an uncomfortable shuffling of feet and an attack of coughs to hide the guffaws. Mixed in between were a few brave souls who didn't bother to hide their grins.

"Why do you ask, Officer Schmitz?" Jason kept his expression sober, his tone serious. "Do you want me to give you a few lessons?"

Officer Schmitz's boot-clad feet dropped to the tiled floor with a thud. He nearly fell out of his chair. Recovering his aplomb, he said, "No, sir. I just couldn't help but notice you on Saturday night dancing with—" he cleared his throat, hiding a grin behind his fisted hand "—Mrs. Conrad."

"Is that right?" Undaunted, Jason lowered himself onto the corner of the man's desk. "And here I thought you were on duty, keeping an eye on the citizens of this fine town, not on the activities of your *police chief.*"

"No, sir…I mean, yes, sir." Officer Schmitz shifted uncomfortably. "I certainly was on duty."

Jason leveled a steady glance at the man and continued, "Even if it's true I was dancing with Mrs. Conrad, what a man does on his day off isn't really anyone else's business but his own. Isn't that right, Officer Schmitz?"

The other man blinked, having the sense not to answer.

Jason went on, "Because I'm sure that an officer who spends his days off playing poker at Tuttle's Tavern—a game of questionable legal repute, I might add—wouldn't want everyone to discuss his winnings and losings the next time he stepped foot into the department."

"No, sir." The man's cheeks flushed a rosy hue. "He certainly wouldn't."

"I'm glad we understand each other." Jason glanced around the room at the rest of the men, who were watching in amused interest. "Anyone else interested in my dancing prowess?"

His challenge got no takers.

Jason smiled. "Good, then why don't we get down to business?"

The subject of his weekend dalliance with the town's favorite waitress temporarily gave way to a reporting of the evening's events. As Jason listened to the report, he silently berated himself for allowing his hormones to rule his judgment. Like it or not, he was the chief of police. His behavior would always be under scrutiny. Not only by his fellow officers, but also by the rest of the town.

Not that he couldn't handle a little razzing from the boys at work. It was the compromising position in which he'd placed Maggie that concerned him. She didn't deserve to be the subject of backroom gossip.

Jason felt the heat of embarrassment as he recalled how close he'd come to giving into his desire and kissing Maggie in the middle of the Spring Carnival's dance floor. A move like that would have given his men even more interesting fodder for the morning's gossip mill.

Betty, the dispatcher, called from her desk, rousing him from his thoughts. "Chief, we've got a call from the principal at the grade school. He says there's a couple of ten-year-old boys who haven't shown up for class yet."

Jason's heart leapt into his throat. His own son's last, fateful trip to school flashed through his mind. As though it were yesterday, he could still see Scott smile and wave goodbye as he walked out the door. He forced the memory from his mind and answered in an even tone, "Has he talked to their parents yet?"

"Yep," she said, nodding, sending coppery ringlets of hair bouncing about her head. "Seems they're pretty upset. The boys left a couple of hours ago for school. They should have been there by now."

"Probably just playing hooky," one of the officers suggested. "It's a mighty fine day out there. If I had a choice, I'd rather spend my morning outside soakin' up the sunshine than inside crackin' open the books."

The suggestion was met with a round of chuckles.

Jason wasn't so sure. He knew firsthand the dangers innocent children faced on a daily basis. "Get a description. Tell the principal we'll start a search for them."

As the dispatcher followed his directions, he snapped out orders to his crew. "Make this a priority. I want everyone out there looking for those boys. Myer, check the hospital for any unreported accidents involving kids. Schmitz, I want you to talk to the parents, make sure the boys aren't hiding out at home, get a handle on their daily habits. Everyone else, patrol the streets and keep your eyes peeled for those boys."

For a moment his men did not move. They seemed surprised, taken aback by his urgency.

"Anything wrong?" he asked, his heart pounding, his voice sharper than he'd intended.

"No, sir. It's just…" Officer Schmitz smiled uneasily. "I, uh…well, I don't think we need to make such a big deal out of this, Chief. The boys'll probably show up at school before we even have a chance to get into our cars."

"I hope you're right," Jason said. He shot a hard glance around the room, challenging the rest of the crew to question his judgment. "In the meantime, I'd suggest you all get moving."

The officers rose to their feet. Conversations buzzed as they gathered their hats and gun belts and headed for the door.

Jason felt numb as he watched them leave. A familiar feeling of helplessness washed over him. He couldn't move; his feet felt like lead. He couldn't concentrate; he was bombarded by images of his son, of the suffering Scott had endured before his tiny bruised and battered body finally gave up the fight.

Scott had lived almost three days after being struck by a car while crossing an intersection on his way to school. The driver had been drunk, coming home after an all-night binge.

Jason's son never had a chance to come home.

The experience had been painful, unbearably so. Jason had wanted to die right along with his son. He didn't know how he'd found the strength to go on alone.

But he had.

Now Jason pushed himself from the desk. He strode over to the dispatcher, listening as she relayed a description of the two boys on the radio. Restlessly he paced the floor between his office and the dispatch desk.

The minutes passed much too slowly, and still there was no word. Ignoring the curious glances from the office staff, he continued his pacing, unable to stop the tension from building inside him.

And then he'd had enough.

Nearly half an hour after the call came in, he grabbed his hat and headed for the door to join the search. He hollered at the dispatcher, "Betty, I'll be in my car. Let me know if you hear anything new."

"Just a minute, Chief," Betty called out, stopping his mad dash. "It's Officer Schmitz. Sounds like he might have found the boys."

Jason's hand rested on the cold metal bar of the door handle. He froze midstep. He stared at her and waited for the news, hoping for the best, dreading the worst.

"Schmitz says the only thing missin' from the boys' homes were a couple of fishing rods." Betty grinned. "Actin' on a hunch, he started checkin' out the local watering holes. He says he found them at Frazier's pond." Her expression softened, her tone gentled. "The boys are okay, Chief. Schmitz is taking them home to their mommas right now."

Relief poured through Jason. His legs felt like jelly, his muscles as weak as a newborn kitten's. The experience had been emotionally draining. He'd come to Wyndchester to find peace. To put the past behind him.

He'd been a fool to think he could ever do that.

Uncertainly he remained at the doorway, feeling adrift, not sure what to do next. After his son's death, he'd relied on the sympathetic ears of fellow police officers to ease his pain.

Now he was the chief of police, someone his men saw as a role model, not someone who broke down over a simple truancy call.

Who could he turn to in Wyndchester when he needed reassurance?

He knew of only one person.

Making his decision quickly, ignoring the dispatcher's surprised look, he said, "Betty, I'm taking a coffee break. If anybody needs to find me, I'll be at Mel's diner."

It was too early for his coffee break.

The morning rush was still in full swing. Frowning, Maggie stared out the front window of Mel's. Panic gripped her as she watched Jason step hesitantly across the street toward the diner.

It was too soon. She wasn't ready to face him yet. Not after what had happened between them on Friday night.

Maggie's pulse quickened, her body warmed as she recalled how good it had felt to be held in Jason's arms. How easily the conversation had flowed between them. How close she'd come to kissing him.

She closed her eyes and drew in a steadying breath. She felt as though she was losing control. As though no matter how hard she tried to push Jason away, the closer they became.

It had to stop. For Kevin's sake and her own, she could not allow Jason to become part of their lives. Forging a relationship with a man who could ultimately destroy what little security she'd found in her life was insane. She was courting disaster.

The bell over the door jangled.

Maggie's eyes flew open.

Jason didn't even make a pretense of his reason for his early visit. With a determined look in his eyes, he headed for the front counter. Wide-shouldered, slim-hipped and long-legged, he proved a formidable temptation. Maggie averted her gaze. She stared at the Formica countertop, steeling herself against an unwanted surge of awareness.

He slid into the stool in front of her. Slowly, almost reluctantly, she raised her eyes and met his gaze.

And knew something was wrong.

Tension etched his handsome face. His jaw was set in a hard line. A vein pulsed at his temple. He looked pale, shaken.

Maggie's resolve to keep her distance melted in a hot rush of concern. Without asking, she placed a cup and saucer in front of him, then poured some coffee and waited.

Jason's hand shook as he reached for the cup. He gripped it so tightly Maggie was afraid it might shatter in his hands.

With the exaggerated care of a man who'd had too much to drink, he brought the cup to his lips and sipped.

Unable to help herself, Maggie cleared her throat. "Is everything all right, Jason?"

"Yeah, I mean...no." He shook his head and gave a bitter-sounding laugh. "I don't know what I mean. I don't know even what I'm doing here." His cup clattered loudly as he dropped it back onto its saucer. Coffee splashed onto the counter. Cursing softly, he rose to his feet. "This was a mistake. I'm sorry to have bothered you, Maggie."

A part of her—the part that would fight tooth and nail to protect her son, as well as herself—wanted to say good riddance. After all, she hadn't asked him to seek her out and drop his problems onto her lap. But another part—the part that remembered how, not too long ago, when the situation had been reversed and she'd been the one in need, Jason had reached out to help her—just couldn't let him go.

"Jason, wait." Without thinking, she put a hand on his forearm, stopping him. Her fingers looked small, delicate against the strength of his arm. His skin felt hot, sizzling to her touch. Maggie gasped as waves of heat rippled through her.

Jason flinched at the sound of her sharp intake of breath. His muscles tightened. He stared at her hand, then his gaze flicked upward to scan her face.

As though she'd been burned, Maggie snatched her hand away. Realizing he was waiting for her to speak, she stammered, "I—I'm due for a break. Why don't we sit down at a booth and talk for a while?"

He hesitated, glancing anxiously out the window at the street outside. For a moment she thought he might refuse. Then, with a sigh, he nodded.

Not giving herself a chance to change her mind, Maggie

grabbed a pot of coffee and called out, "I'm taking a break, Mel."

The kitchen door swung open. Mel poked his head outside. Scowling, he grumbled, "We've still got customers, Maggie."

"Aw, let her go, Mel. I'll take over her station," Dot said, coming to her rescue. The blond waitress placed a hand on her ample hips and gave Maggie a conspiratorial wink. "Enjoy yourself now, honey."

Embarrassed heat rose on Maggie's face. If the residents of Wyndchester hadn't guessed there was something going on between her and the police chief, they'd be sure to think so now. Sitting down with Jason, having a cup of coffee and sharing an innocent conversation with him was like waving a red flag in front of the town gossips. They'd have a hard time resisting the news.

Jason followed her to a booth at the far side of the diner. The table and neighboring booth were empty, giving them some privacy. Setting the coffeepot on the table, she took a seat.

He slid into the bench across from her, his knees bumping hers as he settled himself. Sparks of awareness traveled up her thigh.

"Sorry," he murmured at her sharp inhalation. He frowned. "Did I hurt you?"

"No, I'm fine. It was just—" she crossed her legs, shifting away from Jason's touch, away from temptation "—just a shock."

Silence descended between them. They stared at each other awkwardly. Maggie reached for the coffeepot in an effort to fill the gap. This time, her hands shook as she filled their cups.

The silence continued.

Jason stared at his cup, turning it around and around on

the table before him. Then, without warning, he blurted, ''I had a call this morning. It was about a couple of boys missing from school.''

''Not Kevin?'' she whispered. The words sounded strained, strangled by the sudden tightness of her throat. Her heart thumped wildly in her chest. She searched Jason's face, looking for reassurance that her son was all right.

''No, of course not. Kevin's fine.'' He reached over and covered her trembling hand with his. ''Jesus, Maggie. I'm sorry. I didn't mean to scare you.''

She stared at their joined hands, collecting her scattered poise before facing him again. There was something very reassuring about his touch. It warmed her skin, warmed her heart.

Reluctantly she pulled away, fisting her hands in her lap. She looked up and caught the confusing disappointment in his eyes. Swallowing hard, she said, ''The boys...are they all right?''

''Yeah, they're fine,'' he said with a rueful grimace. ''They were all along. Seems they decided to play hooky for the day. One of my men found them out at Frazier's pond, catching a few fish.''

''Thank goodness,'' Maggie murmured softly. She waited, knowing there was more to this visit than a pair of truant boys. Jason was a man who looked like he'd seen a ghost.

She didn't have long to wait.

Raking a hand through his dark hair, he said, ''I think maybe I've worked too long in the city. It's warped my perception of life. I expect to find the worst in every situation.''

''Like this morning?'' she prompted.

''Yeah, like this morning.'' He sighed. ''I assumed

something bad had happened to those boys. I had my men
out there looking for bodies, not a couple of living-and-
breathing boys playing hooky on a beautiful spring day.''

''You were being cautious,'' she said, choosing her
words carefully, wishing she could erase the pain in his
eyes. ''No one can fault you for that.''

''I overreacted.'' His jaw clenched, then unclenched.
Self-directed anger clouded his handsome face. ''I know it.
And my men know it, too.''

She frowned. ''Why are you being so hard on yourself?
You've only been in Wyndchester a few weeks. You can't
expect to adjust to the ways of a small town so quickly.
No one else expects you to, either.''

Jason didn't answer. He stared at his hands.

She tried a new tack. ''So you made a mistake. You're
human. I've only lived in Wyndchester a few months, but
I've found it to be a town that's willing to give anyone a
second chance.'' When he remained stubbornly mute, Maggie sighed. ''Jason, your men are going to respect you more
for caring too much than too little.''

For a long moment he didn't say a word. Then, just as
she wondered if he'd even heard her, he lifted his gaze and
smiled for the first time. ''A second chance, eh? Is that
why you've come to Wyndchester? For that second
chance?''

The question hit too close to home. Unease settled
heavily against her chest, making it hard to breathe.
''Maybe,'' she said, struggling for an even tone, looking
for a way to direct the conversation back to safer footing.
''How about you? Why did you come to Wyndchester?''

He stared at his cooling cup of coffee. Then, raising a
brow, he asked, ''Do you want the truth?''

She nodded, not trusting herself to speak.

''I came to find a simpler life.'' The hollow sound of his

deep voice sent a shiver down her spine. "To find a reason to restore my faith in mankind."

Pain dulled his eyes. She saw a vulnerability in him she hadn't known existed. And she knew he wasn't telling her the whole truth. Jason carried all the signs of a man who'd been hurt deeply.

What secret pain wasn't he telling her?

Maggie realized, suddenly, they weren't all that different. She and Jason had more in common than she cared to admit. Both had been hurt in the past. Both were looking for a fresh start, a more promising future.

"Have you..." Her voice caught. She swallowed hard. The lump of emotion she felt seemed too big to ignore. "Have you found that reason yet?"

His gaze unwavering, he looked directly into her eyes and said, "Yes, I believe I have."

They stared at each other, neither saying a word. Both waiting for the other to speak. Both uncertain how to deal with the importance of his admission.

Laughter erupted from a group of customers at a table nearby. The sound whipped through the diner, effectively ending the intimate spell Jason's words had cast.

Maggie blinked, coming to her senses. Uncrossing her legs, she scooted out of the bench. "I've got to go."

"Maggie, I—"

"I've taken a long enough break as it is," she said, not allowing him a word, too afraid of what he might say next. She stumbled to her feet.

He started to follow. "If you'd just let me—"

"I'm sorry, but I've really got to run." She stepped away from the booth. "Mel's going to blow a gasket if I don't get back to work."

"Right," Jason said, releasing a defeated breath. "Then I guess I'd better let you go."

Maggie hesitated. She'd been a whisper away from a clean getaway when she made the mistake of looking into his eyes. Those pale blue eyes that mirrored his every emotion. She'd spent the past ten minutes trying to lift Jason's spirits. How in the world could she abandon him now? Not when he looked so miserable.

Nervously she licked her lips. "It's, um, been nice talking to you, Jason."

One corner of his mouth lifted in a half grin. Just enough to make the dimple deepen on his cheek. But not enough to wash the sadness from his eyes. "Thank you for listening, Maggie. You've been a good friend."

Such simple words, yet they caused her heart to stutter. They both knew that there was more than friendship growing between them. There was undeniable attraction.

Jason might be the most gentle, sensitive man she'd ever met. But he'd come into her life too late. So much had happened. She'd struggled too hard to find her independence. She wasn't about to give it up now.

Kevin was the only male she could allow in her life. There just wasn't room for anyone else.

Maggie shrugged and gave a quick smile, trying her best to appear lighthearted. "You don't have to thank me. Looking out for each other—that's what neighbors are for, right?"

As she'd expected, a cloud of disappointment shadowed his face.

Guiltily, before she lost her nerve, Maggie turned on her heel and escaped his tempting presence. Unable to shake the feeling that she'd only delayed the inevitable. That there were forces beyond her control at work here.

That she might have better luck keeping a tornado at bay than keeping Jason at arm's length.

* * *

In less than two weeks, Kevin would be out of school. Other than Jenny Lewis's wedding—a wedding Maggie doubted would even take place—there was nothing to hold her in Wyndchester.

The thought left Maggie feeling oddly unsettled.

Later that evening, as she finished washing the dinner dishes at the kitchen sink, she watched her son sitting on the back porch. His baseball glove in hand, he stared at the house next door, his impatience growing each time he tossed the ball into his mitt. He was waiting for Jason to come outside and play catch.

Selfishly Maggie almost wished their next-door neighbor wouldn't make an appearance tonight.

It would certainly make her life easier.

Sighing, Maggie rinsed a dish and placed it in the drainer. She hadn't seen Jason since he'd left the diner that morning. But truth be told, his image had stayed with her long after. She couldn't stop thinking about him, wondering if she'd hurt his feelings. Wondering if she'd only imagined the sensual undercurrents passing between them. Then knowing she hadn't.

For the first time in years, she found herself thinking of a man in terms other than fear. As much as she hated to admit it, she was physically attracted to Jason. More than that, she genuinely cared about him. Hand in hand, the two emotions were a deadly combination.

Which was why she knew it was time to move on, to leave Wyndchester.

But her heart just wasn't into making the change.

Maggie picked up another plate. She dunked the dish under the sudsy water, watching soap bubbles pop into the air. For the past year and a half, she'd done nothing but keep on the move. She was tired of running away. She wanted a stable life for herself and her child.

In Wyndchester, she'd found her chance at security. She sighed. That is, until Jason came along and disturbed her equilibrium.

Nearby, a screen door slammed shut.

Kevin scrambled to his feet, bounding off the porch like a rabbit roused from its burrow. He hurried across the yard, making a beeline for Jason's house.

A fist of emotion gripped Maggie's heart as she watched Jason's face light up into a smile at Kevin's approach. Dammit, why did he have to be so good with her son? It would be so much easier to distance Kevin and herself from him if he was a cantankerous grouch.

Maggie growled her frustration. What was the matter with her? She should be glad he didn't hold a grudge. Just this morning, he'd made it clear that he wanted more from her than just a casual relationship. And she'd shot him down in no uncertain terms. A lesser man might not have felt up to the task of playing catch with her son.

But, as she was quickly finding out, Jason was no ordinary man.

Somewhere he'd found another glove, as well as a small bat. He held out the bat for Kevin's inspection.

Kevin's small mouth opened in awe. He dropped his glove and reached tentatively for the bat. Running his fingers across its smooth surface, he tested its weight with both hands. A priceless grin stretched across his face.

Speaking words Maggie could not hear, Jason pointed to a spot in the yard.

Kevin, clutching the bat, hurried to take his place as directed.

Maggie held a dripping plate as she watched her son's first attempt with a bat.

He swung and missed Jason's pitch by a mile.

Moaning in commiserative disappointment, she let the

plate slip back into the sudsy water and reached for a towel. Drying her fingers, leaving the dirty dishes for later, she tiptoed outside, careful not to let the screen door bang shut behind her. She sat down on the swing in the back porch and watched the pair at a discreet distance.

"Choke up a little on the bat, Kevin," Jason called out.

Kevin frowned, looking at the bat, then at Jason in confusion.

Jason kept a sober expression, not showing any sign of amusement at her son's lack of experience. Instead, he strode over to Kevin and adjusted the bat in his hands. He tilted his shoulders at an angle and planted his feet in the right direction. Swinging an imaginary bat in his own hand, he showed Kevin the proper form for hitting.

Maggie bit her lower lip to stop a smile when she watched her son's awkward imitation of Jason's slim-hipped waggle and swing.

Nodding and giving a quick smile of assurance, Jason strode back to his makeshift pitching mound. Gently he made another pitch.

This time the bat made contact with the ball. A resounding crack echoed across the yard. The ball sailed high in the air, then fell to the earth at an unseemly short distance from where it had started.

Disappointment shrouded her son's face. He kicked the dirt with his shoe, letting the bat sag to the ground.

"Hey, that's great, you hit the ball, Kevin," Jason said, finding the perfect words of encouragement. "You can't expect to be a home-run hitter the first time at bat. Let's try it again."

Pushing his glasses higher on his nose, Kevin dug the toes of his tennis shoes into the dirt and faced the next pitch with a determined glare.

Maggie crossed her fingers and held her breath, as Jason lobbed her son another pitch.

This time Kevin swung the bat at even keel and made direct contact. With all the force his young body could muster, he sent the ball spinning low and fast toward Jason.

Jason bent down, expecting the ball to be a grounder. But as it neared, it bounced hard off the ground. The force of the impact popped the ball into the air. Jason didn't have time to react. Maggie watched in horror as the ball flew at him, whacking him squarely on the cheekbone just below his eye.

Chapter 8

"Jason!" Maggie gasped, scrambling to her feet. Shock numbed her limbs. She stood frozen in the middle of the back porch, staring as Jason swayed beneath the impact of the ball, apparently too stunned to move.

"Mr. Gallagher!" Kevin dropped the bat. His short legs pumping, he sped toward his wounded hero.

At the sound of her son's distress, Maggie forced herself into action. Stomach churning, she ran as fast as she could to join the pair.

"I'm sorry, Mr. Gallagher." Kevin's voice cracked with emotion. Tears brimmed his eyes, threatening to spill. He reached a tentative hand, patting his friend's arm. "Are you okay, Mr. Gallagher?"

Jason, one hand still cradling his wound, muttered an unintelligible answer.

Maggie gently pushed her son aside to get a closer look. Swallowing her fear, she asked, "Jason, can you hear me?"

"Yeah," Jason mumbled, "I can hear you."

"Think you could look at me?"

Reluctantly he opened one eye, the uninjured one, blinking rapidly.

Frowning, Maggie held up two fingers. "How many fingers do you see?"

He squinted, then scowled and said grumpily, "Well, if the two of you'd stop moving around, there'd only be four."

"Uh-huh. Let's take a look at that eye."

Carefully she pried his hand away from the wound. The ball missed hitting his eye by a mere inch. Unfortunately his cheekbone hadn't fared as well. It was starting to swell, looking red and bruised. There was a small scrape, with blood oozing at the point of impact. She wouldn't be surprised if he ended up with a black eye.

"Kevin," she said, "help me take Mr. Gallagher inside. We're going to have to put some ice on that eye."

"No, no, that's okay. I'll be fine," Jason said, waving off their attempts to help him. "Just give me some room. I can take care of myself."

Maggie wasn't sure how much of his protest was real and how much was a show of machismo. After all, just this morning, hadn't she wounded his male pride? She doubted he would want to appear vulnerable in her presence.

He took a step, then swayed like a drunk.

"Oh, for Pete's sake." Maggie grabbed him around the waist and supported him with her body. Her tone stern, she said, "No arguments. You're coming inside with me so I can take a look at that stubborn head of yours."

"Yeah, Mr. Gallagher," Kevin chirped in, taking Jason's big hand in his own, lacing his small fingers through his. "We don't want you fallin' down and gettin' hurt again."

"I'm not helpless, you know," Jason protested, even as he draped an arm around her shoulders and leaned on her for support. Before she could comment, he narrowed a glance at Kevin, smiling despite his injury. "By the way, nice shootin', Tex. I think you've figured out how to swing a bat."

Kevin grinned, looking proud of his achievement. "Next time I promise I'll try not to hit you."

"Thanks, I'd appreciate that."

Maggie rolled her eyes. "Let's take a look at Mr. Gallagher's eye before we start making any future baseball plans."

The three of them headed for the house, their progress awkward. Angling for better support, Maggie shifted her position, the move bringing them closer.

Jason moaned softly.

Maggie tightened her grip around his waist and glanced anxiously at him. "Are you okay?"

"Peachy keen," he said through gritted teeth.

She frowned. "Are you sure? You look a little flushed."

Instantly his flush deepened. "No, no, I'm fine."

Kevin frowned in obvious confusion, his glance bobbing from one to the other.

Maggie bit her lip, studying her reluctant patient. She was just as confused. There was something odd about Jason's behavior. In fact, he didn't seem to be in quite as much pain as he was enjoying himself. Slowly understanding dawned, and she became all too aware of the intimacy of the situation.

Walking as they were, the sides of their bodies were in close contact. With each step they took, their legs brushed against each other. The worn fabric of his jeans felt buttery soft against her legs. Where she supported him, she had full measure of the powerful width of his shoulders, the narrow cut of his waist and the lean strength of his stomach muscles.

And the big galoot was enjoying every minute of it.

Even worse, so was she. Being so close to him set off an odd stirring sensation deep in the pit of her stomach.

Awareness, pure and simple.

Annoyance sizzled in her veins. If it wasn't for Kevin hovering nearby, she'd dump the big phony in the middle of his backyard and let him fend for himself.

Thankfully they reached the steps of her back porch.

"Kevin, get the screen door," she said, wincing at the strained sound of her voice.

If Jason noticed her discomfort, he had the good grace not to comment. They took the steps carefully. Maggie helped him inside, seating him at the kitchen table. When she released him, the air felt cooler, chilling her. She shivered, hating to admit she missed the heat of his body.

The bump on his cheekbone had grown in size, the skin around it already starting to discolor, rekindling a certain amount of her sympathy. She couldn't deny it, the man was injured. "Kevin, go upstairs and get the first-aid kit out of the bathroom. I need to wash that scrape."

Kevin didn't need to be told twice. He scurried out of the kitchen, his tennis shoes thudding on the linoleum floor. His footsteps on the wooden staircase echoed throughout the house. For a little boy, he could make an awful racket.

Jason winced at the noise.

Maggie moved to the refrigerator and drew a tray of ice out of the freezer. She cracked the cubes into a hand towel, then wrapped it into a tight bundle. Gingerly she laid the ice pack on his cheekbone and held it in place.

Jason didn't protest against her ministrations.

"How are you feeling?" she asked, determined not to think about the close proximity of their bodies or the fact that he seemed to have developed a rapt interest in his eye-level view of her breasts.

"Stupid," he admitted with a sigh. His breath felt warm against her skin. Maggie shivered. "I got KO'd by a seven-year-old. When the crew at the department hears about this, I'll never live it down." He gave a sheepish grin. "That son of yours has got some power behind his swing."

She smiled. "Other than your wounded pride, how do you feel? Still dizzy? Any nausea?"

"The dizziness is going away. And I'm not sick to my stomach." He peered at her from beneath the ice pack, his uninjured blue eye twinkling with mischief. Maggie drew in a steadying breath. Even with a bump on his cheek, the man was too handsome for his own good. "So, what's the diagnosis, doc?"

Surprising him, she reached for his hand resting on the kitchen table. He looked at their twined fingers, then raised a brow, a question in his gaze. Before she lost her nerve, she placed his hand on the ice pack, turning over the nursing duties to him.

"You're probably going to end up with a black eye," she said. "But I think you'll live." Then, on unsteady feet, she moved away from temptation, trying not to think about the disappointment etched in his face.

Kevin bounded into the room, bringing with him a welcome distraction. He held out the first-aid box. "It was on the top shelf. I had to climb onto the end of the bathtub to reach it."

"Thanks," Maggie said, pushing from her mind an unwanted picture of her son falling headfirst into the ancient clawfoot tub. "Mr. Gallagher needs to keep the ice pack on for a few more minutes. While we're waiting, could I interest anyone in a Popsicle?"

"Yeah," Kevin said, taking a seat at the table next to Jason.

Jason shook his head, then winced in pain. "No, thanks. I'm not too hungry right now."

Nodding, Maggie refilled the ice tray with water, feeling the weight of Jason's gaze on her every move. She shoved the tray back into the freezer, splattering water. Ignoring the mess, she took out two Popsicles, a red one for Kevin and an orange for herself. Then, reluctantly, she took a seat at the table.

Handing Kevin his Popsicle, she unwrapped her own and sank her teeth into the frosty treat. She shivered as she swallowed a cool bite. Then looked up and caught Jason still watching her.

She stared at him, not sure what to say.

Fortunately Kevin didn't suffer from a loss of words. "I'm sure glad you decided to move to Wyndchester, Mr. Gallagher. Where did you used to live?"

"Chicago," Jason supplied.

Maggie'd heard at least three different versions of Jason's background at the diner. The only thing the stories had in common were that he was formerly a resident of Chicago. At least the gossips had gotten that much right.

"I've never been there." Kevin took a bite, crunching noisily on the Popsicle. He swallowed hard, then asked, "Is Chicago bigger than Wyndchester?"

Jason shifted the ice pack and chuckled. "You two aren't from the Midwest, are you?"

Kevin shook his head. "Nope, we used to live in—"

"Florida, born and bred," Maggie said, her protective instincts kicking in. No matter how friendly Jason seemed, they just couldn't reveal too much about their pasts to anyone.

Kevin looked at her, blinking in surprise.

"Florida, eh?" Jason said, not questioning her fib. "Then I guess that explains why you're not familiar with

Here's a HOT offer for you!

Get set for a
sizzling summer read...

with 2 FREE ROMANCE BOOKS

and a FREE MYSTERY GIFT!

NO CATCH! NO OBLIGATION TO BUY!

Simply complete and return this card and
you'll get **FREE BOOKS, A FREE GIFT**
and much more!

🌀 The first shipment is yours to keep, absolutely free!

🌀 Enjoy the convenience of romance books, delivered right to your
door, before they're available in the stores!

🌀 Take advantage of special low pricing for Reader Service Members only!

🌀 After receiving your free books we hope you'll want to remain a
subscriber. But the choice is always yours—to continue or cancel
anytime at all! So why not take us up on this fabulous invitation
with no risk of any kind. You'll be glad you did!

345 SDL CPST

**245 SDL CPSL
S-IM-05/99**

Name:
_____
(Please Print)

Address: _____ Apt.#: _____

City: _____

State/Prov.: _____ Zip/
Postal Code: _____

▶ DETACH HERE AND MAIL CARD TODAY! ▶

The Silhouette Reader Service™ —Here's How it Works:

Chicago." He directed his words to Kevin. "It's one of the biggest cities in the United States. Not only that, they've got one of the best baseball teams—the Cubs."

"They do?" Kevin's eyes widened with interest. "Mom, do you think we could go there someday?"

"Ah...I don't know, Kevin."

"Not to live," he added quickly. "Just for a visit."

"Well, maybe—"

"'Cause I don't ever want to move again," Kevin said, not giving her a chance to finish. He crunched another bite of Popsicle. Around his full mouth, he explained, "I'm tired of movin'."

Jason lowered his ice pack, a curious glint in his eyes.

Panic struck like a blow to the chest. Maggie nearly dropped her Popsicle in her lap.

"You've lived in a lot of different towns?" Jason asked Kevin. He kept his gaze trained on Maggie.

"Lots and lots," Kevin said, ignoring her attempts to catch his eye. He shook his head. "Seems like as soon as I start to like a town, we have to leave."

"Kevin, your Popsicle's dripping," Maggie said, desperate to stop him from revealing too much. She rose to her feet, taking the sticky treat from her son. "It's getting late. Time for you to go upstairs and take a bath."

"Aw, Mom," Kevin protested.

"No arguments," she said, her voice sharper than she'd intended. Maggie's heart clutched at the stricken look on her son's face.

Blinking hard, his eyes glistening with unshed tears, Kevin hurried from the room, leaving behind a stunned silence.

Maggie stared at her son's empty seat, letting the melting Popsicles drip onto her fingers, too embarrassed to face

Jason. She didn't want to witness the condemnation in his eyes.

Finally Jason shifted in his seat. The legs of his chair scraped against the linoleum floor. She heard the slow inhalation of his breath, then, "Maggie, I—"

"Excuse me," she said in a rush, not letting him finish. She turned and dropped the Popsicles into the empty side of the double sink, running water onto her sticky fingers. Snapping the tap off with a flick of her wrist, she drew in a deep breath, then turned to face him. "I—I need to talk to my son."

Not waiting for a response, she left the room, desperate to put a distance between her and Jason. No matter how much she wanted to explain, she knew she would never be able to tell him the truth. He could never know the real reason behind their frequent moves.

He, of all people, could never be privy to the secrets that held her and Kevin hostage.

Cold water dribbled onto his hands, chilling him. But it was a minor inconvenience compared to the ache in his heart. Jason held the melting ice pack tightly in his fist and stared at the empty doorway, uncertain what to do next.

Obviously he'd stepped into the middle of a family crisis. The wisest course of action would be to pick himself up and leave Maggie to sort through the problem herself. But no one had ever said he was a smart man, especially when it came to matters of the heart.

For some reason, he just couldn't abandon her or Kevin. Not when the pair was so troubled. Not when Maggie looked so miserable, so ashamed.

No matter what she thought, he knew she wasn't a bad mom. Nor was she prone to making quick, unjust judgments. Until tonight, she'd been the most even-tempered woman he'd ever met. Which made her snapping at her son so much more confusing.

The rebuke had been unnecessary. They'd been talking about Chicago. His former home. A city where the Cubs played baseball. Then Kevin said he never wanted to move again. And Maggie...

Jason sighed. Maggie went ballistic.

Restlessly he rose to his feet, ignoring the dull throbbing of his head. He crossed to the sink, dumping the ice cubes next to the abandoned Popsicles. Turning on the water, he flushed the entire mess down the sink, then tossed the Popsicle sticks into the trash.

He leaned against the counter, crossed his arms over his chest and tried to figure out what the hell was going on. Every time he tried to question Maggie about her past, he saw the door shutting, the protective walls going up around her. The cop in him wondered why. The man in him couldn't help but feel frustrated.

For every step forward they made in their relationship, Maggie took two steps back. He hadn't imagined the pull of attraction between the two of them. Sparks flew whenever they were within ten feet of each other. Yet, despite all of that, she seemed determined to keep him at arm's length.

But not this time.

Jason pushed himself away from the counter and returned to his seat at the table, settling himself in for the long haul. This time he wasn't going to let her push him away.

It was nearly a half an hour before Maggie reappeared. During that time, he'd heard the soothing sound of her voice and knew she was patching things up with her boy. Counting down the minutes, he'd paced the floor, returned to his seat, then paced the floor some more. He nearly lost his nerve, changing his mind at least a dozen times, telling himself it wasn't too late to leave and give them their privacy.

But the memory of the look on Maggie's face when she'd disappeared through the doorway stopped him. That guilty look of shame. He knew in his heart he couldn't leave until she faced him again. Or it would be too easy for her to disappear from his life. Like a puff of smoke, she'd be impossible to hold on to.

Now her footstep faltered when she spotted him sitting at the kitchen table. She stood in the doorway, seeming surprised to see him still there. He was certain she was poised on the brink of turning around and escaping.

"How's Kevin?" he asked, taking the bull by the horns.

"H-he's fine," she said, her voice thick with emotion. Her eyes were red, the skin beneath splotched, proof that she'd recently been crying. She shifted her gaze, looking too embarrassed to face him. Instead, she stared at a point beyond his shoulder.

A sledgehammer of emotion hit him squarely in the gut, making it hard to draw a breath. It took every ounce of willpower he possessed not to stand up and reach out to her, to try to console her.

"Maggie," he said. Leaning forward, elbows on his knees, his hands clasped in front of him, he willed himself to say the right thing. "I know how hard it is to raise a child. Sometimes, when a person's tired, they say things they don't really mean."

Maggie remained stubbornly mute.

He didn't let her silence deter him. Keeping his voice even, his tone soothing, he said, "Kevin's a smart boy. I'm sure he doesn't expect his mother to be perfect all the time."

Maggie rolled her eyes, giving a mirthless smile. "I'm far from perfect."

"Maybe not, but you are a good mom."

She looked at him, finally meeting his gaze. "And how do you know that?"

"Because I've seen you with Kevin. I've seen the love in your eyes when you look at him. And I've seen the care with which you treat him. He's a lucky boy to have you for a mother."

"Not so lucky." Tears misted her eyes. Maggie blinked hard, staving off the flow. "He deserves much more."

Jason pushed himself to his feet, the chair scraping against the linoleum floor. He took a step toward her, then stopped at the alarmed expression on her face.

"He's got your love, Maggie," Jason reminded her, unable to keep the frustration from his voice. "What more could you give him?"

"It's not that simple," she said, raking a wayward strand of hair from her eyes. "Kevin...he hasn't had it easy. Not since—" She stopped abruptly, the light fading from her eyes.

"Since your husband died?" he prompted, desperate to keep her from withdrawing.

She didn't answer. She refused to look at him.

"Kevin's not the only one who hasn't had it easy," he reminded her. "Is that why you've had to move so often? Because times were tough? Were you looking for a job?" *Or were you just trying to run away from the past?* Wisely the last question remained unspoken. Her silence was unbearable. He took another step toward her. "Maggie, talk to me."

"I—I can't," she said, the words so quiet he could barely hear them.

Frustration churned inside him. Refusing to back down,

he closed the gap between them until they were mere inches apart. "Why not, Maggie? What's so bad that you can't talk about it?"

She shook her head, refusing to say a word.

His voice gentled. "Don't you see? I care about you. I just want to help." He reached out a hand and stroked the velvety smooth skin of her cheek.

Maggie flinched at his touch. Panic filled her eyes. Pushing herself away from the door frame, she looked ready to flee.

"Maggie, don't..." His voice broke. The words caught in his throat. "Don't leave me, not yet."

She hesitated, clinging to the door frame and looking at him with wide-eyed uncertainty.

"I'm sorry," he said. "I didn't mean to frighten you. I just..." Frustrated with himself, with the hopelessness of the situation, he shoved his hands in his pockets and released a sighing breath.

He'd tried to take things slow. He'd tried to be patient. But all he ever seemed to accomplish was to scare her away.

Perhaps it was time for honesty.

He looked into her eyes, almost losing his nerve at the wariness in her gaze. "Maggie, I'm not going to lie to you. The truth is, I'm attracted to you. I've never felt this way before. Whenever I'm near you, I want to touch you, to hold you." He swore softly beneath his breath. "Dammit, Maggie, I want to make love to you."

She held herself unnaturally still, like a deer caught in headlights, facing down certain disaster.

"And I don't think it's my imagination—or wishful thinking—but I believe you feel the same way," he said, unable to keep the challenge from his tone.

He paused for a steadying breath, waiting for her to respond. She neither confirmed nor denied the statement.

Encouraged, he said gently, "I'm not your late husband, Maggie. I never have and I never will hurt a woman. Right now, all I want to do is kiss you. If you've got a problem with that, just tell me." He pointed at the screen door leading outside to the night-darkened yard. "Because if you do, I'll walk straight out that door without another argument. And we'll just forget this whole thing ever happened."

Maggie swallowed hard, a battle obviously being fought behind those beautiful green eyes of hers.

Jason held his breath and waited.

Finally she cleared her throat. Her gaze flitted over him. She looked as nervous as he felt. "I guess I...I don't really want you to go, either. Not yet, anyway."

Jason gave a silent prayer of relief. He stared at her, not sure what to do next. Now that he'd been given permission to indulge his wants, he hadn't a clue where to begin. Feeling as awkward as a teenager on a first date, he couldn't decide what to do with his hands. Although he'd like nothing more than to pull her into his arms and hold her tight, he was almost afraid to touch her. To do anything that might scare her away.

Instead, he hooked his thumbs in the pockets of his jeans. With the chasteness of a proper first kiss, he leaned forward and brushed his lips against hers. And it was enough. It was everything he'd imagined and more.

Her lips were soft and full, warm to his touch. Other than a tiny breath of surprise when their mouths met, she didn't fight off his advances. Instead, once the deed was done, she seemed to relax, accepting the inevitable.

Still not touching her, Jason deepened the kiss. He angled his head for better access to her mouth. Maggie matched his move with one of her own. She tilted her chin upward and let the pressure build between them.

At the brush of his tongue, her lips parted. And he sought the sweet heat of her mouth. Moaning softly, Maggie placed a hand on his shoulder. To steady herself or to push him away, he wasn't sure which.

Not giving her a chance to do the latter, Jason untangled his hands from their self-imposed handcuffs and reached for her. He pulled her toward him.

Her body tensed for just a moment. Then, with a breathy sigh, she relaxed. She melted against him, letting him support her slender weight. Her breasts felt warm and heavy against his chest. Her stomach grazed his zipper, making the heat pool in his groin and his body harden in response.

Jason groaned. He felt weak with desire. Stepping back slightly, he sought the solid strength of the door frame, needing its support to hold him. Then they broke apart.

Gasping for air, their chests rising and falling with the effort, they stared at each other. To his relief, instead of fear, passion glittered in Maggie's eyes.

Then, with a contented smile, he pulled her back into the circle of his arms. Indulging himself, he sampled her mouth again. He nibbled at the corners of her lips, moving restlessly across one lightly freckled cheek, seeking the sensitive skin beneath her earlobe.

She dropped her chin, closed her eyes and drew in a deep breath.

Jason buried his fingers in the silky strands of strawberry blond hair, lifting her face to his for another kiss. When he hesitated, she opened her eyes, looking confused.

He grazed her lips with his, then before he lost his nerve, he said, "You are so beautiful. I want you, Maggie. I want to know everything there is about you—and that includes your past."

He felt her body tense, the intimacy of the moment slipping away. Her brow wrinkled into a worried frown. She brought a hand between them, placing it on his chest, trying to push him away. Her withdrawal felt like a slap on the face. "Jason, I can't—"

"I know, I know, it's too soon," he whispered. Stubbornly he pulled her closer, unable to face the recoil he knew would be in her eyes. He brushed his whiskery cheek against hers, relishing the delicate softness of her skin. "Someday, whenever you're ready…I just don't want you ever to feel ashamed or that you can't talk to me. Trust me, Maggie, there's nothing you can tell me that I haven't already heard. I'm not here to pass judgment. I just want to help you."

Before she could protest, he kissed her deeply. His demands were gentle yet urgent, revealing all his fears for their uncertain future. Long before he'd had his fill, he ended the kiss and looked into her eyes. There he saw myriad telling emotions: uncertainty, disappointment, but most devastating of all, fear.

Unexpected anger flared in him. Not at Maggie, for she was an innocent, unable to control the circumstances that had led to this situation. His anger was directed at a man who was long gone. A man unable to answer to his crimes.

With his death, Maggie's late husband had taken away the most precious gift any man could give the woman he cared about—trust.

Even in the most intimate of situations, Jason could feel the gap loom between them. Was he fighting a hopeless battle? Would there ever come a time when Maggie would let down her guard and give herself completely to him?

Suddenly, with a trembling hand, Maggie reached out, tenderly touching the forgotten bump on his cheek. "You're going to have an ugly bruise."

"It won't be the first."

She smiled. And he studied her lips, now swollen from his kisses. "Thank you."

He frowned, feeling confused.

"For being so patient with Kevin...and me." A flush of color touched her cheeks. "You've been a good..."

She hesitated.

Jason lifted a brow. "Neighbor?"

"No, friend," she said, her tone sincere. Her face softened as she amended her statement. "Much more than a friend."

Jason felt the stirrings of hope. It wasn't much. But for now it would have to do.

"You're making it hard for me to say good-night, Maggie." He brushed the tips of his fingers over her cheek.

For once, she didn't flinch at his touch. Instead, her smile deepened. "Good night, Jason."

He struggled to keep from pulling her into his arms and not ever letting go. With all the strength he could muster, he left her then, with only the memory of her smile to keep him warm that night.

Chapter 9

"So what do you think?" Jenny Lewis pointed to a picture in the bridal magazine. "Yellow or blue?"

"Hmm, I don't know." Maggie frowned, studying the picture, finding it hard to concentrate on picking out a bridesmaid's dress. Especially since buying an expensive dress might be a waste of money. She still doubted the wedding between Jenny and Joe Bosworth would take place.

"Mrs. Bosworth said this is absolutely the last day to order the dresses if we want them to be in before the wedding," Jenny said, her expression worried. "If we wait any longer, it might be too late."

The bell above the diner's entrance sounded. New customers filtered into the diner. The lunch hour was beginning.

Maggie sighed. "Why don't you just pick one, Jenny? As long as it isn't hot pink and doesn't clash with my hair, I'm sure it'll be fine."

Dot ambled over, bumping Maggie aside with her hip. She eyed the magazine and arched a brow. "If you want my opinion, you should go with something a little flashier. Something with sequins or lace. That dress is plain boring."

"It's not boring," Jenny protested. "Joe's momma says it's tasteful."

"So's one of Mel's blueberry pies. But that doesn't mean I want to wear it."

Maggie bit her lip, smothering a smile.

Jenny scowled, raising her chin in indignation. "Dot, you're not helping at all. Every time I tell you the wedding plans, you've got one smart comment after another."

"If they were *your* wedding plans and not Mrs. High-and-Mighty Bosworth's, I'd keep my lip buttoned," Dot said, shaking her head in disgust. "That woman's got you hopping every time she snaps her fingers. Honey, you're bending over backwards to do everything she wants. Don't you want your wedding to be special? To be all yours?"

Jenny's lower lip trembled and tears brimmed in her eyes. The heat of her self-righteous anger fizzling fast, she glanced around the diner, lowering her voice so she wouldn't be overheard. "I don't have a choice, Dot. The Bosworths are paying for the wedding. You know I couldn't afford to do this on my own."

"I don't care if the Bosworths are footin' the bill. It still don't make it right. You should have some say in the plannin' of your own wedding." Dot tapped an impatient foot on the tiled floor. A stubborn scowl pursed her lips. "Tell her I'm right, Maggie."

Maggie shifted uncomfortably. Too many bitter memories were associated with her own wedding. She didn't want her disappointing experience to cast a pall on her young friend's special day. "It's not my decision. It's Jenny's."

Jenny stared at the bridal magazine, a distant look in her eye. "I've always dreamed of having a big church wedding. You know the kind, me in a gorgeous white gown, tons of flowers and candles around and organ music playing in the background." Her lips trembled as she gave a wan smile. "Well, this is my chance. My dream come true."

Maggie's heart thudded hollowly. She shot a worried glance at Dot. For once, the blond waitress looked at a loss for words. Even she couldn't bear to burst Jenny's bubble, no matter how misguided the young girl's intentions might be.

The doorbell jangled again.

Maggie looked up to see Jason, accompanied by Officer Stan Wilson, walk into the diner. Her pulse quickened. A familiar warmth sifted through her veins as memories of their kiss flashed through her mind.

A week had passed since they'd shared that intimate embrace in the kitchen of her home. He still wore the shadow of a bruise beneath his eye, although the injury was healing quickly. It served as a constant reminder of what had happened between them. No matter how much she wished it wasn't true, things were different. There'd been a shift in their relationship, an irrevocable one.

And Maggie was at a loss as to what to do about it. She felt in limbo, torn in two by indecision. Her mind knew full well the risk she was taking. Logic told her to flee, to take her son and seek the safety of anonymity. But her heart told her to stay. The part of her that craved the closeness of a warm body and a caring relationship just wouldn't let her abandon this chance at happiness.

So, while her mind and heart warred, she stayed. Only, whenever she saw Jason, she didn't know how to act, how to greet him. She couldn't feign an indifference that didn't exist, not after the wantonness of her behavior. Nor could she bring herself to open her heart to the uncertainties of a love affair.

She didn't know if she was strong enough to risk another heartbreak.

Despite the emotions churning inside her, she found herself smiling as he approached the counter.

Smiling back, Jason slid onto a stool at the counter in front of them. "Good afternoon, ladies."

Stan Wilson followed at a slower pace. Dragging his feet, he took a seat next to Jason. His gaze darted self-consciously around the diner until finally coming to rest on Jenny. Then, with a challenging glint in his eyes, he stared at her.

Oblivious to the undercurrents rippling around him, Jason nodded at the magazine still lying open on the counter. "Something's caught your attention. Good news, I hope."

"Well..." Maggie glanced uncomfortably at Jenny and Dot.

Jenny's cheeks flushed a deep red.

Dot snorted, her chest heaving with barely controlled laughter.

Stan Wilson glanced sharply at the magazine, his eyes narrowing on the bridal pictures.

Jason looked confused. "What? Did I say something wrong?"

"No, Chief Gallagher," Jenny said, picking up the magazine, clutching it protectively to her breasts. She looked at Stan, her gaze defiant. "We were just picking out the bridesmaids' dresses. My wedding's just around the corner."

Stan's jaw clenched, then unclenched. His battle with self-control was obvious. But his gaze didn't waver. He continued to stare at Jenny, refusing to retreat.

"Ah…I see." Jason's smile faded. Frowning, he shot a wary glance at his officer.

"Time to get back to work," Dot suggested, giving Jenny a nudge toward the kitchen. "Mel's going to be bustin' a gut if we let the orders stack up."

With a stubborn stomp of her foot, Jenny whirled away from the counter and marched toward the kitchen. Rolling her eyes, Dot followed the younger woman. Maggie glanced at Stan and wondered how to soothe the officer's ruffled feathers.

Her worries were for naught. Looking as though he'd been sucker punched, Stan rose to his feet. "Chief, I just remembered. I've got some paperwork to catch up on. I'll, uh, meet you back at the department when you're finished with lunch." Turning on his heel, he strode out of the diner.

Jason stared after him, releasing a whistling breath. "This is going to be a rough summer."

Observing Stan Wilson's angry progress across the street, Maggie shook her head. "Nobody ever said falling in love was easy."

After a heartbeat of a pause, Jason said, "No, it's not."

Maggie whipped her gaze around at the solemn tone of his voice. Jason was no longer watching Stan. His gaze was focused on her. An unspoken emotion glittered in his pale blue eyes.

And Maggie knew he was talking about more than the state of his officer's heart. He was talking about his own.

Seconds passed. A palpable tension stretched between them. Swallowing hard, knowing she was taking the coward's way out, she said, "Wh-what can I get you for lunch?"

Disappointment flickered across his face, just before a carefully schooled smile slid into place. "Well, I was going to order the special. But maybe I'd better get a couple of club sandwiches to go. Stan's mood is going to be bad enough this afternoon. He doesn't need an empty stomach making it worse.''

Maggie nodded, then, feeling the heat of his gaze, she headed for the kitchen to place the order. As she did so, she noticed a customer take Stan's vacated stool and begin talking to Jason.

Breathing a sigh of relief, Maggie busied herself delivering other orders until his sandwiches were ready. Out the corner of her eye, however, she watched Jason. A concerned look crossed his handsome face as he listened to the man at his side. He nodded and spoke, his tone low and confiding. Finally the other man stood and placed a hand on Jason's shoulder. He smiled and said something more. When Jason laughed, her stomach did a flip-flop. Her hands shook as she packed his bag with the sandwiches, pickles and chips before returning to where he sat.

She placed the bag on the counter. Her heart lurched at the expectant look in his eyes. ''Your lunch is ready.''

At her brisk, businesslike tone, Jason sighed. He stood, reaching for the wallet in his back pocket and placed enough money on the counter to cover the cost, plus a generous tip. With a bittersweet smile, he said, ''I guess I'll be seeing you around, Maggie.''

He turned to leave.

Unwilling to let him go, not with things so unsettled between them, she blurted, ''Jason, wait.''

He stopped, swinging around to look at her. His wide shoulders tensed. He remained standing very still, focusing all his attention on her as he waited for her to speak.

Daunted, Maggie took a deep breath for courage. ''Kevin has a ball game tonight at the park. You're...you're welcome to come if you'd like.''

Relief eased the lines of tension around his eyes. "What time's the game?"

"It starts at seven."

"I'll be there," he said, not giving his answer a second thought.

"Good," Maggie said, gripping the edge of the counter until her fingers were white-knuckled from the exertion. "Kevin'll like that."

He nodded, a knowing smile playing on his lips. It was as though he'd read her mind and had understood how difficult the invitation had been for her to make. "I'll see you tonight, Maggie."

A weight pressed against her chest, making it difficult to breathe as she watched him leave. She'd taken that first step. She'd opened the door to her heart.

From now on, there was nothing she could do to keep it from slamming in her face.

Jason wasn't coming.

Maggie checked her watch. Seven forty-five. There was less than fifteen minutes left in the game. She tried not to let her disappointment show. But with each slam of a car door and each voice of a new arrival, her hopes rose and fell.

She glanced around the grounds. It was a beautiful spring evening. The sun was just beginning to set across the green fields of the city park. Tree limbs, heavy with new leaves, swayed in the light breeze. The stands surrounding the ball field were filled with cheering parents.

Maggie sat alone, waiting anxiously for a man who wasn't going to come.

Memories of the past crowded her mind. Too often, she'd been disappointed by her ex-husband. The only attention he'd paid to Kevin was one of irritated disapproval, and even that dubious regard was given in small quantities. Most of the time he ignored his son. Kevin had been born a small child. His fine bone structure and shy temperament was a constant annoyance to his father, a man who was strong, confident and aggressive.

A part of her had been relieved by her ex-husband's indifference. The less time he spent with Kevin, the less chance he had to become abusive to their son. Another part of her, however, couldn't help but be disappointed. Her own childhood had been devoid of a male presence. She'd wished for so much more for Kevin.

And whether she wanted to admit it or not, she thought she'd found that something more in Jason.

He'd been so attentive, so encouraging, so supportive of Kevin's attempts at baseball. Maggie sighed. That was what made his absence so much harder.

"Y'rrr out," the umpire called, demanding Maggie's attention.

Three outs. With a shuffling of feet and kicking of the dirt, the teams exchanged places. They were now in the bottom of the last inning. Kevin's team was up at bat, with the other team two points ahead. And if her calculations were correct, Kevin would soon be hitting.

Parents of other children on the team were exchanging words of encouragement, knowing just the perfect thing to say. She had no clue about what advice to give her son. Instead, she caught his eye as he stood in the dugout and gave him a thumbs-up. He smiled, then turned his attention back to the game.

Maggie drew in a steadying breath, trying to calm the butterflies in her stomach. The first batter approached home plate. With enthusiastic swings, the young hitter struck out. Leaning forward on the bench, elbows on her knees, her fingers laced, Maggie concentrated so hard on the game she didn't hear the approach of another fan. Not until he placed a hesitant hand on her shoulder. Startled, Maggie whirled to meet Jason's apologetic glance.

He was still in full uniform, and his face looked haggard. His hair was mussed, unruly curls falling onto his forehead. There was an unmistakable weariness in his stance. "I'm sorry, Maggie. There was a bad accident. Some tourist made a wrong turn on Main Street and hit a van full of kids. I couldn't get away until we got the mess sorted out."

Relief poured through Maggie. Not at the accident that had claimed his attention. But at the fact that, despite the demands and the toll his job had taken, he still found the time to be with her son.

"I'm glad you came," she said softly, her smile hesitant.

The corner of Jason's mouth lifted into a half grin. "So am I."

Their gazes held for a long moment. Then the crack of a bat and the cheer of the crowd broke the intimacy of the moment. Maggie watched as the ball sailed into the outfield and the batter made it safely to first base.

Jason glanced around the field, taking in the scene. "How's Kevin's team doing?"

"Well, it's close. We're in the bottom of the last inning, and his team's only two points behind." Quietly she added, "There's one out and Kevin will be up soon."

Jason nodded, staring at the dugout. "I'll be right back."

She watched as he strode with his usual long-legged confidence to the dugout. Her heart caught as Kevin's face lit up with unfettered delight at Jason's presence. Jason knelt down on one knee, speaking to him at eye level. Kevin nodded, listening intently. Then, patting him on the shoulder, Jason returned to the stand. He slid into the space next to her, his leg brushing hers.

She felt the sinewy strength of his muscles beneath the

stiff fabric of his pants. The heat of his body warmed her. Inhaling sharply, she breathed in a mixture of scents that was purely male: spicy cologne, the oiled leather of his gun belt and the sweat of hard work. She found it difficult to concentrate on the baseball game and not on the man beside her.

The pitcher threw wild, hitting the next batter on the leg. Once it was assured the player wasn't injured, the little boy took his base. The next batter hit a high fly into the air, allowing the shortstop to catch it with ease.

Two outs, two men on base—and it was Kevin's turn to bat.

Maggie moaned beneath her breath.

Jason chuckled and covered her hand with his. "Don't worry, Maggie. He'll be fine."

"How can you be so sure?"

"Because for the last five days we've been practicing hitting in the backyard. His swing's improved and so has his accuracy." Squeezing her hand gently, he repeated, "Like I said, he'll be fine."

Kevin hitched his pants up on his slender hips as he strode to the batter's box. With a determined scowl on his face, he tapped the tip of the bat on home plate, took a couple of practice swings and stared down the pitcher, who had to be at least twice his size.

Maggie gripped Jason's hand tightly, forgetting all the reasons she should be keeping a distance between them, needing his reassuring touch even more.

On his first attempt, Kevin tried too hard. He swung, his bat whistling as it sliced the air. Strike one.

Maggie glanced at Jason. He smiled at her, seeming unperturbed, his confidence in her son unwavering.

The second pitch was high. But Kevin got a piece of it. The ball went up, up, up into the air. Calls of "heads up" peppered the stands. The foul ball landed smack dab in the middle of the bleachers. Strike two.

Jason chuckled at her cry of dismay.

Maggie held her breath and waited for the next pitch.

It was a perfect throw, just the right height and speed for someone Kevin's size. With a satisfying crack of the bat, the ball sailed into centerfield.

Maggie jumped to her feet, with Jason following.

Dropping his bat, Kevin ran for first base. The ball continued to fly, up and over the outfielder's head. Kevin and his teammates rounded the bases. First one, then another, made it into home. The score was now tied.

Kevin hesitated on his way to third base.

In the outfield, two players had collided while trying to catch Kevin's hit. Regrouping, they picked themselves up and ran for the ball. The third-base coach was waving Kevin on.

Glancing anxiously at the outfield, he ran for broke. He rounded third base, heading for home, the tie-breaking run resting squarely on his small shoulders. The boy in centerfield picked up the ball, tossing it to his cutoff man at second. Kevin and the ball were now at a dead heat.

At home plate the catcher raised his glove, his feet straddling the base, readying himself to tag Kevin out.

Maggie's heart thudded wildly in her chest. Joining the other parents in yelling words of encouragement, she jumped up and down on the narrow metal footspace, nearly losing her balance and toppling forward. Jason reached out a steadying hand, smiling indulgently at her show of enthusiasm.

Kevin neared home as the second baseman tossed the ball to the catcher. With the reckless spirit of youth, he threw himself at the plate, sliding under the catcher's feet as he jumped up to catch the ball. A hush fell on the crowd as they watched Kevin touch the base—a split second before the catcher, ball in hand, brought his cleated foot down squarely on Kevin's outstretched arm.

And Maggie's world tilted beneath her as the snap of Kevin's bone breaking echoed across the field.

A collective gasp arose from the crowd.

The color drained from Maggie's face. She opened her mouth, but no sound was emitted. She swayed, looking as though she might faint as she stared at her son.

Kevin lay on the ground, holding his arm awkwardly in front of him, his body curled protectively around his injury.

Jason's grip tightened at her waist. "Maggie, are you okay?"

She drew in a choppy breath. "I've got to get to Kevin."

He nodded. Jumping down from the stands, he reached out to help her. He felt the tremors racking her body as he lifted her to the ground. His own heart thumped so hard he could barely hear the excited buzz of the crowd around them. Pushing his way through the throng of players and coaches, glad for once of the respect his uniform afforded, he led Maggie to her son at home plate.

By the time they reached him, Kevin's coach was kneeling beside him, shouting orders to his assistants. "We need ice. Somebody get an ice pack out of the cooler."

Somewhere in the commotion, Kevin had lost his glasses. As Jason approached, he saw the tears making tracks on his dusty cheeks. But the boy wasn't crying out in pain. Instead, he bit down hard on his trembling lower lip, keeping up a brave front.

Hiding her fear, Maggie dropped to the ground beside her son. With the same air of self-assuredness Jason had seen her assume when Bob Williams had his heart attack, Maggie spoke to her son. "Kevin, I'm going to have to look at your arm. Do you think you could hold it out for me?''

Kevin nodded, still not saying a word. He slowly lifted his arm from the protective cradle of his chest.

The arm wasn't swollen, yet, but Jason could clearly see the imprint of the catcher's cleats. The skin at the point of impact looked red and tender. And the set of bones looked off-kilter, somehow, as though one side were shorter than the other.

Jason heard Maggie's sharp intake of breath as she stared at Kevin's arm. Swallowing hard, she gently probed the injury with two fingers. When she reached the point where the cleat marks were at their deepest, Kevin cried out in pain for the first time.

''I'm so sorry, honey. I'm all finished now,'' she murmured, her voice soothing. Tears glazed her eyes. She blinked rapidly, not allowing her son to see her distress. Then, carefully, she replaced Kevin's arm against his chest. Jason felt the full impact of her concern when she turned her troubled gaze to him. ''His arm's broken. He needs to go to the hospital.''

Once again, without question, Jason accepted her diagnosis. ''I've got a first-aid kit in my patrol car. There's an air splint. We can put it on him before we move him.''

''That would be great.''

Her voice sounded strained, hollow. Wishing he could do more to reassure her, Jason forced himself to move, heading for his patrol car with rapid strides. By the time he returned with the first-aid kit, Maggie was holding an ice pack on Kevin's arm. The coach had cleared a space around them, keeping curious parents and players away.

Without asking, Maggie opened the kit, inflated the air splint and anchored it around Kevin's arm. Jason watched with a growing unease. This wasn't the first time he'd witnessed Maggie's nursing skills. It seemed as though she knew exactly what to do, as though she was a trained medical professional.

Jason pushed the thought brusquely from his mind. If Maggie was a nurse, why in the world was she working as a waitress? It just didn't make any sense.

The coach tapped him on the shoulder, interrupting his troubled thoughts. "Kevin's glasses. I found them in the dirt by home plate. They're a little scratched, but not broken."

"Thanks," Jason said, slipping them into the breast pocket of his shirt.

"Finished," Maggie announced, a weary note to her voice. "Kevin and I...we walked to the park. I didn't bring my car. I don't..." Her voice broke and she closed her eyes. When she'd regained her composure, she said, "I don't know how I'll get him to the hospital."

"I'll drive you," Jason said quietly, unable to keep the concern from his gaze. "Are you ready to go?"

Maggie nodded.

Turning to Kevin, he looked into the boy's pain-filled face and felt his stomach clench. Memories of his own son's last days of suffering flooded his mind. Brushing the terrible images away, he said, "I'm going to carry you to the patrol car, Kevin. Moving around is probably going to hurt a little. Think you can handle it?"

Kevin nodded, blinking back the fear in his eyes.

Carefully, after directing Kevin to hold his injured arm against his chest, he lifted the boy. His weight was easy to bear. With Maggie close at their side, they headed for the patrol car.

Concerned parents and anxious players cleared a path for them. Unexpectedly a cheer arose from the crowd. Fans from both teams clapped as they left the field.

Kevin's eyes widened, looking confused by all the attention.

Maggie frowned and placed an anxious hand on her son.

"Don't worry, Maggie," Jason whispered. "They aren't glad Kevin got hurt. They're just showing their support. After all, he did win the game for them."

"I did?" Kevin said, speaking for the first time. He grinned with pleasure, despite his injury.

Jason chuckled, catching the bemused expression on Maggie's face. Their mood lighter, they headed for the car. After depositing Kevin in the back seat under his mother's care, Jason slung himself into the front seat. He gunned the engine and pulled out of the parking lot, then sped to the hospital. Once there, they were overwhelmed by the frenetic activity of the emergency room.

Belatedly Jason remembered the accident on Main Street. Due to the number of teenagers in the crowded van, there'd been numerous minor injuries. No doubt the hospital staff was still dealing with the overflow of patients.

Kevin was placed in a wheelchair and whisked down the hall to an examining room.

Maggie started to follow.

A heavyset nurse stepped in front of her, stopping her. She gestured Maggie toward the reception desk. "You're going to have to fill out some forms first."

Maggie released an exasperated breath. "Now? Can't it wait?"

The nurse raised a brow. "You do want your son to be treated, don't you?"

Maggie's eyes narrowed. Her chin jutted out. She looked like a mother lion ready to pounce to protect her cub.

Jason placed a calming hand on her arm, pulling her back. "It'll only take a minute, Maggie. The sooner you get it over with, the sooner you can be with Kevin."

For a moment Jason thought she might argue. But finally she sucked in a deep breath and nodded. The soles of her tennis shoes squeaked impatiently against the tiled floor as she headed for the reception desk. Grabbing a pen and clipboard, she hurriedly filled out the forms. A few minutes later, she slammed the pen onto the desktop and handed the clipboard to the waiting nurse.

"Your son's in examining room three," the nurse said as she shuffled through the forms.

Without a backward glance, Maggie turned on her heel and rushed down the hall, leaving Jason standing awkwardly at the reception desk. He stared after her, not sure what to do next. More than anything else, he wanted to follow her, to be with her and Kevin. His concern for the pair throbbed in his chest like an untended wound.

But he didn't know if his presence would be welcome.

His decision was made for him.

The nurse at the desk blew out an irritated breath. "For goodness' sake, she forgot to sign the release form." Grumbling, she leaned heavily on the desk and began heaving her ample girth from the chair.

"Keep sitting," Jason suggested, taking advantage of the opportunity. "Why don't you let me collect her signature?"

The nurse eyed him suspiciously, scanning him from head to toe. Whether it was the uniform or the eager look in his eye, he passed muster. She handed him the clipboard. "The form's on top. She needs to sign both sides."

"Yes, ma'am." He took the form, careful not to appear too anxious, then strode toward the examining rooms.

His step faltered midway down the hall as he glanced at the forms and realized he held a gold mine of personal information about Maggie in his hands. There was no denying that his curiosity was piqued. Since meeting Maggie, the one thing that frustrated him most was that he'd been unable to get her to share her past. Now, staring him in the eye, was an opportunity to slake his curiosity.

None of your business, Gallagher, he told himself sternly, slapping the clipboard against his thigh. When the lady wanted to share her past, she'd tell him herself.

But would she?

The unsettling thought needled him, burrowing into his conscience and not letting go. He had known Maggie for over a month. In that time, they'd become close friends very quickly. They'd seen each other through some pretty tough situations. And had even taken a step toward intimacy.

Yet she still held a part of herself aloof, stubbornly guarding her past. Something about her just didn't gel. Uneasily he recalled the self-assuredness with which she handled her son's injury. She knew exactly how to treat a broken bone, taking charge without relying on anyone else's advice. It was as though she'd done it many times before.

Jason paused a few feet from the examining room, glancing uneasily down the busy hall. Gripping the clipboard in his hand, he flipped through the pages, seeking anything that might shed a clue about Maggie's past. On the third page, he froze as he scanned the sheet. The papers rattled as he held them too tightly in his hands.

On the form, she'd listed her birth place as a small town in California. Her social-security number was from California, as well. But a week ago she'd told him she'd been born and bred in Florida.

Why would she lie?

Jason closed his eyes and muttered an oath beneath his breath. If he hadn't been so damned curious, none of this would be happening.

Now what the hell was he supposed to do?

Releasing a ragged breath, he opened his eyes and stared

at the entrance to room three. Through the open doorway, Maggie's reassuring voice drifted out to greet him. He heard Kevin's anxious tone…and felt as though he were being ripped apart with indecision.

Maggie had deliberately deceived him. But he couldn't believe there was anything illicit behind her reason for doing so. He'd seen the fear in her eyes, her protectiveness toward her son. These were primal instincts, not the traits of a woman comfortable with the art of deception.

Maggie was an innocent; he'd stake his reputation on that. Someday soon she would tell him the truth, and he'd look back on this moment and laugh at his own fears.

But until she did, that didn't mean he couldn't do a little checking on his own. He had a friend on the police force in California. A simple phone call would clear up any questions he might have about Maggie and her past.

Carefully sorting the papers back in place, Jason drew in a steadying breath and stepped forward to join Maggie and Kevin.

Chapter 10

"Six weeks!" Stretching out on the lumpy old couch in their living room, Kevin lifted his broken arm and squinted at the cast, his gaze myopic. Somewhere in the excitement at the ball park, he'd lost his glasses. "I have to wear this thing for six weeks?"

"Kevin, you're lucky it wasn't worse." Maggie dropped a kiss on the top of his head and breathed in the scent of baby shampoo and soap. Fresh from a bath, he'd washed away the grime of the baseball field and looked less disreputable. Yet he still appeared tired, in pain, and terribly vulnerable. Unwanted tears stung her eyes. She pulled away. "It was a clean break. You'll heal fast. Don't be so upset."

"But the baseball season will be over before I can play again."

Maggie's heart ached at the forlorn expression on her son's face. It did seem a shame that Kevin's first victorious game of the season would also be his last, especially since he'd worked so hard on his skills. She offered a wan attempt at consolation. "There's always next year."

"Yeah, but only if we're still living in Wyndchester," he said, heaving a miserable sigh.

She stared at him, unable to think of a response. She couldn't promise him anything, for she wasn't sure where they'd be living twelve days from now, much less twelve months.

The doorbell rang, saving her from having to answer. Peeking out the living-room window, Maggie's pulse quickened at the sight of Jason standing on her front porch. Earlier, at the hospital, he'd proved invaluable. He'd sat by her side and kept her company while Kevin had been getting X-rayed. Quietly he'd held her hand while the doctor had set the fractured bone. And he'd entertained Kevin with knock-knock jokes as they'd plastered his arm in a cast.

When he'd dropped her and Kevin off less than an hour ago, she hadn't wanted him to leave.

Now her heart was thumping with relief that he'd returned. Her hands felt clumsy as she unlatched the chain and opened the door. Overwhelmed by a flood of confusing emotions, she simply stared at him through the open doorway.

He wore faded jeans and a light blue T-shirt that matched his eyes. His dark hair was wet, as though from a recent shower. She detected the telltale scent of soap, shampoo and spicy aftershave. In his hand, he held out a pair of child's glasses. "I found these in my pocket when I was changing out of my clothes. Kevin's coach gave them to me before we left the park. Sorry—I forgot all about them until now."

"Oh, thank goodness. I was afraid we'd have to get a new pair." She reached for the glasses. Her fingers brushed against his palm, igniting sparks of awareness. Her fingertips tingled at the point of contact. Flustered, she snatched her hand away. At his searching gaze, she knew he'd been aware of her reaction. A blush warmed her cheeks as she mumbled a quick thank-you.

Jason shifted uneasily, the soles of his tennis shoes making a soft scraping sound on the porch floor. He nodded toward the light in the living room behind her. "How's Kevin doing?"

"Still awake and still hurting. But not for long. He just took one of the painkillers the doctor sent home with him. In another few minutes, he won't be feeling a thing."

"Good." She heard the inhalation of his breath, felt his gaze as it lingered on her and sensed the hesitation in his stance. He looked as though he'd like to say something more. Finally, sighing, he said, "Well, I guess I'd better be heading on back."

"So soon? Would you like to come in?" she blurted, panicking at the thought of his leaving. Embarrassed, she added, "You could tell Kevin good-night."

"I'd like that."

Despite the pain and weariness clouding his young eyes, Kevin managed a smile when he saw Jason enter the room.

"How are you doing, Kevin?" Jason asked, his voice laced with concern. He stepped toward the couch.

"Okay," Kevin said with a shrug. "It still hurts a little."

"That's to be expected. It won't be long, though, before the worst is over." He took a seat at the far end of the couch, careful not to jar Kevin's arm. "Pretty soon you'll be bugging your mom to get that cast off your arm so you can play again."

Maggie smiled. "He's already been complaining about missing the baseball season."

"I don't blame you a bit," Jason said. "The team's going to be missing their star player."

Kevin grinned. But not for long. His smile faded as his mouth widened into a yawn.

Maggie and Jason both laughed.

"That's my cue to put you in bed, young man," she said.

Kevin didn't argue. Instead, he swung his legs off the couch and rose wearily to his feet. When he swayed, she stooped to pick him up. "How about a ride, squirt?"

"Do you need some help?" Jason asked, frowning as he pushed himself to his feet.

"No, I can manage." With Kevin safe in her arms, she glanced at Jason, noting for the first time the agitated look in his eyes. He seemed overly concerned by her son's injury. Granted, he'd been coaching Kevin in the evenings, helping him with his baseball skills. Surely he didn't blame himself for Kevin's accident. "This won't take long. There's lemonade in the refrigerator. Help yourself. I'll be back in a little while."

Jason nodded, but he didn't move. She felt the weight of his troubled gaze as she carried her son from the living room. He was still on the couch when she returned, his elbows on his knees, his hands clasped in front of him. So lost in thought, he didn't hear her until she was almost at his side.

He glanced up, his eyes wide and startled. Then, with an embarrassed grin, he stood. He towered over her, making her feel petite. "Is Kevin asleep?"

"Yes," she said, ignoring the butterflies fluttering in her stomach. "It only took about three seconds after his head hit the pillow. I don't think he'll have any problems sleeping through the night. The hospital prescribed some strong painkillers."

With a nod, Jason shoved his hands in his back pockets and released a ragged breath. A commiserative pain glittered in his own eyes. "I hate to see anyone hurting, especially Kevin."

Maggie felt a rush of concern. Kevin's injury didn't warrant such distress. Once again, she wondered if Jason felt responsible in some way for Kevin's accident. "Jason, I...I wanted to thank you."

He raised a questioning brow.

"For helping me at the ball field and the hospital. Usually I'm pretty good in a crisis. But if you hadn't been there...I would have fallen apart." She gave a self-deprecating grimace. "I guess it's hard to be rational when it comes to your own child."

He didn't answer right away. Instead, he stood very still and stared down at the faded rose pattern of the rug beneath his feet. Finally, drawing in a deep breath of air, he said, "Believe me, Maggie. I know exactly how you feel."

Instinctively she knew he was speaking of his own son, the child who wouldn't need his baseball glove anymore. This wasn't the first time Jason had alluded to the boy. She remembered how upset he'd been the morning the two boys had played hooky from school. When they'd turned up unharmed, what was it he'd said? *So often things turn out differently.*

"Your son," she said softly, unable to stop herself, "was he hurt?"

He flinched as though he'd been struck. Raising his head, he looked at her in surprise. "H-how'd you know about Scott?"

"The glove—Kevin told me it belonged to your son. I was just curious about him."

Jason stared at her numbly. Her heart clutched at the hollow emptiness of his eyes. Bluntly he said, "Scotty died."

"Oh, Jason, I'm sorry." She felt tension thrumming

through his body when she placed a hand on his arm. Hesitantly, a part of her still afraid to get too close, she pulled him down on the couch beside her. "Tell me, how did it happen?"

For a long moment he remained silent. Maggie was afraid she'd overstepped her bounds. Perhaps she'd misjudged the situation. She thought he needed someone to confide in. Now she wondered if she was invading his privacy.

Jason stared at his hands, his jaw clenching and unclenching. Then, in a flat, emotionless tone, he said, "It happened almost two years ago. Scott wasn't much older than Kevin at the time. His mother and I had divorced when he was a baby, but we lived a few miles apart so we could share custody. He was staying with me at the time. Scott's school was only four blocks from my house, but he had to cross an intersection to get there. He was so proud the first time I let him walk the distance by himself." The memory brought a bittersweet smile to his lips.

Maggie didn't say a word, afraid to interrupt, knowing the worst was yet to come.

"That morning, when I sent him off to school, he was in a hurry. He'd forgotten to bring his math book home the night before. He wanted to get to school and finish the assignment before classes started. I barely got a hug goodbye before he ran out the door." Jason swallowed hard, giving himself a moment before continuing. "The next thing I know, there are two uniformed policemen on my doorstep telling me Scott was hit by a drunk driver. The bastard didn't stop, not even after he sent my son's body flying through the intersection."

Maggie closed her eyes, trying to blot out the horrible images, images that Jason lived with every day. Unable to find the words to comfort him, she reached for his hand.

His fingers felt cold as they covered hers. He held on tight, as though she'd thrown a lifeline to a drowning man.

"He lived for three days," Jason said. His voice sounded thick, hoarse with emotion. "He never regained consciousness, but I could see the pain written on his face. He suffered more than any child should have to, and there wasn't a damn thing I could do to stop it."

Maggie didn't think twice. With unguarded tears in her eyes, she lifted her arms, wrapped them around his neck and held him close. She rocked him slowly, comforting him without words, letting the warmth of her body still the cold tremors shaking his.

Sighing, he lowered his head and buried his face in her hair. She shivered as his breath fanned her neck when he whispered, "I'm sorry, Maggie. You've got enough on your mind with Kevin. I shouldn't have bothered you. Not tonight."

"Shh." She pulled away, far enough to see the pain in his eyes, and pressed a finger to his lips. They felt soft to the touch. And she remembered how gently he'd kissed her.

Jason trusted her enough to share the demons of his past. She wished she could reciprocate, to tell him the truth about her situation with Kevin. But something held her back. Even now, when she'd never felt closer to a man, her protective instincts were too strong. She couldn't open herself up completely. She couldn't allow herself to be vulnerable, not even with Jason.

But that didn't stop her from wanting him, from needing to feel his body close.

He shut his eyes and appeared to be struggling for control.

Slowly she lowered her hand, tracing the lean contours of his face with the tips of her fingers. A slight dimple creased his cheek, and she wished he would smile so that she could watch it deepen. His skin felt smooth, freshly shaven, with only the barest hint of a whisker. Her fingers glided over his strong jawline, stopping at the vein pulsing in his neck, measuring the rapid beat of his heart.

Then, unable to help herself, she brought her lips to his and kissed him. A gentle, tender kiss, meant to heal, as well as to satisfy.

A deep moan rumbled from his chest. His eyes flew open. Then he gripped her shoulders and pushed her away. The rush of cool air chilled her skin. Instantly she missed the heat of his body.

His voice harsh, he said, "I didn't come here for this. It's not a good idea, Maggie."

She felt the sharp sting of rejection. Embarrassed heat flooded her skin. She glanced away, unable to face him. "I—I'm sorry."

"No, don't be," he said, his voice filled with frustration. He hooked a finger beneath her chin, forcing her to look at him. "You don't understand, Maggie. I need this…I need you too damned much. Once I start, I'm afraid I wouldn't be able to stop."

Her stomach churned with trepidation. A weight seemed to press against her chest. For some reason, she couldn't breathe in deeply enough to fill her lungs. "I—I wouldn't want you to stop."

He stared at her, his eyes searching her face. "Do you know what you're saying?"

"I'm saying I need you, too," she said, her voice whisper soft. "I want you to hold me, to kiss me. Make love to me, Jason."

She held her breath, waiting for his response. It didn't take long. With a growl of frustration, he plowed his fingers through her hair and tilted her head back. Taking a second to study her face, he lowered his mouth and kissed her deeply.

Feeling weak, she anchored her hands on his shoulders for support.

He tore his mouth from hers. Restlessly, his lips explored her face. He grazed her mouth, her cheekbones, her chin, the tip of her nose. His hands dropped to her waist. She felt the searing heat of his fingers as he slipped them beneath her T-shirt.

He hesitated, glancing at the lace curtains that covered the windows. "Your curtains are very pretty, Maggie, but they don't give us much privacy."

"We could…" She cleared her throat, feeling brazen and reckless. "We could turn off the light."

Without a word, he reached for the table lamp, and with a flick of his wrist, the room was cast in darkness, leaving only the muted light from the kitchen.

Kissing her once again, he traced the outline of her breasts with his fingers, then his hands slid to her waist. He gripped the hem of her T-shirt. She gasped when he pushed the fabric up and over her head and the cool air hit her passion-warmed skin.

Lowering her back against the couch, he placed a kiss on her bare stomach. And Maggie quivered beneath his touch. For once she didn't mind the discomfort of the couch. He loosened the clasp of her bra and she heard the growl of desire deep in his throat as he looked down at her.

With incredible tenderness, he cupped her breasts, rubbing his thumbs across the sensitive nubs, watching her face as they hardened beneath his caress. Her back arched off the couch when his lips followed and he took one taut nipple into his mouth, and then the other.

Feeling clumsy and inept, she wasn't sure what to do with her hands. "Making love" had been a misnomer when applied to what she'd shared with her ex-husband. There had been no give and take, only her husband's demands.

But this was different. Jason was different.

She wanted to please him as much as he pleased her.

Maggie wove her fingers into the thick curls at the back of his head, cradling him against her as he suckled her breasts. Heat pooled low in her stomach; an ache throbbed deep inside her. When she could bear no more, she raised his head and claimed his mouth with a greedy kiss.

As their tongues mated, she raked her fingers down his back, molding her hands against the hard muscles of his body, stopping at his narrow waist. Impatiently she tugged at his shirt, needing to feel his skin against hers.

Ending the kiss, he shucked his shirt with an economy of motion and tossed it on the floor. She stared at him for a long moment, drinking her fill, marveling at the perfection of his body. A light mat of dark hair covered his chest, narrowing to a point at his waist before disappearing into the waistband of his jeans. There was a jagged, white scar on his shoulder, and given his occupation, her imagination leaped to a number of frightening conclusions.

Tentatively she reached out and touched him. The hair on his chest felt springy. His skin sizzled with heat. His body was all rock-hard muscle and velvety smooth skin. Her fingers grazed his nipples and they hardened in response.

Groaning, he gathered her into his arms and held her close, flattening the aching fullness of her breasts against his chest, reclaiming her mouth with his. Maggie felt as though she might explode with the sensations flowing inside her.

His free hand fell to her waist, and he unfastened the top button and pulled down the zipper. Her shorts fell open and he pushed them and her panties down, running his hands silkily over her thighs and legs.

When he stood and struggled out of his own clothes, kicking his shoes and jeans out of the way, Maggie felt the first jolt of panic. He was towering, and in the shadowy light, the lean strength and power of his naked, aroused body both exhilarated and frightened her. She sucked in shallow breaths, willing herself to be calm.

He returned to the couch, lowering himself beside her, his body half-covering hers.

The room spun. An unwanted bubble of fear rose in her throat, choking her. Her muscles tightened reflexively and she struggled to push him away. "I—I can't."

Jason flinched. He raised himself on his elbows, holding himself still, looking at her with obvious confusion. "What's wrong? Did I hurt you?"

"No," she said, shaking so hard she barely got the word from her mouth. "I—I'm just afraid."

"Aw, Maggie." He sighed, pulling away. Even with the fear racking her body, she missed his reassuring warmth. She wanted to pull him back into her arms and pretend that everything was all right. Sitting up, he looked down at her with such regret her heart ached. "I thought you knew I'd never do anything to hurt you."

"I do know that," she said, reaching a tentative hand to his face. "I still want you. I…I just don't know if I can do this. I can't stop thinking about…" She hesitated.

"About your husband," he said flatly. For the first time anger flickered across his face, his jaw tightening with the intensity of the emotion. Swearing softly, he gently cupped her face in his big hand and said, "Listen to me, Maggie. I'm not your late husband. I'd never force you to make love to me." Sighing, he fell back against the cushions, cradling her in his arms. "As long as it takes, I'll wait until you're ready."

For a long moment he held her close, enveloping her in the warmth of his body. With her ear pressed against his chest, she heard the erratic pounding of his heart, the frustrated sigh of his breath. Being this close did little to still the fire of passion.

Then he kissed the top of her head, and pulled away, reaching for his clothes scattered on the floor. And Maggie knew he meant every word he'd just said. He wasn't angry with her. He still wanted her. He would wait until she was ready. Confusing emotions tumbled about inside her, but strongest of all was relief.

Before he could rise to his feet, she propped herself up on one elbow and placed a hand on his back. "Jason," she said softly. "I don't want to wait."

He looked at her, studying her carefully. "Are you sure, Maggie?"

"I'm positive."

"Then we'll make it right for you," he promised. The whisper of fabric filled the room as he dropped his jeans back onto the floor.

He lay down on the couch beside her, slipping his hands beneath her and lifting her body as though she were as light as a doll. In one fluid motion, they shifted places on the couch until she was straddling him, looking down into his sparkling eyes.

"You're in charge, Maggie. Tell me what you want."

"I want to touch you."

"Then do it."

Hesitantly, she ran her fingers over his chest, his flat stomach, smoothing both hands along the sides of his hips. She grazed the tip of his manhood and felt a bead of moisture. Nervously she moved her hands away, sliding them down the length of his sinewy thighs, the hair on his legs scratching her sensitive skin.

Timidly she raised her hands and cupped him.

"Maggie," he said on a sharply indrawn breath of air. He swelled at her touch, and she marveled at the velvety strength of his body.

Emboldened, she stroked him, giving him the pleasure she'd first denied.

He stilled her hand and nodded toward his jeans on the floor. "If I admit I've come prepared, will you still believe me that I didn't plan on any of this happening?"

She raised a brow skeptically.

"I can't help it if I've been hopeful, Maggie." His smile was so innocent she couldn't help but believe him.

Awkwardly she reached for the jeans, searching the pockets until she found the foil packet. Her hands trembled as she tore it open and slipped it into place.

Jason reached out, his palms flattening her breasts. He ground them lightly, raised his head and licked the swollen tips.

Her body quickened and Maggie raked her fingers through his hair as she opened herself to him and sheathed him with her body. He arched his back and buried himself deeper. Blood, hot and thick, coursed through her veins as she moved above him, slowly at first, then faster.

He held her hips in his hands, guiding her through wave upon wave of sensation, watching her face as heat blossomed inside her. And when she finally reached the peak, her body shaking with the tremors of passion, he soon followed. She felt his pulsing climax deep inside her.

When it was over, exhausted, she rolled over, snuggling against his side. Their bodies were hot and damp with perspiration, the couch small and uncomfortable, but she didn't mind. She rested her head on his shoulder and felt a contentment she'd never experienced before.

Tangled in his arms, she felt safe…and loved.

Long minutes passed. The heat of passion waned and the air cooled about them, chilling him. But Jason didn't move. He was too afraid to do anything that might burst the bubble of contentment that surrounded them.

With Maggie in his arms, he felt complete. In her, he'd found a perfection no other woman had ever matched.

She was innocence and passion rolled into one. She made his heart sing, his body hum. She brought out every primal need, every protective instinct that he possessed.

And yet, she had lied to him. He pushed the thought from his mind, unwilling to spoil this perfect moment.

She shifted in his arms, yawning sleepily. Her full breasts rose and fell, pillowing against his chest. Once again, he felt the stirrings of arousal. Making love to Maggie had only whetted his appetite. He doubted if he would ever tire of her intriguing body.

But it was late. And Kevin was upstairs, asleep in his bed. He didn't need to wake up in the middle of the night and find them together. Sighing, Jason sat up, reluctantly ending the embrace. "I need to go."

"Already?" she asked, her voice drowsy.

"It's late." He brushed a strand of hair from her eyes, smoothing the curl behind her ears. "I've got to work in the morning."

"And Kevin will be up early," she said, sitting up on the edge of the couch next to him. With an embarrassed grimace, she glanced at the clothes scattered across the living-room floor. "It looks like a tornado hit this room."

"A small cyclone at least." He stood, feeling not in the least bit uncomfortable about his nudity. Maggie, on the other hand, had succumbed to modesty. Pulling on his briefs and jeans, he watched as she hurriedly dressed herself, panties first, then shorts. Leaving her bra on the floor, she pulled her T-shirt over her head.

She gave an impatient breath, when her shirt tangled in a bunch about her shoulders.

Chuckling, he reached out and smoothed the snarled fabric. "In my opinion, it seems a shame to have to cover such a beautiful body." Once finished, he pulled her snug against him and planted a kiss on the end of her freckled nose. "I'll have you know it took a great deal of willpower to help you without taking advantage. You owe me."

A blush bloomed on her face.

He smiled, amused by her embarrassment. Moments ago she had abandoned her inhibitions and given herself to him fully. Now she seemed shy and awkward.

Just when he thought he had her figured out, she surprised him once again.

The thought settled uneasily in his mind.

His smile fading, he pulled on his shirt and picked up his shoes. Leaving his feet bare, he tiptoed into the kitchen, with Maggie following close behind. At the back door he indulged himself with one last, lingering kiss.

"Good night, Maggie," he said, rubbing a thumb along the delicate curve of her mouth. He memorized the sweet expression on her face, storing it in his mind's eye to recall later, when he was trying to fall asleep in his lonely bed. Before he changed his mind and refused to leave, he stepped out of her warm embrace and into the cool night air.

The cold, damp grass was a shock to the system. He quickened his step, already missing the coziness of Maggie's house, the warmth of her embrace. He wished he didn't have to go.

With each step he took across the night-darkened yard, his confidence slipped another notch. He'd never felt so close to a woman. And yet, what did he know about her?

They'd just made love. They'd become intimate in the most basic of ways—but he still had no clue to Maggie's past.

Climbing the steps of his porch, he paused, glancing across the yard to the house next door. He'd trusted her enough to open up to her, to confide his past and share the circumstances of Scott's death. He'd seen the pain in her eyes when he told her of his son's suffering, and he knew she cared.

But she still didn't trust him.

Or surely she'd have felt comfortable enough to tell him about herself. She wanted to, though. He'd seen the hesitancy in her eyes and knew she'd been on the verge of telling him the truth.

But at the last minute she'd changed her mind.

What could be so bad that she felt she needed to hide it from someone who'd become her lover?

A number of answers crossed his mind, none of which eased his fears. Setting his jaw in a stubborn line, Jason swore to himself that he'd get to the bottom of Maggie's secret past.

His reasons were purely selfish. He was losing his heart to the woman next door. He didn't want anything to get in the way of his chance at happy-ever-after.

Chapter 11

"**E**venin', Chief," the dispatcher said as Jason strode into the Wyndchester Police Department late the next day. Betty stood, stretching the kinks out of her back and covering a yawn. Her night replacement hovered nearby, coffee cup in hand, looking anxious to take over.

"Have a good evening, Betty. I'll see you in the morning," Jason said as he passed her desk with a smile on his face, his step light and his mood...well, to say his mood was good would be an understatement.

Betty eyed him thoughtfully. "You're looking awfully peppy this evening, Chief. Must have slept good last night."

"Like a baby," he lied, pausing at her desk. The truth was, it was late before he'd gotten home from Maggie's house. Even later before his hormones unwound enough to allow him to relax and fall asleep. Despite his lack of rest, he'd never felt better or more content. "I guess I'm finally getting used to how quiet a small town can be in the middle of the night.''

"You need noise to put you sleep? Just wait until the weather warms up," she said, opening a drawer and taking out her purse. "Then you'll have the cicadas and the bullfrogs singing you a lullabye.''

"Or driving you crazy," Officer Schmitz said with a snort. He slammed a file drawer closed, shaking his head in disgust. "I've lived here all my life and I can't stand the racket. It's like 'surround sound' without the advantage of a volume button. My advice is to buy some earplugs, Chief.''

"I'll keep that in mind," Jason said, chuckling, as he turned to continue on to his office.

"Oh, Chief, I almost forgot. You got a call," Betty said, grabbing a memo slip from her desk. She squinted at the paper in her hand. "A Tom Burns from Meridia, California, called a few minutes ago. He says he wants you to call him back ASAP.''

Jason's heart gave a lurch. His good mood fizzled like a balloon deflating at the end of a party. Earlier this morning he'd placed a call to his old friend in California. His request: run a check on a name and social-security number. The person's name: Maggie Conrad. Such a simple request, yet it had taken all the strength he possessed to make it.

He'd expected Tom to return his call hours ago, but he hadn't. With each passing minute, second thoughts had hounded him. Last night, he'd resolved to settle the questions about Maggie's past once and for all. He'd told himself that they couldn't have a future until they put the past where it belonged—behind them.

Now he wasn't so sure he wanted to know.

The truth was, he was afraid of what he might find out. Maggie hadn't been at the diner today. They'd told him at Mel's that she'd taken the day off to be with her son. He'd missed her shy smile and reassuring presence. At least ten different times during the course of the day he'd reached for the phone to call her, just to hear her sweet voice.

Something had stopped him.

They'd come so far these past weeks. It had been a slow, uphill battle to win her trust. Now, he was afraid that she'd hear the guilt in his tone, that somehow she would know he'd betrayed her faith in him.

"Chief?" Betty's voice snapped him out of his troubled thoughts. Jason blinked into focus the curious expression on his dispatcher's face. "You okay, Chief? I thought I lost you there for a minute."

"I'm fine," he said. Forcing himself to move, he reached for the memo. "Thanks, Betty."

Crumpling the note in his hand, he strode to his office, closing the door firmly behind him. He tossed his cap on the desk and blew out a tension-releasing breath. Sitting down heavily in the swivel chair, he stared at the wrinkled memo.

It was too late to change his mind. He'd already set into motion the steps that would bring him either peace or further discontent. Delaying the inevitable would accomplish nothing. He gave a mirthless laugh. Nothing but raise his anxiety level, that is.

Jason scowled. What was wrong with him? Why was he ready to assume the worst? Who said the news would necessarily be bad?

With that thought in mind, he pulled the phone toward him and punched in the digits for Tom's number. Impatiently he drummed his fingers on the scarred wood of his desktop, counting off each unanswered ring—three, four, five.

Then, on the sixth ring, just as he was about to hang up, the phone was answered. A gravelly male voice barked, "Meridia County Sheriff's Department."

"Detective Tom Burns, please."

"One minute."

It seemed like an eternity before he heard a familiar voice answer, "Detective Burns, Homicide."

"Tom? Jason Gallagher here."

"Jason, I'm glad you caught me. Sorry I didn't get back to you sooner. It's been a zoo here today. We had a double shooting on a bus this afternoon. Can you believe it? We've got at least twenty witnesses, but nobody saw a thing. It's gotta be gang related. Everybody's too scared to put their necks on the line and make a statement." He heaved a weary sigh. "I sure could have used your help, partner."

Tom and Jason had worked together in Chicago's south side five years earlier. Since then, Tom had transferred to his home state of California, settling in Meridia County, one of the many districts making up the Los Angeles area. Jason's life had been turned upside down, as well. With his son's death, everything had changed.

Except Jason hadn't realized just how drastic that change would be. He made a mental list of the calls he'd had today. The most demanding of them was a dispute between two neighbors, culminating into a frantic call from one of the elderly gents. Once the man was calm enough to speak, he'd explained to the police that his neighbor of twenty-some years was attacking his tree with a buzz saw. All because his neighbor had tired of the seed pods that fell into his yard every spring. The saw had been confiscated. The dispute had been settled with an agreement of a mutual cleanup.

Not quite as exciting as a double homicide, but Jason wouldn't trade the slower pace for anything in the world.

He'd burned out on the senseless crime and violence of the city. He needed to know there was still a place in the world that a person could feel relatively safe.

"Sorry, Tom. I'm happy right where I'm at."

"You're happy in Podunk, USA? I can't believe it."

"It's true. I'm here for the long haul."

"Well, I can't say I blame you. One of these days, my ulcer's going to burn a hole big enough to drive a freight train through. Then I'll be looking for a place to kick back and relax, too. Maybe I'll join you in Podunk, and we'll do a little fishing on our days off."

Jason chuckled, unable to imagine his old friend anywhere but behind the desk in a homicide division. He hesitated, then asked, "Did you come up with anything? On that name and social-security number I gave you?"

"Yeah, I sure did." Papers rustled over the phone line. Clutching the phone tightly, Jason waited, his heart thudding against his ribs. "It all checks out, the name, birthplace, social-security number..."

Relief poured through Jason. He exhaled slowly, then refilled his burning lungs, not even realizing he'd been holding his breath. He almost smiled at the foolishness of his unwarranted fears.

"There's only one problem," his friend said, the words catching Jason off guard. "Our Maggie Conrad died as an infant twenty-eight years ago."

The statement hit like a sledgehammer to Jason's gut. He opened his mouth, but couldn't form the words to answer. He felt poleaxed by the implications of the news.

"Did you hear me, Jason? Whoever your lady in Wyndchester is, she's using a fake ID."

"I heard you," Jason said finally. His voice sounded strained, oddly hollow in the quiet office.

Slowly Tom asked, "What do you want to do now?"

"I don't know."

"If you think this is a criminal case—"

Jason's head throbbed. He kneaded his temple with the tips of his fingers.

"—we can always run a fingerprint check. If the lady's on the run, we'll probably have her on file somewhere. Why don't you give me a description and I'll run her through the computer, see what comes up—"

"Dammit, wait a minute," Jason said sharply.

There was a stunned silence on the other end of the phone line.

Jason muttered an oath beneath his breath. "I'm sorry, Tom."

His friend cleared his throat. "No problem."

"It's just…I'm not sure how I want to handle this yet."

"I understand."

"No, I don't think you do." Jason swallowed the bitter taste of disappointment rising in his throat. "It…it's personal."

Tom sighed. "I figured it might be. Look, I'll leave this to you. Just let me know if I can be of any more help. All right?"

"Yeah, thanks."

"And Jason…" Tom hesitated. Jason could almost see the worried frown creasing his friend's face. "Take care of yourself."

"I will."

After saying their goodbyes, Jason returned the phone to its cradle. He stared at his hand, still closed around the receiver, struggling with the urge to pick up the instrument and toss it across the room. Slowly he released his grip and pushed himself away from the desk.

He strode to the window, lifted the slatted blinds and stared across the street at Mel's diner. Breathing in deeply, he tried to ease the pain gripping his heart. It was useless. He hadn't felt this bad in years. Not since...

Not since he'd lost Scotty.

With the news of Maggie's deception, something inside him had died. Hope.

Jason closed his eyes, blotting out unwanted images of Maggie from his mind. Yet they still came, quick and hard, filling him with dizzying confusion.

Maggie...the beautiful temptress whose smile was so shy and sweet, who looked so fresh and innocent with all those freckles dusting her skin, that he couldn't resist her charms.

Maggie...the frightened woman who'd shied away from even the slightest overture of friendship and who'd brought out a protective instinct in him he'd forgotten he possessed.

Maggie...the loving, passionate woman who'd flourished beneath a steady diet of gentle patience. The woman who'd had his hormones tied in knots from the first minute he'd met her.

Maggie...the woman who'd looked him in the eye and deliberately lied.

Jason snapped the blinds shut with a decisive flick of his wrist. Turning his back on the view of the street, he leaned forward and gripped the edge of his desk, fighting the need to strike out, to hurt someone, to make them feel as badly as he felt at the moment.

He closed his eyes and released a ragged breath. Dammit, what was he supposed to do now?

How could he face her again and not demand to know the truth?

Just who in hell are you, Maggie Conrad?

Maggie turned off the hall light and stepped softly down the wooden stairs, not wanting to disturb her sleeping son. Kevin had had a restless day and evening. His arm had ached with a relentless pain. The cast had been clumsy and difficult to maneuver. She'd given him a painkiller a few minutes earlier, and he had finally found relief in a drugged sleep.

She only wished there was a miracle cure for what ailed her—old-fashioned second thoughts.

Since making love to Jason the night before, she hadn't heard a word from him. He hadn't phoned or stopped by to see her or Kevin. His lack of attention both surprised and worried her. Normally he was a very caring man. She couldn't help but wonder if he might be regretting what had happened between them.

Maggie entered the kitchen. The air felt hot, the room unbearably still. Her bare feet padded noiselessly against the linoleum floor as she crossed the room and stepped outside. Twilight had descended on the yards, yet it had brought little relief from the day's heat. Summer would be here soon, reminding her that she hadn't planned to stay this long in Wyndchester.

She hadn't planned on a lot of things.

Glancing across the yard, a fist of unease tightened around her heart. Jason's light shone brightly in his kitchen window, telling her he was finally home.

There was no denying she wanted to see him again.

If only she knew what his greeting might be.

Gathering her courage, Maggie tiptoed down the wooden stairs of her back porch. The damp grass tickled the soles of her feet as she crossed her yard and stepped onto Jason's property. Glancing down at her old denim cutoffs and faded shirt, she almost turned around, wishing to look her best for Jason.

She forced herself to continue. A string of expletives salted the air as she stood outside his back door. The sound of a pan banging on the stovetop, followed closely by the distinctive odor of burned food, told her all was not well.

Perhaps this wasn't the best time for a visit. She almost turned around and left. But then the clatter stopped abruptly. Maggie's breath caught as she spotted Jason standing stiffly in the middle of his kitchen, staring at her through the screened door.

Swallowing hard over the lump of emotion in her throat, she forced a smile. "May I come in?"

For a long moment Jason didn't answer. He didn't move, either. He just kept looking at her, as though seeing her for the first time. Then, with a curt nod, he said, "Of course. Where are my manners?" He opened the door and stepped aside, allowing her to enter.

Her shoulder brushed his outstretched arm as she went past him. A shiver of awareness traveled the length of her body. Her breathing uneven, she stood awkwardly in the middle of the kitchen, not sure what to do now that she was there.

Jason's kitchen was stark, utilitarian. Missing were all the whimsical touches that make a home cozy and warm. The pan that held the scorched remains of a can of stew stood on an unlit burner. Noticing the direction of her gaze, Jason grabbed the pan and strode to the sink. With a grimace, he said, "Now you know why I eat at Mel's diner so much."

Maggie smiled and watched as he dumped the stew in the sink and turned on the disposal. The fabric of his white T-shirt stretched and molded the muscles of his back as he moved. He still wore his uniform pants, but he'd shucked off his shoes and socks. There were dark circles under his eyes. Standing before her half-dressed, he looked tired, rumpled and irresistible. She desperately longed to reach out to him, stroke his temples and wipe away the lines of weariness, but she dared not.

He finally turned off the disposal and looked at her. Maggie's heart stuttered. His face remained impassive, devoid of expression. But his eyes told a different story. They were troubled, brimming with unspoken emotion.

Her chest tightened. She should have trusted her instincts. She shouldn't have come. Nervously she stammered, "Kevin and I...we had chicken salad for dinner. There's plenty left over if you'd like—"

"No," he said, with a brusqueness that startled her. Sighing, he crossed his arms and leaned against the counter. "I'm not really that hungry tonight."

An awkward silence filled the room, the tension between them almost palpable. If Maggie had wondered before, she was certain now. There was something terribly wrong.

Last night Jason had been a tender and gentle lover. He'd acted as though he never wanted to leave her. Now he acted as though he was uncomfortable being in the same room with her.

"How's Kevin?" he asked, forcing her out of her troubled thoughts.

"Still hurting," she said, glancing out the back window and across the yard to her own house, feeling the overwhelming urge to run to safety. "I probably should get back...in case he needs me."

"Was there something...?" He hesitated, shifting his weight from one foot to another. Rubbing the back of his neck, he gave her a look of utter defeat. It sent a shiver down her spine. "Why did you come, Maggie?"

Emotion filled her chest, making it hard for her to breathe. Looking into his eyes, she saw the silent plea and knew she couldn't lie to him even if she wanted to. "I...I didn't hear from you today. I was worried that...that something was wrong."

His silence spoke volumes.

"Obviously I was right," she said, striving for a nonchalant tone but failing miserably. Embarrassed heat scorched her skin. Averting her gaze, she stepped past him toward the door. "I—I'm sorry to have bothered you. I won't take up any more of your time."

"Maggie, wait." He stepped in front of her, reaching a hand to stop her. His fingers felt hot against her skin. His grip strong, unrelenting, biting into the tender flesh of her upper arm.

She glanced at his hand, then met his gaze, unable to hide the fear in her heart.

Muttering an oath, he immediately loosened his grip, dropping his hand to his side. "I'm sorry. I don't want you to leave. We need to talk."

His apology only added to the tension building in her. Despite the little voice in the back of her mind screaming at her to run—not walk—out that back door, she knew if she left now, it would be over. The fragile trust they'd built between them would be gone. There would be no chance for a future with Jason.

Dragging in a deep breath, she said, "All right. I'll stay, but only for a little while. I need to get home."

"Have a seat," he said, motioning toward the round oak table and matching chairs. "What would you like to drink? I have soda, beer...plenty of water."

"Nothing, thank you."

"No, I insist." He smiled for the first time. But even now, it seemed a forced and empty gesture. "What kind of a host would I be if I didn't offer you something to drink?"

"Soda, I guess," she said, with a shrug as she slipped into a chair. The last thing she wanted was a drink. She wanted this conversation to be over. She wanted things to be the same between them as they were last night.

Jason grabbed a glass from the cupboard and a soda from the refrigerator. He handed her the glass and set the soda on the table in front of her. Murmuring a thank-you, she placed the glass on the table beside the soda, leaving the drink untouched.

To her dismay, Jason remained standing. He towered over her, making her feel vulnerable and even more uncomfortable. Unable to help herself, she blurted, "I know there's something wrong. Just tell me what it is."

At first she thought he might deny the accusation. He looked down at his bare feet. When finally he raised his head, she saw regret shining in his eyes. "Things have been moving a little too fast. I need some time to think about…well, about us."

She sat stiffly in the chair, feeling the walls close in around her. "I see."

"We hardly know each other, Maggie."

It hadn't made a difference last night, she wanted to scream. Instead, she remained silent, sitting like a stone in the middle of his kitchen.

"I need to take things slowly, get to know you better," he explained, his voice so soft she almost didn't hear.

A familiar panic rose up inside her. She didn't know what frightened her more—losing Jason or revealing herself to him. "Wh-what do you want to know?"

"Everything," he said. The hair stood up on the back of her neck as he moved closer. He squatted down next to her chair, bringing himself to her eye level. Maggie felt herself shrink back as his intense gaze searched her face. "Do you trust me, Maggie?"

"Y-yes." The word seemed to stick to the roof of her dry throat. "Of course I do."

"Then tell me about yourself." His smile was gentle, encouraging. "I want to know the good and the bad—everything that's made you the woman you are today."

The good and the bad. He sounded so sincere. The temptation to confide in him was overwhelming. Was it so much to ask? Didn't he deserve to know the truth, all the sordid details of her past?

And if she did confide in him, what would happen next?

In the short time she'd known him, she'd come to realize that Jason was a man of uncompromising integrity. Asking him to keep her secret, that she was a woman on the run, would be like asking him to give up a part of himself. The part she loved and admired the most.

Love. The thought sent a chill through her body. For the first time she realized just how deeply her feelings for Jason ran. They went beyond caring. Somewhere along the line she'd fallen in love with him.

Her vision blurred as tears of regret threatened. She cared too much about him. She couldn't allow him to be hurt by any of this. Not if she could prevent it from happening.

Blinking away the emotion, she said flatly, "There's nothing more I can tell you."

The tenderness drained from his face. A hard mask of indifference slipped into place. An unexpected anger flickered in his eyes. Without another word, he rose to his feet and stepped away, turning his back to her. She felt his withdrawal like a cold slap in the face.

"I'm sorry, Jason," she said, pushing herself from the table, stumbling to her feet. Tears clouded her vision as she stared at his stiff shoulders. She wanted to run her hands along their width and measure their strength. She wanted to rest her head against them and feel his support.

Not allowing herself the chance to change her mind, she

turned and hurried to the door. Her hand was on the door-knob when he stopped her.

Grabbing her shoulder, he swung her around to face him. His eyes glittered with a fierceness she'd never expected. Before she had time to react, he clamped a hand around her waist and pulled her close. With smooth, swift move-ments, he stepped forward and pinned her against the wall with his big body.

Fear squeezed her chest, and a protest rose in her throat. Before she had the chance to utter it, he lowered his head and took her mouth with his.

There was no tenderness in his kiss. Raking his fingers through her hair, he tilted her head back and parted her lips with a flick of his tongue, delving into her mouth with a clear and complete show of possession. The kiss was harsh, meant to punish. His late-day beard abraded her skin. It was as though he wanted to hurt her as badly as she'd wounded him.

She gasped for air when he finally tore his mouth from hers. Holding her tight, he stared at her, his eyes glazed and wild. Someone else, not the gentle man she'd come to know, demanded, "Who are you, Maggie?"

She shook her head, unable to find the words to answer.

With a growl of frustration, he buried his face in her hair. The words sent a shiver down her spine as he whis-pered over and over, "Who are you? Who are you?"

Cold tendrils of fear curled up in her chest. At that mo-ment she realized there was more to his anger than pure male pride. Somehow he'd figured out the truth. He knew that she'd lied to him. That she wasn't the woman she had led him to believe.

For the first time Maggie was afraid of Jason.

"Jason, stop," she said, the words bubbling up in her throat. Vainly she tried to push him away, but he was too strong. As she fought, the pressure of his arms tightened, nearly smothering her with his weight. It was as though he couldn't, or wouldn't, hear her. Desperately she cried, "Jason, please. You're hurting me."

The stark fear echoing in her voice finally seeped into his consciousness. Immediately he loosened his grip, backing away, giving her room to breathe, room to escape.

Sucking in choppy breaths of air, she stared at him. He looked almost as stunned as she was by what had just happened.

"I—I'm sorry, Maggie."

Maggie was unable to stop the hot tears of disappointment that coursed down her cheeks. All the regret she felt in her heart spilled out in a rush. Without another word, she turned on her heel and ran.

The screen door banged shut behind her as she stumbled outside. She didn't look back. Nor did she stop running, not until she reached the safety of her own house. Once inside, she bolted the door behind her and leaned her shaking body against its solid frame.

Then the strength leaked out of her limbs. Like a rag doll, she sank slowly to the floor. Weak, useless sobs racked her body as she buried her face in her hands.

Oh, God. What was she going to do now?

Jason stared at the empty doorway.

He was in love with Maggie. And yet he'd forced himself on her. He'd used his brute strength to take something that he'd wanted, not caring that it wasn't his to take. How could he have hurt her that way?

Appalled at his volatile reaction, he turned his back to the door. The kitchen felt as empty and hollow as his heart.

"Dammit," he muttered, his voice echoing in the quiet

room. He squeezed his eyes shut and willed the pain throbbing in his chest to stop.

He was fighting a losing battle, he realized, opening his eyes. His actions had put them both in a tenuous position. He knew she was using a false ID. Instead of confronting her, he'd hoped against hope, had given her the chance to open up to him.

But she hadn't.

She'd continued to lie, betraying his trust. Even now, the anger and bitter disappointment roiled up inside him. He wanted to march over to her house and demand she tell him the truth.

But in his heart, he knew she had to be the one to initiate the confidence.

Either she trusted him or she didn't.

With a defeated sigh, he glanced at the table. The can of soda remained on the tabletop, untouched. But Maggie had held the glass in her hand.

At that moment he knew what must be done. Before he could change his mind, he strode to the counter and withdrew a plastic bag from a drawer. Returning to the table, he carefully picked up the glass and slipped it into the bag.

Maggie's fingerprints would be clear on the smooth surface. If she were a criminal, her prints would be on file. Once and for all he would know who she really was, what she was hiding.

It was his only chance at finding out the truth.

So why did it feel as though it was too little too late?

Chapter 12

The bed shifted beneath her, waking her. Maggie squinted against the brightness of the sunlight pouring in through her bedroom window to see her son sitting cross-legged on the bed next to her.

"Hi, Mom. Whatcha doin'?"

"What time is it?" She blinked the grit from eyes that burned from lack of sleep and too many tears shed the night before. Her head felt thick, as though stuffed with cotton.

Careful of his broken arm, Kevin scooted to the head of the bed for a closer look at the alarm clock. The ancient mattress rocked drunkenly in his wake. "It's seven o'clock."

"Oh, great," she moaned, struggling to sit up. "I'm going to be late for work."

"It's Sunday, Mom." Kevin frowned, giving her a puzzled look. "You don't have to work on Sunday."

"You're right," she said, falling back against the covers, letting her eyes drift shut. She gave herself a chance to regroup before she tried to move again. Her encounter with Jason the night before had left her emotionally and physically drained. She needed more time to recover.

Seconds later mother's guilt took aim and struck a clean blow to the heart. Her eyes flew open. She raised herself on one elbow and looked at her son. "How are you feeling? Is your arm still sore?"

"Yeah," he said, giving a half shrug, feigning indifference. "It feels kind of hot. And it's like it's got a heartbeat or somethin'. It keeps thumpin' inside my cast."

"Oh, Kevin, I'm sorry." She sat up straight, brushing a hand across his forehead. He felt warm, feverish. "I think you're running a temperature."

"Is that bad?"

"It means I should probably call the doctor."

He made a face. "Is it going to hurt?"

"No worse than it already does," she promised, wishing she could do more to ease his pain. She swung her legs over the side of the bed and pushed herself to her feet. "Let me get dressed, then I'll take your temperature."

Kevin scanned her body from head to toe and grinned. "You're already dressed."

Embarrassed heat flushed her skin as she glanced down at her clothes. She still wore her denim cutoffs and the faded shirt from the night before. Last night she remembered falling into bed fully clothed and crying herself into an exhausted sleep. She'd been so tired she hadn't bothered to get up and undress.

Heaving another weary sigh, she said, "You can stay in my bed, if you want. I'll change in the bathroom."

He didn't argue. Instead, he took her spot on the bed, burrowing himself in the lingering warmth of her pillows. His skin looked pale beneath the flush of his fever.

She grabbed a fresh pair of shorts and a T-shirt out of her dresser. Forcing a smile, she said, "I'll be right back."

Kevin nodded, his glasses glinting in the sunlight.

She hurried into the bathroom. When she looked into the mirror, she cringed inwardly. Her eyes were puffy, the skin beneath blotched, all remnants of last night's crying jag. Turning on the faucet, she doused her face with cool water, wishing she could wash away the memories of Jason just as easily.

Impossible, she told herself, letting the icy water trickle through her fingers. She would never be able to forget the anger and disappointment she saw in Jason's eyes. Somehow he'd guess the truth. That the widow, Maggie Conrad, was nothing more than illusion. That her whole world, everything she had told him, was a lie.

If only she had followed her instincts and left town weeks ago, none of this would be happening now. She wouldn't have been forced to share close quarters with the town's chief of police. She wouldn't have risked her and her son's safety.

She wouldn't have risked losing her heart.

In the wee hours of the morning, she'd convinced herself that she had no choice but to leave Wyndchester. Now, in the light of day, she wasn't sure how she could. Obviously Kevin wasn't ready to travel. Until his arm healed, he needed to be under a doctor's supervision.

Not only that, Jenny's wedding was less than a week away. She was depending on Maggie's support. Despite their efforts to the contrary, she and Kevin had made friends in Wyndchester. Good friends who cared about them.

For her that was no small feat. Most of her adult life, she'd been wary of forming any close relationships. Her mother and then her husband had reinforced her belief that letting someone into your life, opening your heart to them, only led to pain. Out of necessity, she'd learned to become self-sufficient and independent. But the experience had hardened her.

Jason had been the first to break through her protective shell. She had trusted him. More than that, she'd fallen in love with him. Completely and irrevocably in love.

How could she ever leave him?

Her vision blurred as new tears threatened. If he knew the truth, would he even want her to stay?

Maggie switched off the water. She unbuttoned her shirt and slipped it off her shoulders, letting it slide carelessly to the floor. The denim shorts soon followed. Picking up the clean T-shirt and shorts, she dressed quickly.

Later, when she had more time to think, she would decide how to handle the mess she'd made with Jason. She picked up a hairbrush and attacked her snarled curls with unnecessary roughness. Right now she had a son who was in pain. He needed a strong, confident mother to take care of him.

Kevin's well-being, his happiness, had been the driving force in her life since the day he was born. He was the sole reason she'd finally found the courage to leave her husband. His safety was most important. Nothing else mattered.

Nothing else mattered?

Maggie's hand froze midbrush. She stared at her reflection in the mirror, catching a frightening glimpse of her future. A future of being constantly on the run, never settling down, never forming another close relationship.

A future of always being alone.

Later that morning, Jason entered the Wyndchester Police Department carrying a plain manilla envelope. The offices were eerily quiet, unnerving him. The weekend dispatcher looked up from his desk and nodded a hello. Jason returned the silent greeting.

A few other officers milled about, sipping coffee and looking bored. Duty calls would be few and far between today. It was Sunday, a day of rest, even for the bad guys. Only a skeleton staff was needed this morning. Most of the crew were home with their families.

Which suited his needs just fine. For the job he had in mind, he didn't need an audience.

Striding into his office, he closed the door behind him with a firm click. Earlier this morning, in the privacy of his own home, he'd taken the prints from Maggie's drinking glass. He'd been careful, touching only the rim. Dusting the smooth surface with powder, then lifting the prints with a sticky tape had been easy. In a matter of minutes he'd had a clear imprint of Maggie's thumb and her first three fingers.

Now he was faced with a more difficult task.

Once again, he had to find the strength to betray the woman he'd come to care for.

Jason carefully placed the manilla envelope that contained Maggie's prints on the middle of the desktop. He stood staring at the envelope, unable to move as memories of last night flooded his mind. It had been as though someone else, not him, had grabbed Maggie and pinned her to the wall. Once again, he felt the anger that had spurred him to act in such a brutish way. He saw the terror in her eyes, knowing he'd been the cause of her fear.

Jason closed his eyes, blotting out the images. His behavior had been inexcusable. By allowing his emotions to get the better of him, he'd hurt Maggie. He doubted she would ever be able to forgive him.

Not that he deserved her forgiveness.

But that didn't mean he would ever stop hoping. Stubbornly he still believed that if only he knew the truth, the real reason behind Maggie's deception, then he might be able to help her—and to help himself hold on to her.

Slowly he opened his eyes. Before he lost his courage, he picked up the phone and punched in the number for the Meridia County Sheriff's Department. A woman's voice answered this time, taking his call with polite efficiency. Within minutes he was connected with his old friend, Tom Burns.

"Hey, Jason," Tom said. "How'd you know I'd be working this morning?"

Jason smiled despite himself. "I was your partner, remember? When we were in Chicago, not only did you insist on working seven days a week, but you dragged me along for the ride, too."

"Dragged is right." Tom chuckled. "You were always complaining about something, like sleep or some such nonsense."

"Yeah, well, now it looks as though we're both turning into workaholics."

"Work, right," Tom said with an exaggerated sigh. "I knew this wasn't a social call."

"No, it isn't. Something's come up," Jason said. His voice sounded hoarse as nerves tightened his throat. "I need you to run some prints for me, after all."

"Are we talking about the same woman? This..." He paused, and Jason could hear papers being shuffled. Jason waited, his heart ticking off the passing seconds with uneven thumps. "Maggie Conrad, right?"

"Right," he said softly. "That's the one."

There was an awkward silence. It seemed like an eternity before Tom finally asked, "You're sure this is what you want, Jason?"

"No, I'm not sure," Jason admitted. He sat down hard

on the edge of his desk, the strength going out of his limbs. "But it's what I've got to do."

"Okay," Tom said, asking no further questions. "Look, go ahead and fax me the prints. But it might take a few days before I can get the results. Our lady isn't a flight risk, is she?"

The thought stunned Jason, stealing the breath from his lungs. Maggie wouldn't...she couldn't run away. Not even allowing himself to consider the possibility, he said, "No, I—I don't think so."

"Good, because I want to use a friend of mine to help us out, someone I can trust. He's on vacation right now. He'll be getting back later this week. I'll have him get on it as soon as he returns."

"Trust?" Jason frowned, concern prickling his skin. "What's going on, Tom? You got some problems in your department?"

"No more than the usual."

Jason's unease grew. "Maybe you'd better explain exactly what you mean."

Tom sighed again. "Look, it's nothing to worry about. This is a big department with a lot of employees. Some I know well, some I don't. I don't have to tell you about a policeman's salary. We don't get paid enough for the risks we take. There's always going to be a few rotten eggs looking for a way to pad their income."

Jason's grip tightened on the phone. "Look, Tom, maybe this was a bad idea. I don't want to cause you any trouble."

"Me? Trouble? Are you kidding? I'm like a cat. I always land on my feet." Tom grunted. "Just send me the prints, all right?"

"All right," Jason said, ignoring the little voice in the back of his head telling him to stop before it was too late. "Give me your fax number and I'll have these out to you in a few minutes.'' He hesitated, then added quietly, "And, Tom, when you get the results, remember they're for my eyes only. No messages."

"Whatever you say, partner. By the way, what happens if we do turn up something on this Maggie Conrad?"

The question caught him off guard. To tell the truth, he hadn't considered his legal obligations if he discovered Maggie was hiding a criminal past. His only goal had been to help her, not harm her. Vaguely he answered, "I'll deal with that when the time comes."

Jason jotted down the fax number, then the two men said their goodbyes. The department was still quiet when he emerged from his office. As he headed for the office's communal fax machine, Stan Wilson entered the building.

Off duty, Stan wore civilian clothes. His jeans and faded polo shirt emphasized his lean, lanky body. A baseball cap with the Cardinals' logo hid all but the edges of his blond hair. He looked like a teenager, not an officer of the law.

"Mornin', Chief," he said, strolling up beside him. He leaned an elbow on the cabinet housing the fax machine, making himself comfortable. "Kinda quiet here today."

"Looks that way," Jason agreed. Short of appearing rude, how was he going to get rid of his junior officer? Sighing, Jason inserted the fax with Maggie's prints attached into the unfamiliar machine, then punched in the connection for the Meridia County Sheriff's Office. Suddenly a high-pitched squeal went off, telling him he'd done something drastically wrong.

"Whew. I think you hit the wrong switch, Chief." Stan grinned, then punched a button, immediately quieting the cantankerous machine. "Why don't you let me help you out?"

Embarrassed heat warmed Jason's skin. The last thing he wanted was for anyone to know he was using the department's equipment to check out his next-door neighbor. Averting his gaze, he mumbled, "No, that's okay. I can handle it."

"Chief, listen," Stan said, leaning close, his tone confiding. "This machine's fickle. It needs a gentle touch, that's all. It's nothing to be embarrassed about. Now just give me the fax number and I'll send it right off."

Jason shifted uncomfortably from one foot to the other. He glanced around the office, looking to see if anyone else was listening. Once assured they wouldn't be overheard, he lowered his voice and said, "This is personal, Stan. It's not something I want everyone to know about."

Stan closed an imaginary zipper across his lips, locking it with an invisible key. "My lips are sealed, Chief. Now give me the number."

With the technical efficiency of youth, Stan sent off the fax with no further problems. When the paper fed itself into the machine and emerged on the other side, he whisked it out and handed it to Jason, not sparing it a second glance. "Here you go, Chief. All signed, sealed and delivered."

"Thanks," Jason murmured, folding his copy of the fax in half so that the fingerprints remained unseen. He took a second glance at his officer. "What brings you to the office this morning, Stan? I thought you were off duty today."

"I didn't have anything better to do," Stan said with a shrug, his tone nonchalant. But Jason noted the agitated look in his eye and the restless tapping of his foot on the floor. He was anything but calm.

"Everything okay, Stan?"

"Everything's just great, Chief." Stan's attempt at a laugh fell flat. He stared blindly out the window, shaking his head at something only he could see. Softly he said, "The wedding's less than a week away. She's really going to marry the son of a—'' He stopped, releasing a long, whistling breath.

Jason sighed, too. He didn't need to ask who the "she" was. Knowing he was the last person who should be handing out advice to the lovelorn, he struggled to find the right words. "Stan, sometimes things happen…people do things we'll never be able to understand. We just have to accept it and get on with our own lives."

As he said the words, he realized that the advice was something for himself to heed, as well. No matter how much he wanted to, he couldn't solve all of the world's problems. There was a real possibility he wouldn't be able to help Maggie, either.

"I don't know if I can do that, Chief," Stan said, his troubled voice rousing Jason from his own self-absorbed musings. "I just can't sit back and watch Jenny make the biggest mistake of her life."

"You may not have a choice."

Stan didn't answer. He just kept staring out the window, refusing to meet his gaze.

Jason blew out a frustrated breath. "Look, I'm finished here. What do you say we go out and get ourselves an early lunch?"

"No, thanks, Chief. I'm not too hungry." Stan slapped his thigh and pushed himself away from the cabinet. "I guess I'd better be going. I'll see you tomorrow."

Jason nodded. "Take care of yourself, Stan. Stay out of trouble, you hear?"

"Sure thing, Chief." With a mock salute, he strolled across the office and disappeared out the front door.

Jason headed for his own office. How could he expect his junior officer to listen to his advice when he wouldn't even pay attention to it himself? The smartest thing for him to do would be to let Maggie go...to give up on their future together.

But he just couldn't do that. Jason sighed. When it came to the matters of the heart, he never had been too lucky. Or too smart. All he could do was follow his instincts and hope for the best.

For now, work would keep his mind off his problems. He intended to spend the rest of the day catching up on paperwork. Until he heard from Tom Burns and knew exactly what he was up against, he didn't think he could face Maggie again.

It was late when Jason finally left work. Darkness pressed against the windows of his Jeep, heavy clouds blocking out any trace of moonlight. A damp breeze filtered in through an open window, doing little to soothe his frazzled nerves. Thunder growled in the distance, warning him of an approaching storm. He almost laughed. It seemed an appropriate end to such a dismal day. A day he'd spent unsuccessfully trying not to think about Maggie.

But she had invaded his thoughts at the most unexpected times. In the middle of filling out a tedious form, while fetching a drink from the coffee machine and while giving his officers instructions on how to handle a call, she had popped up in his mind, never giving him a moment's rest.

Now he was on his way home, where less than twenty feet away Maggie would be asleep in her bed.

His headlights fanned the front of the house as he pulled into the driveway. He frowned as he caught a flicker of movement in the shadows of the porch. His cop instinct on full alert, he parked, turned off the ignition and waited. Once again, he saw the shadows move. Squinting against the darkness, he barely made out the shape of a person's body.

Someone was waiting for him.

He rolled up his window and climbed out of the Jeep. His gun was in its holster at his hip. Within easy reach, if needed. But he didn't feel as though he was in danger.

His instincts were proved correct when Maggie emerged from the shadows. Leaning against the porch railing, she watched his approach. Jason's heart thudded against his ribs. She wore a white sundress, the color of innocence. And he realized just how much he wanted it to be true, just how much he wanted to believe she had done nothing wrong. He stopped a few feet away and stared at her, feeling rooted to the spot by uncertainty.

Neither of them spoke. Instead, they studied each other with equal amounts of wariness. The stillness of the night surrounded them, cocooning them in a false sense of peace, broken only by the rumbling of more thunder and the ragged inhalations of their breaths.

Lightning streaked the sky, startling them.

Maggie flinched, stepping back further onto the porch.

Jason shot a worried glance at the heavens. If he was a superstitious man, he'd say he'd just been delivered an omen. Pushing the thought from his mind, he directed his gaze to Maggie. "It's late."

"I know," she said, finally finding her voice. "There's something I need to tell you."

The words were like a death knell, working to agitate his nerves even further. Judging from the somberness of her tone, whatever she had to say, he knew he wasn't ready to hear it. "Where's Kevin?"

"At home. Jenny's with him." She drew in a deep breath, her full breasts rising and falling from the exertion. "She's feeling a little jittery about the wedding and needed some company. I wasn't sure how long I'd be, so she…she volunteered to stay the night and keep an eye on him."

Jason gave himself a moment to digest the implications of her admission. "Have you been waiting long?"

"An hour or so."

"Then it must be important."

"Yes, it is."

Jason allowed himself a resigned sigh. He felt a weariness in his bones that went beyond mere physical tiredness; it was a weakness of the spirit. Unable to fight the inevitable, he closed the distance between them and sank onto the top step of the porch. Glancing up at her, he patted the space beside him. "Have a seat."

She hesitated only for a moment. The skirt of her sundress swirled against his thighs as she sat down. She stirred the air with her movements, and he caught the flowery scent of her perfume. Up close, her skin shimmered like fine porcelain in the dim light. His hands itched to reach out and touch her.

Not allowing himself the pleasure, he leaned forward, elbows on his knees, and clasped his hands in front of him. "Before you say anything, Maggie, I...I want to tell you that I'm sorry about last night. I never meant to hurt you. I don't know what got into me."

"It's okay, Jason."

"No, it isn't." He forced himself to look at her, to face the condemnation he knew must be in her eyes. To his surprised relief, there was none. "It was inexcusable. I promise you, Maggie, it'll never happen again."

"I know that," she said, her voice whisper soft.

He gave a harsh laugh, shaking his head in disgust. "How can you know that? How can you trust me, trust any man after what you've been through with your husband? I don't care if he *is* dead. I just don't want you thinking that all men..." He released a breath on a sigh. "That *I'm* like him."

The strength seemed to go out of her body. Her shoulders slumped. She dropped her chin to her chest and stared at her sandal-covered feet. "That's what I need to talk to you about—my ex-husband."

Jason frowned, feeling confused. "Ex-husband? I thought you said—"

"I told you he was dead. But he isn't. He's very much alive and living in California."

Lightning flashed, followed closely by an earth-trembling crash of thunder. Nature's show of force went almost unnoticed as Jason stared at Maggie, not sure what to say. He didn't know what he'd expected her to tell him, but it certainly wasn't the resurrection of her dead husband. Silently he waited, giving her the time she needed to explain.

"Everything else I told you about him is the truth," she said, still unable to look at him. Nervously she smoothed a hand along the skirt of her sundress, her fingers worrying over the pleated hem. "He's a powerful, influential man. But he's also very violent. For years I took the abuse he'd dealt out, believing that somehow it was my fault, that I wasn't good enough...special enough to make him h-happy." Her voice broke. And Jason's heart clenched.

Swallowing hard, she continued, "It wasn't until he started taking out his anger on Kevin that I woke up and saw him for what he really was—a bully."

Unable to help himself, Jason reached out and covered her hand with his. To his relief, she didn't push him away. She laced her fingers through his and clung to him, seeming to draw strength from the contact.

Her voice stronger, she said, "I divorced him. And that's when the trouble really began." Her eyes glittered with sudden tears. She blinked hard, not allowing them to fall. "He took me to court and sued for custody of Kevin. Not because he really wanted his son, but because it was just one more way to punish me.''

A strong wind swept the yard, bending the limbs of the trees. Jason frowned, ignoring the volatile skies. "Surely no judge would allow a man who has a history of domestic abuse to have custody of a child.''

"There was no proof of his attacks on me," she said, her voice so quiet he almost didn't hear her.

His frown deepened. "I don't understand. Didn't you report the abuse?''

The corners of her mouth lifted in a bitter smile. "Oh, I reported it all right. But like I said, my husband was an influential man. He had connections, both legal and illegal, that reached as far as the police department. For most of our marriage, my calls for help went virtually unanswered. Once the police realized who my husband was, they looked the other way. In court all the reports came up missing. In the end it was my word against his.''

"My God.''

"No, God had nothing to do with this. It was pure evil, corruption through and through. The judge was a friend of my ex-husband's. He ruled in his favor. He gave him sole custody of Kevin.''

"Aw, Maggie,'' Jason said, struggling to find the right words to comfort her, knowing, no matter what he said, it would be inadequate.

She shook her head. "You have to understand—I couldn't let it happen. I couldn't let him have Kevin.''

"Of course you couldn't.''

"I didn't have a choice. He'd already threatened to kill me. I have no doubt he would have hurt Kevin, as well.'' Her voice shook with emotion. Her body trembled as the words spilled out. "There was no one I could turn to. No one I could trust.''

He touched a finger to her lips, stilling the disjointed words. He lowered his hand, rubbing a thumb along the delicate line of her jaw. Gently he said, "What are you trying to tell me, Maggie?"

The tears she'd been fighting so hard flowed freely down her cheeks. Looking him straight in the eye, she said, "In the eyes of the law I'm a criminal because I refused to turn Kevin over to his father. I spent time in jail for contempt. When they finally released me, I took Kevin away. I defied a court order and abducted my own son. For the past nineteen months, I've been running, because I'm sure there's a warrant for my arrest in California."

Jason's world tilted. His head reeled with the news. "Your name isn't Maggie Conrad."

"No, I've been using a fake ID," she said, shaking her head. "My real name is Margaret Stuart."

"And your job? Have you always been a waitress?"

She sighed. "Being a waitress is convenient. It's a job that's easy to find when you're new to a town, and the pay's all right. But no, I was an emergency-room nurse in California, before I married my husband."

The last pieces of the puzzle fell into place. Now it all made sense. No wonder she was so frightened when she first saw him standing on her doorstep. She probably thought he was there to arrest her, not welcome her as a new neighbor. Her reluctance to get to know him was a matter of self-preservation, not a reflection of her true feelings toward him.

The realization did little to comfort him. He'd gotten his wish. He finally knew the truth.

In doing so, his worst fear had come true.

Maggie was a fugitive from justice. And it was his duty to uphold the law. But if he carried out his duties and turned her over to the authorities in California, he'd be putting her life, as well as Kevin's, in jeopardy. Whatever chance they might have had for a future together would be gone. Their only chance at happiness would be over.

The wind gusted, sending fat drops of rain splattering against the sidewalk. The sky had finally opened up, releasing its burden. He barely noticed the wet drops dampening his skin, making dark splotches on the legs of his pants and the sleeves of his shirt. He felt too numb to feel anything.

"I'm sorry, Jason." Maggie tore her hand from his, pushing herself away and rising to her feet. "I shouldn't have told you. I should have just left—"

"Maggie, wait." He rose to his feet, as well, stopping her. He gripped her shoulders, holding her tight, afraid to let her go.

She looked at him, her eyes so wide and trusting he felt lost in their depths. "I—I didn't know what else to do, Jason. I just couldn't lie to you anymore. I wanted you to know the truth. Whatever you want to do, how you want to handle this, it's up to you. All I ask is that—" she swallowed hard "—if you decide to turn me in, you'll give me enough warning. My ex-husband can't find us. I won't...I can't lose Kevin."

"Maggie..." Jason shook his head, unable to form the words for what he felt inside him. He felt as though he were being ripped in two, torn between his job and the woman he loved.

"Maggie, I..." His throat tightened, robbing him of his voice. And then he knew what it was he had to do. There was no other choice. No other course for him to follow.

With a frustrated growl of resignation, he pulled her into his arms and kissed her, letting his actions speak his decision for him.

Chapter 13

The wind gusted, whipping the skirt of Maggie's sundress around her legs. Rain fell from the heavens, splattering her upturned face, her skin. Yet she barely noticed as she stood with Jason on the steps in front of his house, locked in an intimate embrace. The fury of the storm that surrounded them paled in comparison to the passion churning in their hearts.

Yet Maggie felt no fear. Not from the weather. Not from the man who held her. Deep inside, she felt a release. A sweet letting go of the fears that had haunted her most of her adult life. For the first time she allowed herself to hope, to wonder at the possibility of a happy future.

Breathlessly Jason tore his lips from hers. Lightning streaked the sky, and the electricity was reflected in his pale blue eyes as he searched her face. He stepped back, putting an unforgivable distance between them, and held out his hand. "Come with me."

The simple request sent a shiver down her spine. Slowly

she shook her head. "Are you sure you know what you're getting yourself into?"

"It'll be all right," he said in a voice so calm, a tone so certain, she couldn't help but want to believe him.

Fate had dealt her one too many blows. Stubbornly she held her ground. "How do you know?"

"I'll make it right."

Maggie stared at him, at the hand he extended. Stinging drops of rain pelted her skin, chilling her. She clenched her jaw to keep her teeth from chattering. Then, wordlessly, she reached out and accepted his hand.

Together they dashed up the stairs, finding safety from the storm in the covered porch. Her heart in her throat, she watched as Jason fumbled with the key to the front door. Soon the door swung open and they stepped into the quiet of the night-darkened house.

He flipped on a switch and the living room emerged from the shadows. Briefly, as he led her through the room, she noted an oversize couch, books stacked on a pine coffee table, CDs scattered nearby. Unlike his kitchen, the room had a comfy, lived-in look. She could almost see him stretched out on the couch, book in hand, relaxing as he listened to soft music after a long day at work. The innocent image, the insight into his private life, was almost provocative, heightening the intimacy of the moment.

They entered a narrow hall. The wooden floorboards whispered a protest beneath their feet, setting Maggie's heart pounding.

He dropped her hand as they stepped into another dark room, which she assumed must be a bedroom. She hesitated in the doorway, watching as he strode across the room and switched on the bedside lamp, the pale light illuminating his large body.

Wordlessly he unbuckled his holster. Wrapping the

leather straps around the gun, he tucked it into the drawer of the nightstand. The bedsprings creaked beneath his weight as he sat down on the edge and took off his shoes. His socks soon followed. He stood, then slowly unbuttoned his wet shirt, his eyes never leaving her face.

An erotic thrill coursed through her veins as she watched him slip the shirt off his shoulders. Her body trembled—from the chill of her damp clothing or from anticipation, she wasn't sure which. She clung to the door frame, needing its support.

Shirtless and barefoot, he made his way toward her. "You don't know how many times I've dreamed of having you in my bedroom."

"Well, here I am," she said, striving for nonchalance, but the effect was ruined by the breathless quality of her voice.

"Yes, you are," he said, and closed the distance between them. He reached out and stroked her face with his knuckles, sending shivers of delight throughout her body.

Gone was the urgency that had consumed them only moments ago. It was as though, instinctively, they knew they had a lifetime to enjoy this moment. He weaved his fingers through her damp hair, cradling the back of her neck with his hand. Placing his other hand on her waist, he drew her against him and claimed her mouth in a kiss.

She lifted a hand, running it across the expanse of his chest, raking her fingers through the light matting of hair. His skin felt warm, the muscles beneath strong. Flattening her palm on the center of his chest, she felt his heart pounding erratically.

The mood began to shift. His kiss grew restless, more demanding. Shockwaves of awareness skittered through her body as he lowered his hands, skimming her waist, not stopping until he cupped her derriere and brought her flush against him.

Evidence of his desire pressed hard and full against the softness of her belly. Maggie tore her mouth from his and drew in a steadying breath. Not missing a beat, he lowered his mouth, trailing butterfly kisses down the length of her neck, over the swell of her breasts.

Impatiently he fumbled with the buttons of her sundress. Cool air hit her skin as the dress fell open. He slid the damp fabric from her shoulders, allowing it to fall carelessly to the floor. Within seconds, he unfastened her bra, sliding it out of his way. Her nipples puckered beneath the impact of the cold air and his searing gaze.

Hooking his fingers into the waistband of her panties, he lowered them to the floor, then dropped to one knee in front of her to slide off her sandals. With his hands, then his mouth, he caressed her. Not an inch of her body went untouched. The callused pads of his fingers glided over her calves, her thighs. His hands slipped between her legs, parting them.

Maggie's breath caught when he found her moist, warm center and stroked her. His lips soon followed, his tongue thrusting, his mouth suckling. Her body trembled. The strength left her limbs. Closing her eyes against the sensations pulsing deep inside her, she clung to his shoulders for support and bit her lip to keep from crying out.

When she thought she could stand no more, he rose up before her, lifting her off her feet as though she were weightless. Before she could react, he lowered his head and closed his mouth around one aroused nipple. He sucked gently first, then hard. Unable to stop herself, Maggie cried out with the intense pleasure. Wrapping her legs around his waist, she buried her fingers in his hair, tilted his head back and claimed his mouth with a hungry kiss. With a frustrated growl, he carried her to the bed.

Together they fell across the mattress, their bodies tangled. Jason pulled away only long enough to yank off his pants and briefs, kicking them out of the way. They came together in a rush, touching, arousing, giving each other exquisite pleasure.

Maggie never wanted the moment to end. Yet, as the heat built inside her, she felt impatient for much more. She lost all sense of reason, all inhibition. Nothing else mattered. Not the past. Not the future.

Only now. Only this.

As though sensing her impatience, Jason rose above her. His eyes dark and hooded with desire, he looked down on her. She met his gaze without wavering, feeling nothing but complete and utter trust. Then, bracing himself on his elbows, he slipped inside her, filling her. And Maggie nearly shattered beneath him.

He moved, slowly at first, finding a gentle rhythm. But it wasn't enough. Impatience and desire took over. Soon the pace was fast and furious. Maggie watched as the muscles of his neck corded. His expression tautened with the intensity of the moment. Instinctively she raised her hips, taking him deeper inside her, meeting him thrust for delicious thrust.

Suddenly her world splintered into a thousand points of light and heat as her climax consumed her. Her pleasure only grew as seconds later she heard Jason's hoarse cry and felt his pulsing release.

They collapsed on the bed, their bodies still entwined. A fine sheen of perspiration dampened her skin. Overwhelmed by the emotions billowing inside her, she felt tears mist her eyes. Embarrassed, she turned her face into the hollow of his shoulder.

"Maggie, what's wrong?" Concern laced his voice. He pulled away, far enough to lift her chin, forcing her to look at him. Stiffening with sudden tension, he ran his hand across her tear-dampened face. Muttering an oath, he said, "If I've hurt you—"

"No," she said, pressing a finger to his lips, stilling his fears. "I can't explain. It was so...so perfect." Heat flushed her face. "I'd never imagined I could feel that free...that complete."

His chest rose and fell with his sigh of relief. He pulled her close, cradling her in his arms. "It's the way it should be. And if I have anything to say about it, it's the way it will always be."

Despite the tears, she smiled. The beat of her pounding heart returned to normal. A lethargy stole over her limbs. Secure in Jason's arms, she felt her eyelids grow heavy. Too many restless nights had finally taken their toll. Feeling safe for the first time in months, she fell into an exhausted sleep.

Jason watched as her face softened into the lines of slumber. The air around them grew cold. Reaching for the blanket, careful not to disturb her, he covered them, wrapping them into a cocoon of warmth.

He wished he could cocoon them from all the problems he knew they would soon face. He'd promised her a future together. He'd promised to keep her safe.

How the hell was he supposed to accomplish the task?

A rush of cool air woke him. Feeling groggy, disoriented, he blinked his bedroom into focus and knew something wasn't right. The lamp was still on, even though traces of dawn glowed through the cracks of the miniblinds. A single blanket covered his body. His sheets were tangled and twisted at his feet. And his bed felt cold and empty.

He sat up and saw Maggie slipping on her clothes. Trying not to let his disappointment show, he asked, "What time is it?"

"It's early, but I need to go home," she said, buttoning her sundress. "Kevin will be waking soon."

He pulled back the covers, rising to join her.

"You don't have to get up," she said. "Stay in bed. I can see myself out."

He shrugged as he reached for a pair of jeans and stepped into them. "I need to get to work soon, anyway."

"Work..." she murmured.

His heart caught at the wistful tone of her voice. At his gaze she glanced away, biting her lip, looking troubled.

In three quick strides, he was in front of her. Gripping her shoulders, he forced her to face him. "There's no need for second thoughts, Maggie. We will find a way to work this out."

"And what if we can't?" she asked, her chin jutting, her gaze steady and defiant. But the trembling of her lower lip belied her show of confidence. "Are you willing to look the other way for the rest of your life? Can you live with yourself, knowing that you'll be breaking the law right along with me? If you don't turn me in, you'll be harboring a fugitive, Jason."

His grip on her slender shoulders tightened. He felt a surge of fruitless anger rise inside him. "I'll do whatever's necessary to keep you and Kevin safe."

She sighed, the fight going out of her eyes. "I know you will."

Unease tightened his chest. The defeated expression, the resigned slump of her shoulders, the sadness tinting her green eyes, all spelled a woman ready to give up. He couldn't lose her, not now. "Maggie, you have to trust me. Everything will be all right."

"I do trust you, Jason," she said with a bittersweet smile. "It's fate I don't trust. It has a way of screwing up even the best-laid plans."

"So what are you saying? That you're ready to give up without even a fight?"

She shook her head. "I don't know what I'm saying."

"Promise me you won't leave, Maggie," he said, unable to keep the desperation from his tone. "You have to give me time to sort this out."

Closing her eyes, she nodded. "I promise."

He breathed a quiet sigh of relief and pulled her into his arms. Burying his face in her strawberry blond curls, breathing in her sweet scent, he never wanted to let her go.

After a long moment Maggie pushed away. "I really do need to get home."

He nodded. "I'll walk you out."

The air felt cool and crisp against his skin as he stepped outside. Everything looked fresh from last night's cleansing rain. A mourning dove bid him good-day, singing its plaintive song from a nearby treetop. Barefoot, he crossed the backyard to Maggie's house, holding her hand tightly in his.

When they paused at the steps of her back porch, he leaned down for one last kiss. Wishing he could tell her everything he felt in his heart, but uncertain if she was ready to know how much he cared, how much he loved her, his true feelings remained unspoken. Instead, he released her, whispering, "Have a good day, Maggie."

The tension eased from her face long enough to allow a half smile. Then, without another word, she turned away and disappeared into her house.

Jason hesitated, standing in the dew-ladened grass, as a chill stole over him. Maggie trusted him. But perhaps he didn't deserve that trust. She didn't know the whole truth. She didn't know about his call to Tom Burns in California.

It was too late to turn back now. Because of his own insecurities, he very well might have set into motion the events that would uncover Maggie's secret. His friend in California would undoubtedly be concerned that Jason had become involved with a fugitive. He would press him to do something about it.

His hands fisting at his sides, Jason turned from Maggie's house. He had less than a week to figure out damage control. Somehow he had to assure his friend that all was well, that it had been nothing more than a misunderstanding. That there was no need to be concerned.

No need to be concerned.

If only it was true.

Five days later, on a bright and sunny Friday morning when Jason stepped into the police-department offices, he was met by a flurry of frantic activity.

"Thank God, you're here," the dispatcher said, pressing a hand to her ample chest. "We've been trying to reach you on the radio."

Jason's face warmed with embarrassment. Up until an hour ago, he'd been asleep in Maggie's arms. After a quick shower, he'd headed for work. His mood was so good he hadn't wanted to ruin it by listening to any bad news on the radio. So he'd done the unforgivable and turned it off on his way into work.

"What's wrong?" he asked, frowning.

"We're in deep trouble, Chief," Schmitz said, coming up from behind him. "Homer Bledsoe is gone."

"Gone?" Jason blinked, feeling confused. "What do you mean, gone?"

Homer Bledsoe was a backwoodsman and a mean-spirited alcoholic, who'd gotten drunk a couple of weeks ago and beaten his wife unconscious. Leaving her bruised and bleeding, he'd gone into town to celebrate with a few more drinks at Tuttle's Tavern. When the bartender refused to serve him, he'd broken a chair over the man's head. Then he'd proceeded to tear up the rest of the tavern.

Taking him down had been a difficult and costly task. Somewhere along the way, he'd found a shotgun. After unloading his supply of cartridges at two of Jason's officers, Homer had thrown down the gun and tried to fight his way out of the situation. Officer Schmitz still wore the scar of a jagged cut on his forehead as his reward for finally subduing the dangerous drunk.

Denied bail, Homer had been in the city jail awaiting trial on a long list of charges. Due to the seriousness of his rampage and the fact that this was not his first offense, he was guaranteed to serve time in the state penitentiary. Bitter and blaming everyone but himself for his troubles, he was the last man Jason wanted to see out on the streets.

"It was a mistake, Chief," Schmitz explained quietly. "Burt Johnson was supposed to be released last night. Somehow the paperwork got mixed up and Homer got out, instead. We didn't realize there'd been a mix-up until a little while ago."

"Do you mean to tell me we just let him walk out that door?" Jason said, jabbing a finger at the entryway. His voice sounded calm. But inside, he was churning with irritation.

More officers gathered around, looking worried.

Schmitz gave a curt nod. "That's the way it looks, Chief."

"How in Sam Hill did something like this happen?" Jason growled.

"We don't know that for sure," Schmitz said, shooting

a sidelong glance at the night guard. The guard's face flushed a deep red and he dropped his gaze to his feet. Schmitz continued, "But we're still looking into it."

Jason raked a hand through his damp curls. "Dammit, did anyone tell Homer's wife yet? You know he blames her for everything that's happened. He swore he was going to kill her when he got out."

"Yes, sir," another officer said. "She's all right. Stan's on his way out to her house right now to pick her up. He's dropping her off at a safe place until her husband's been recaptured."

"Good." Jason drew in a deep breath, giving himself a moment to gather his thoughts. "We'd better call the sheriff in on this. Homer's a backwoodsman. He's going to go underground. We'll need the county's help to flush him out."

"I'll get right on it, Chief," Betty called out, putting on the telephone headset.

"Call everybody in. Night shift, as well as day," Jason said, turning to Schmitz. "We're going to need all the help we can get. Make sure they bring their bullet-proof vests. I don't want to take any chances."

"Right," Schmitz said, moving toward his desk.

The rest of the men scattered, hurrying to get ready.

Jason headed for his office. He hadn't had time for breakfast. His empty stomach burned, feeling on fire. Damn, he muttered to himself, massaging his belly, what a way to start the day.

"Don't forget your messages, Chief," Betty said, waving a stack of papers in her hand.

He sighed again. Grabbing the messages, he continued on to his office. He didn't get far, however. One message caught his eye and stopped him dead in his tracks. He strode back to the dispatcher and held out the message. "Betty, when did this message come in from California?"

She squinted at the note. "Must have been last night, Chief, after I left. I wasn't the one who took it."

Tom Burns had been trying to get hold of him since Wednesday morning. During that time, Jason had done his best to avoid contact with his old friend. Unforgivably he'd ducked his calls and didn't return his messages. It wasn't that he was taking the coward's way out, he told himself. He just wasn't sure yet what he would say.

This message was different, however. It was marked "urgent," and the word was underlined twice. He sighed, knowing he couldn't avoid talking to Tom forever. As soon as he got a chance, he'd give him a call. Jason crumpled the note in his hand. Until then he had a job to do, a fugitive to catch. One that was a *real* threat to society.

Unbidden, Maggie's image came to mind. Even though he'd had time to get used to the idea, he still couldn't bring himself to call her a fugitive. There was no comparison between the crimes Homer Bledsoe had committed and the one Maggie had been forced to commit in the name of love for her son.

In his eyes, Maggie could never be a criminal.

Later that afternoon, Maggie shivered as she looked out the window of Mel's diner, unable to shake the uncanny feeling that someone was watching her. It was a Friday afternoon, the unofficial beginning of the weekend. Already the street was filled with tourists, all hurrying to their various destinations: the antique shops, the ice-cream shop, the historical homes. No one appeared to be standing on the street staring at the diner.

Maggie sighed. The truth was, she'd been feeling jumpy ever since she'd confessed her secret to Jason. Not that she had a reason to be skittish. Jason had been nothing but supportive. In the past few days, he'd spent as much time as possible with Kevin and her. With every word he spoke, each action he took, he tried to ease her fears. He tried his best to make her believe they had a chance at a future together.

Beneath Jason's persistent attention, Kevin had flourished. His arm was healing faster than she'd expected. So fast he was able to go to Tommy Marshall's house, where Tommy's mother had agreed to watch him now that school was out for the summer and Maggie still had to go to work. It was hard for Maggie to trust Kevin to someone else, but she had to begin sometime. And somehow Jason had become a vital part of their family, the positive male influence she'd longed for her son to have.

Life seemed perfect. Too perfect.

She wondered how long the illusion would last.

Maggie turned away from the window, trying vainly to push the bleak thoughts from her mind. Too often in the past she'd expected the worst, always waiting for the other shoe to drop. It was as though she believed she didn't deserve to be happy.

But all that had changed, she told herself, when she'd met Jason. He'd made her believe in the power of love. He was the only man she'd ever trusted so completely.

"Maggie, it's time to close up," Mel announced, startling her out of her troubled thoughts. He pulled his chef's hat off his head, revealing his shiny, bald pate.

"Already?" Maggie blinked at him in surprise. The lunch-hour rush had barely ended. There were at least two more hours left on her shift.

"Jenny's getting married tonight, isn't she?" he said, untying his apron.

"Well, yes, but—"

The twinkle in Mel's eye belied his gruff expression. Purposefully he strode to the front door, turning over the Closed sign and slapping it in place. "Then we'd better get ready for the party, don't you think?"

"What's this?" Dot sashayed to the counter. "Is the high-and-mighty slave driver *really* giving us the afternoon off?"

"Watch it, Dot," Mel growled, "or you'll be cleaning out the fat vats."

Dot winked, snapping her gum. "You don't scare me, you ol' softie." Then she leaned across the counter and planted a kiss on Mel's cheek, leaving a crimson imprint of her lips. "I'm wise to you."

Mel's face turned bright pink. "Skedaddle, both of you, before I change my mind."

"Thanks, Mel." Maggie grinned and tugged off her apron. With a wave of her hand, she headed for the door. "I'll see you all tonight."

"I can't wait to see you in your fancy dress," Dot called after her. "But watch out, I've got dibs on the bride's bouquet."

Maggie laughed as she stepped out into the bright sunlight—and then felt a chill run down her spine. Her smile faded. Her step faltered as she glanced around. Cars lined both sides of the street. Pedestrians crowded the sidewalk, parting in a V as they made their way around her.

Maggie could see no one lurking nearby. No one to bother her.

Rubbing her arms, she fought the urge to cross the street and pay a visit to the town's chief of police. She was a grown woman, after all, she thought. She'd been taking care of herself for some time. There was no need for her to become dependent on Jason. She forced herself to continue on home.

As she left the town square, the crowd thinned. Turning down the quiet residential street where her house stood, she felt another prickling of unease. She turned, glancing sharply over her shoulder, and caught a late-model gray car turning the opposite corner.

The shaded windows blocked her view of the driver. And the car was gone before she could look at the license. Maggie stood frozen to the spot, staring at the empty street. Then, with a nervous laugh, she shook her head.

What was wrong with her?

Tonight was Jenny's wedding. She was just the matron of honor, not the bride. She had no right to have a case of prewedding jitters.

Maggie lifted her face, letting the sunshine work its magic in banishing the chill around her heart. There wasn't a cloud in the sky. A soft breeze stirred the air. And, to lift her spirits, she had a beautiful new dress waiting for her at home. It promised to be a wonderful night and an even more special ceremony.

She didn't need to spoil the evening with a case of unfounded apprehension.

Pushing all thoughts of doom and gloom from her mind, she moved off down the sidewalk to her house.

Chapter 14

"Careful he doesn't hit his head," Jason said, watching as two officers pulled Homer Bledsoe out of the back seat of a patrol car.

After spending most of the day combing the woods of the Missouri Ozarks for their fugitive, they'd finally caught their man thanks to the help of a local Realtor, who'd discovered a broken lock on one of his lakeside rental properties. Instead of investigating on his own, the Realtor had wisely alerted the police. Within minutes, the county and city police departments had swarmed the remote cabin.

Bledsoe had given up with only a token fight. If the empty bottles of whiskey strewn about the cabin—compliments of the owner's well-stocked liquor cabinet—were any indication, Homer was in no shape to stand on his own two feet, let alone defend himself.

Now, emerging from the car, Bledsoe listed drunkenly.

Simultaneously, the two officers tightened their grip beneath Homer's shoulders. Supporting him on either side, they half-led, half-carried their prisoner into the police department. The rest of the officers involved in the manhunt followed closely, anxious to assure themselves of Homer's imminent incarceration.

Everyone but Officer Schmitz, that is. He stood by his patrol car, peering inside, shaking his head in disgust.

Jason hesitated, frowning. "Is there a problem?"

"The son of a—" Gritting his teeth, Schmitz struggled to control his temper. "Our prisoner threw up in the back seat of my patrol car."

Jason felt the tension ease. He bit back a smile. "A hazard of the job. Look on the bright side—at least we got our man."

Schmitz did not seem comforted by the thought. He narrowed his gaze and set his lantern jaw into a displeased line.

Jason grinned at him, "It's going to be a warm evening. If I were you, I'd hose that car down ASAP. No telling how long the scent will linger if you don't."

Ignoring the grumble of curses falling from Schmitz's lips, Jason strode into the police department. A scene bordering on the lines of a party filled the offices. Men were laughing and retelling stories of the day's activities. A few stood at the counter, watching as Homer was rebooked. Others lingered by the coffee machine, embellishing on their parts in the capture.

Noticeably missing from the group was Stan Wilson.

Belatedly Jason recalled that this evening was Jenny Lewis's wedding. A wedding he'd promised Maggie he'd attend with her and Kevin. Jason glanced at his watch. A wedding for which he was going to be very late if he didn't get home soon.

Stan was a big boy, he assured himself. No doubt he would deal with the upcoming nuptials in his own way.

And after spending the day tromping through the thick underbrush, he felt hot and gritty. His shirt was drenched in sweat. Cockleburs were snagged in his pant legs. Jason sighed. All he wanted to do was go home and stand beneath a long, hot shower.

"Maggie Conrad called, Chief," Betty announced, demanding his attention. "When I told her you were out looking for an escaped prisoner, she told me to tell you not to worry about rushing home. That she'll meet you at the church for Jenny's wedding."

Catcalls sounded across the room.

Jason felt the back of his neck warm with embarrassment. The phone rang, sparing him from any further unwanted announcements from his dispatcher. He took advantage of her distraction and headed for his office.

But not quickly enough. "Chief, it's that Tom Burns from California," Betty said, stopping him once again. Her brow furrowed into a frown. "He really sounds agitated, Chief. He says he needs to talk to you immediately."

Tension tightened Jason's throat. Swallowing hard, he said, "Thanks, Betty. I'll take the call in my office."

His feet felt heavy as lead as he forced himself to move. He'd been delaying the inevitable for the past three days. It was time to face the fallout of his own actions. Stepping inside, he closed the door behind him. Then he picked up the phone and punched in the blinking light. "Hi, Tom."

"Where the hell have you been?"

Jason blinked, taken aback by the anger in his ex-partner's voice. "We had a prisoner escape. I've been tied up all day with a manhunt."

"I'm talking about the rest of this week. I've been trying to get hold of you since Wednesday."

"Look, I know I should have called—"

"You're damn right you should have called me back.

All hell is breaking loose over here. Do you have any idea who your mystery lady in Wyndchester is?''

"Slow down, Tom," Jason said, his head reeling with confusion. "What's this all about?"

"Your Maggie Conrad's real name is Margaret Stuart, the former wife of a local businessman, Gerald Stuart. We've been looking for her ever since she disappeared almost two years ago."

"I know that," Jason said, overwhelmed by the extent of his friend's displeasure. What was going on here? He'd expected Tom to be concerned for his welfare, not to be so agitated. "Maggie told me about taking her son, that there was probably a warrant out for her arrest."

"That isn't the half of it," Tom said sharply. "Gerald Stuart is under investigation in connection with organized crime. Money laundering and racketeering are only a couple of the charges pending against him. We also believe he's guilty of conspiring to murder in at least two separate cases. He wasn't the trigger man, but he was one to give the orders. Except, at the moment, the prosecutor's case is in limbo. Its fate is hinging on the testimony of the state's star witness—your Maggie Conrad."

Jason sat down hard on the edge of his desk. He felt numb inside, unable to form the right words to respond. It was too much, too soon. He couldn't think, couldn't make sense of the news. Why hadn't Maggie told him the truth, that she was a state witness?

"We've been looking to put Gerald Stuart away for a very long time. Until now, nobody's been able to get close enough to do the job. We've got to get his ex-wife back to California, Jason," Tom persisted. "She's too important to the case to let her slip away again."

"Wait a minute," Jason said, a hot surge of anger thawing his frozen tongue. "If you think I'm going to just hand her over, you're crazy. She isn't a criminal. She's scared to death, trying to protect her son."

"Nobody's blaming her motives, but—"

"Look, I don't understand any of this. Maggie's not the kind of woman to just up and walk out on an investigation. If the prosecutors wanted her as a witness, why weren't they protecting her and her son?"

"Well, because—" Tom hesitated "—she wasn't exactly slated to testify at the time."

"What does that mean, *exactly?*"

Tom sighed. "It wasn't until after she left town that the prosecutors started looking seriously into the case. The custody trial was messy, all over the papers out here. During the hearing, her attorney alluded to her ex-husband's criminal activities, stating that Maggie had been a witness to some of these activities. Unfortunately the judge dismissed the allegations, not allowing them to be aired in court."

"That's because the judge was a friend of her ex-husband's," Jason cut in, unable to keep the bitterness from his voice.

"Gerald Stuart has a lot of friends. That's part of the problem." Tom released a terse breath. "We came up with a hit on Maggie's prints on Wednesday. Once I figured out who we were dealing with, I couldn't keep a lid on the news. I didn't have any choice but to tell my supervisor."

Jason muttered an oath. His innocent little background search had snowballed into an out-of-control avalanche of bad news.

"There's more, Jason," Tom said quietly. The somber tone of his voice sent a shiver down Jason's back. "Gerald Stuart's been missing since Thursday morning. We have reason to believe that the news of his ex-wife's reappearance was leaked to him by someone in our department.

There's a possibility he's on his way to Wyndchester. Hell, he might be there already.''

Jason's heart slammed against his rib cage. The blood roaring in his ears, he lurched to his feet. "Why didn't you tell me this in the first place?"

"Calm down, Jason. Now can you understand why we need to get her back to California? She's got to testify—for her own sake. It's the only way we can protect her."

"The only thing I understand is that your department has alerted a dangerous man to the whereabouts of an innocent woman and her child." Jason's voice shook with barely suppressed anger. "You've put their lives at risk. If anything happens to them, it'll be on your shoulders, partner."

He slammed the phone back in its cradle, the crash reverberating throughout the quiet office. Yanking open the door, he stepped outside into the mayhem of the department. Ignoring all attempts to get his attention, he stormed through the office, not stopping until he was outside in the fading evening sunlight.

Officer Schmitz lifted his head from the back seat of his patrol car. A wad of paper towels in hand, he frowned and said, "Everything okay, Chief?"

"No, everything's not okay," Jason said, striding to his Jeep. He opened the door and slung himself behind the wheel.

Schmitz blinked, looking confused. "Where are you going, Chief?"

"To a wedding," he said, slamming the door shut. Grinding the key in the ignition, he popped the Jeep into gear. Tires squealing, he pealed out of the parking space. Beneath his breath, he added, "God help me, I just hope I'm not too late."

"How are you feeling?" Maggie asked, studying her young friend in concern.

Her face as pale as the bridal gown she wore, Jenny sighed. "Still a little queasy. But I guess I'll be okay."

"Of course she's all right," Mrs. Bosworth, Jenny's future mother-in-law, cut in. "The wedding's about to start. There can't be any delays."

"She's ill, Mrs. Bosworth," Maggie said, appalled by the woman's lack of compassion.

"It's just a mild case of prewedding jitters." Mrs. Bosworth gave her perfectly coiffed blond head a dismissive shake. "We've discussed this before, Jenny. As Mrs. Joe Bosworth III, you have a reputation to uphold, an image that must be maintained." She flashed a quick, impersonal smile. "There won't be any more problems, now, will there?"

"No, ma'am," Jenny whispered, dropping her gaze to the bridal bouquet she was clutching. Like the rest of the wedding, the starkly formal arrangement of arum lilies seemed unsuited for such a sweet, down-to-earth young woman.

"Good," Mrs. Bosworth said, lifting her chin, her face lighting in an expression of triumph. "Now, I must take my place in the church." With that announcement, she swept out of the dressing room on a cloud of expensive perfume.

Missing Jason's reassuring presence more than ever, Maggie sat down next to her friend and placed a hand on her trembling shoulders. "Jenny, are you sure this is what you really want? If you're having second thoughts..."

"It's too late," Jenny said, her voice shaking with emotion.

"Honey, it's never too late. All you have to do is say no."

"I can't," Jenny said, her eyes filling with tears. "Mrs. Bosworth—she's made so many plans, spent so much money. She'd be very upset if the wedding didn't take place.''

Carefully Maggie said, ''Getting married only because you're afraid of disappointing your future mother-in-law is not a good enough reason.''

''You don't understand. No one says no to her. Not her husband, not Joe.'' She shook her head. ''And certainly not me.''

''Jenny, please. I wish you'd reconsider—''

A knock sounded and the door of the dressing room swung open. Strains of ''The Wedding March'' wafted in as Mel stood before them, looking uncomfortable in his tux and bow tie. Jenny's father hadn't been a part of her life for a long time. Mrs. Bosworth had insisted that tradition must be upheld, that Jenny must be given away by a male member of her family. With no one else to turn to, Mel had graciously volunteered for the job. Flexing his big shoulders, he said, ''Time to get this show on the road, ladies.''

Jenny rose unsteadily to her feet.

Reluctantly Maggie followed her lead. Every instinct told her to do something, anything, to stop this farce of a wedding. Jenny was no more in love with Joe Bosworth than she was suited to meeting the demands of the snooty Mrs. Bosworth. Her dream of a better life was turning into a nightmare. The marriage would be a disastrous mistake.

But Jenny was too scared to listen. Short of tying the bride to the nearest chair, Maggie had no idea how to stop the wedding.

The wedding planner Mrs. Bosworth had hired to make sure the ceremony went smoothly breezed into the dressing room. With a critical eye, she glanced at Maggie's elegant but boring blue silk dress. With a snap of her fingers she said, "Matron of honor, you're holding up the wedding. Let's get in line, pronto."

With one last troubled glance at Jenny, Maggie fell into step. From that moment on, the wedding took on a surrealistic quality. Everything around her seemed out of focus, moving in slow motion, like a film gone bad. It was as though someone else, not her, was marching up the aisle. Faces of people—some familiar, many not—stared at her, their gazes curious, unsmiling. She searched the crowd for Jason, but came up disappointed. Even after spotting Kevin's smiling face as he sat next to Dot, Maggie still felt exposed, on display. If she was this uncomfortable, how was the fragile bride holding up?

As Maggie took her place at the altar, she turned to watch Jenny walk up the aisle. In the white dress with its many sequins and beads and its long, satin train, Jenny looked overwhelmed, as though she was about to collapse. Beneath the veil of lacy netting, her expression seemed void of all emotion. Leaning heavily on Mel's arm for support, she seemed small, frail and completely unprepared for the wedding.

Frowning his concern at the bride, the minister began the ceremony. The words blurred together and Maggie felt a chill of apprehension run down her spine. Surreptitiously, she glanced around the church, looking for a reason for her uneasiness, but she saw nothing untoward. Attributing her fears to her concern for Jenny's well-being, she forced her attention back to the ceremony.

The vows were exchanged. Joe's voice rang out loud and clear. Jenny's was barely above a whisper. Finally the minister turned to the guests and announced, "If there be anyone who has just cause for this wedding not to take place, let him speak now or forever hold his peace."

A hush fell on the crowd.

Maggie held her breath, waiting, hoping for a miracle.

Her miracle was granted in the form of a disheveled, wild-eyed Stan Wilson.

Striding up the aisle, his long legs closing the distance between him and Jenny, he said in a loud voice, "I have just cause."

A buzz of shocked murmurs arose from the pews.

Jenny turned to face the newcomer, her eyes wide, her mouth forming an O of surprise. For the first time since the wedding began, she showed a spark of emotion.

The groom's face reddened in anger.

In a nearby pew, his mother's expression hardened with disapproval.

Undeterred, Stan climbed the steps of the altar. Shaking his head, he said simply, "Jenny, you can't marry this man—not when you're in love with me."

"Don't be ridiculous," the groom said, laughing in amusement at the very idea. "Jenny, tell him he's crazy."

Jenny didn't answer. Instead, she stared at Stan, her eyes filling with tears.

"Jenny?" Joe Bosworth turned to her.

Stan's eyes never left Jenny's face. His smile was gentle, coaxing. He held out his hand. "Come on, Jenny. It's time to go."

A trembling smile touched Jenny's lips. Without a word, she placed her hand in his and followed him down the steps of the altar.

The crowd watched their escape in stunned silence.

The pair had gotten about halfway out of church before the groom finally seemed to realize what was happening. Storming down the aisle, his groomsmen right behind, he bellowed, "Wilson, you bastard. You're going to pay for ruining my wedding."

The guests began to spill out of the pews, following the bridal party outside.

Maggie lingered behind by the altar. The church was now empty, and from outside she heard scuffling and the angry sounds of shouting. She'd had enough violence in her life. She was in no hurry to be a witness to more.

Jenny's expensive bridal bouquet, lying on the floor, abandoned and forgotten, caught her eye. Maggie stooped to pick it up. As she rose, she heard footsteps on the marble floor in the aisle behind her. Half expecting, half hoping it was Jason, she smiled and whirled to face him.

Her smile faded. Her heart stuttered as she stared into a pair of cool, deceptively placid, blue eyes. Her worst fear had finally come true.

After all her months on the run, her ex-husband had finally found her.

Chapter 15

His fault. If anything happened to Maggie, it would be his fault.

The thought settled heavily on Jason's shoulders. Guilt pressing hard against his heart, he tromped on the gas pedal, pushing the Jeep as fast as he dared through the evening traffic. Weekend tourists, as well as locals looking to relax and unwind with a night on the town, filled the streets, slowing his progress to the church.

Growling in frustration, Jason braked for a red light. Knowing that technically this was not an emergency call, he flipped on his lights and siren and nudged his Jeep through the intersection.

He had been the one who hadn't trusted Maggie enough. Instead of simply asking her to tell him the truth, he'd gone behind her back and sought to slake his curiosity by using the contacts of his job. In doing so, he'd put her life, as well as Kevin's, in jeopardy.

Unbidden, memories of his son's death crowded his

mind. The pain of losing him. The helplessness he'd felt watching him die and being unable to do anything to prevent it. The guilt he'd felt at still being alive and healthy and able to continue on alone, while his son's life was cut short. All of these emotions washed over him, overwhelming him. It had taken him years to accept that he'd lost Scotty because of circumstances beyond his control.

This time things were different.

He'd be damned if he'd lose Maggie and Kevin because of his own stupid mistake.

The Jeep teetered precariously, threatening to roll over, as he turned the next corner too sharply. Straightening the wheel, he sped up again, keeping the church steeple within his sights.

Maggie's beautiful face flashed before his eyes. Her sparkling green eyes, her shy smile, the dusting of freckles on her nose and cheeks, the strawberry blond hair that was like cornsilk to the touch—he couldn't get the images out of his mind. His pulse quickened. Nor could he shake the feeling that something was terribly wrong.

That Maggie was in danger.

A crowd jammed the front steps of the church, spilling out onto the sidewalks. A few people glanced his way when he pulled up to the church with his lights throbbing and his siren blaring. In the center of the crowd, the focus of the group's rapt attention, was Stan Wilson.

Obviously Stan had taken his matter of the heart into his own hands. Literally.

Before him, a fist fight ensued involving Stan and the groom, Joe Bosworth, the son of the town's leading citizen. No doubt there'd be hell to pay in the morning. Joe's father was an alderman, one of the men who'd hired Jason, one who could also fire him. Mr. Bosworth was still displeased at Jason's arrest of his youngest son for the possession of alcohol during the school's Spring Carnival. If he stood back and did nothing to stop this fight, his job might be on the line.

But none of that mattered to Jason now. Stan's battle for the woman he'd loved would have to go unassisted.

Jason had to find Maggie.

Cutting the siren, he threw open the door of the Jeep and stepped outside. He scanned the crowd, searching for Maggie's sweet face. Instead, he spotted a familiar head of brassy blond hair, topped with a feathered purple hat. Weaving his way through the crowd, he reached to Maggie's friend, Dot.

When he tapped her shoulder, she reeled around in surprise. Pressing a hand to her ample bosom, she exclaimed, "Chief Gallagher, you scared me half to death."

"Sorry, Dot. I'm looking for Maggie and Kevin."

"Why, Kevin's right here." She turned, frowning at the empty space beside her. "Well, he *was* here just a minute ago."

Jason schooled his face, revealing none of his concern. "Have you seen Maggie?"

Dot shook her head, causing the feathers of her hat to billow in the air. "Well, not since the wedding was, uh, cut short. I guess she must still be inside. Maybe Kevin went in to find her."

Jason nodded, turning to leave.

"Chief," Dot called, stopping him. She waved a hand at the battling suitors. "Aren't you going to do something about this?"

He glanced at the two men, watching as Stan ducked just in time to miss a blow to the chin. Recovering quickly, Stan rose and landed two sharp punches on Joe Bosworth's jaw.

Jason shrugged, allowing himself a slight grin. "Looks

as though Stan's doing just fine without me. I don't think he needs my help.''

Dot's crimson mouth curved into a smile. Her throaty laughter followed him as he headed toward the church.

"Gerald," Maggie whispered, staring at the man before her. Tall, blond and handsome, he hadn't changed much since the day she'd first met him. He still possessed an aura of confidence, of power—of intimidation and danger. An impression that was reinforced by the gun he held in his hand.

"You still recognize me," he said with a smooth smile. "I suppose I should be grateful for that...after all this time.''

"H-how...?" Fear tightened her throat. The words refused to form. She hated herself for feeling so scared, so weak.

His smile deepened. "How did I find you? I have to admit it wasn't easy. It took me longer than I expected.'' He chuckled, the hollow sound sending a chill down her spine. Despite the controlled tone of his voice, there was a maniacal glint in his eyes. She'd never seen him look more crazed. This time, she told herself, he would certainly kill her. "I had to wait until you slipped up. Obviously you trusted the wrong person. Someone was checking up on you, my dear. Your fingerprints were scanned through the police files in California. It didn't take long for the word to get to me.''

Maggie's heart stuttered. The church suddenly grew colder. She shivered, realizing it must have been Jason who had betrayed her. Who else would have access to the police files?

No, she refused to believe that Jason would do anything to harm her. There had to be another reason for her ex-husband's appearance, she told herself, as her heart ached with uncertainty. She felt helpless, more alone than she had in months.

Pushing the troubling thoughts away, unwilling to go down without a fight, she shook her head, gripping the bouquet of arum lilies more tightly. "You'll never get away with this, Gerald. We're in a church. There's a big crowd just outside the doors."

His gaze sweeping the altar, he said, "If you're waiting for an act of God to save you, I wouldn't hold my breath. I've long given up hoping for His influence in any way." He inclined his head toward the entrance. "As for your friends, I believe they're otherwise occupied. I sincerely doubt anyone will notice our departure."

Unable to help herself, Maggie glanced down the aisle toward the entrance. Then she wished she hadn't. A fear so great it nearly overwhelmed her trembled through her body. She wanted to shout, to cry out a warning. But she was afraid her calls for help would only aggravate an already explosive situation.

Instead, she watched, frozen to the spot, as Kevin slowly made his way toward them.

He wore a light blue suit and tie. His arm was still in its cast and sling. His face was pale. There was fear reflected in his young eyes.

After years of watching Gerald abuse her and being abused himself, Kevin's self-esteem had been eroded. Only after months of being away from his father's destructive influence, after the patient positive reinforcement with which she'd plied him and his fledgling relationship with Jason, had he regained some of his confidence.

In the past Kevin might have run away, too terrified to face his father.

But not tonight.

* * *

Even in his worst nightmare, Jason could not have imagined a more frightening scene.

Moments ago he had slipped into the church. Immediately he was struck by the eerie stillness of the building. It was a stark contrast to the mayhem outside. His heart sounded too loud as it pounded in his chest. His footsteps against the marble floor seemed to echo throughout the church. Reflexively he tiptoed through the vestibule, making his way quietly toward the altar.

He stopped dead in his tracks at the sight before him.

Maggie stood at the altar, facing him. A blond man stood a few feet away from her. In his hand he held a gun, which was trained on Maggie. Not far behind, inching his way closer to danger, was Kevin.

For God's sake, Jason moaned silently, it was a disaster waiting to happen.

How was he supposed to save them both?

Forcing himself to move, he unfastened his gun, slipping it out of his holster. Quickly, quietly, he crept up behind the small group.

A flicker of recognition lit Maggie's eyes. Their gazes caught and held across the length of the chapel. She drew in a sharp breath of relief, unconsciously alerting her ex-husband to his presence.

The man tensed, whirling around to face him. Simultaneously he spotted Kevin. Frowning with confusion, he raised his gun, pointing it directly at his son.

Outrage rose in Jason's throat. The force of the emotion stopped the words from emitting. Hurling himself toward the pair, the world spinning around him, all he could muster was a single, bellowed word. "Noooo..."

Things happened very quickly.

Kevin, tucking his head down and raising his shoulders

like a miniature football tackler, threw himself at his father, clipping him at his knees.

The gun went off, spewing its bullet in an upward arc, sending a shower of plaster and wood chips raining from the choir loft.

Gerald fell back, struggling to regain his balance as his feet were caught on the first step of the altar. All the while he reached out, trying to grab hold of Kevin.

With a grunt of exertion, Kevin rolled out of the way, scrambling to his feet.

Her son safe, Maggie raised the thick bouquet of flowers and swung with all her might, landing a blow on one side of her ex-husband's head.

The blow stunned him but didn't stop him. It did, however, give Jason the time he needed to close the distance between them. Just as Gerald whirled around to face Maggie with a livid, frenzied expression on his face, Jason moved in.

Tucking his gun in his holster, he clamped a hand around Gerald's wrist, lifting the man's arm and his gun out of harm's way. With a strength he hadn't realized he'd possessed, he squeezed his grip until he heard the other man's cry of pain. The gun fell from Gerald's hand, clamoring noisily on the marble floor.

Quickly Maggie bent to pick it up. Her hands shaking, she held the gun, pointing it at her ex-husband. Kevin used the distraction to clamber up the steps of the altar, finding safety behind his mother, watching, horrified, as he clung to her silky skirt.

Wishing he could spare the boy any more violence, but knowing he had to act quickly and forcibly, with his free hand, Jason landed a roundhouse punch to Gerald's gut.

Gerald's breath escaped in a whoosh. He bent over, gasping in pain. Taking advantage of his weakened state, Jason unhooked the cuffs from his belt and clipped them on Gerald's wrists.

Suddenly there was a commotion at the entryway. Jason glanced over his shoulder and spotted Officer Schmitz and a handful of other policemen running down the aisle toward him. Frowning with confusion, he said, "How did you know?"

His face grim, Schmitz grabbed hold of one of Gerald's arms. "When you left, you said you were going to the church. From the look on your face, I knew it had to be bad news. I figured it was about Stan, until Betty told me you'd just talked to that guy in California, the one whose phone calls you've been dodging all week. Then I knew there had to be more to it." He shrugged his massive shoulders. "So I got a few guys to follow me, thought maybe you could use some help."

"Yeah, I can," Jason said, standing numbly, unable to move. The impact of what had just occurred, of what might have happened, struck him like a blow. His breath caught in his throat. The strength drained from his muscles. All he wanted to do was take Maggie into his arms and hold her tight, reassuring himself she was safe.

"Chief," Schmitz said.

Jason glanced at him, frowning.

Schmitz nodded toward the altar. "I think we've got another problem here."

He whirled around to find Maggie standing at the altar. Her face was drained of color, causing her freckles to stand out. She looked lost, her expression distant, haunted. But that wasn't what troubled him most. In her shaking hands, she still held Gerald Stuart's gun.

And it was pointed directly at Gerald Stuart's head.

"Maggie," Jason said, keeping his voice soft, his tone

nonthreatening. Slowly he stepped toward her. "Maggie, honey, give me the gun."

"He was going to hurt Kevin," she said, her voice trembling, her eyes never leaving her ex-husband's face.

"Will somebody do something about her?" Gerald Stuart snapped. His face was red, his breathing harsh. "The bitch wants to kill me!"

Schmitz wrenched Gerald's arm back, evoking a cry of pain. "Say another word and I'll personally shut you up."

Jason ignored the pair. He moved closer, stepping into her line of vision. "He can't touch you now, Maggie."

She shook her head. "He'll find a way."

"No, Maggie. This time he's going to jail for what he's done. His power over you is finished." Jason stepped between her and her ex-husband. He lifted his hand, reaching for the gun. "He won't hurt you or Kevin ever again."

Moisture filled her eyes. She blinked, sending a stream of tears down her cheeks. She stared at him, as though seeing him for the first time. Then, looking down at the gun in her hand, her face crumbled and she released a pitiful cry of pain and suffering.

Jason took the gun from her limp grip, handing it over to a nearby officer. Then he pulled her into his arms, cradling her against his chest. Her tears, hot and damp, stained his shirt. Her warm breath fell in rapid puffs against his skin. Heart-wrenching sobs shook her slender body. And all he could do was hold her close.

Officer Schmitz led Gerald Stuart away, motioning for the other policemen to follow.

In the sanctuary of the altar, Jason continued to hold Maggie, rocking her gently until the sobs lessened. Until he heard a small voice say, "Mom?"

Jason loosened his hold on Maggie, turning to find Kevin

standing at his side. His expression was one of fear mixed with concern.

"Kevin?" Maggie said, pushing herself away. She dropped to her knees, running her hands over her son's face, his hair, gently touching his wounded arm. "Oh, honey. Are you okay?"

He nodded, looking too upset to speak. Tears glittered in his eyes, magnified by the lenses of his glasses. Sniffing loudly, he swiped impatiently at the offensive teardrops.

Mindful of his broken arm, Maggie pulled him close, enfolding him in her arms. Together, mother and son, they formed a tightly woven bond of love.

Jason stepped away, feeling suddenly out of place, as though he didn't belong. Because of him, Maggie and Kevin had been traumatized, endangered. If he'd trusted her, believed in her, he wouldn't have called his ex-partner in California.

It was his fault that Gerald Stuart had found them.

It would have been his fault if Maggie or Kevin had been hurt, or worse.

He stared at the pair, thankful for their safety, wishing he could explain why he'd done the things he had, but knowing the words would be inadequate.

Once Maggie knew the truth, would she ever be able to forgive him?

Chapter 16

Ronald P. Evans, acting on behalf of the Meridia County District Attorney's Office and representing the state of California, paced the floor of the judge's chambers, making clear his impatience with the speed of the proceedings.

Judge Walter Hornblower, a tall, thin man with a narrow face and beaklike nose, sat behind his desk and peered at him over the rim of his reading glasses. ''Mr. Evans, would you mind sitting down? You're distracting me.''

The attorney blew out an exasperated breath, but did as requested.

Maggie, sitting in a chair opposite Evans, glanced across the room to where Jason stood at the door. His smile was brief, but did not touch his eyes. The exchange did little to reassure her.

In the past three days, since the arrest of her ex-husband, the only contact she'd had with Jason had been of a legal nature. Even then, he'd seemed so formal, so distant. Not that she blamed him. As the chief of police for Wyndchester, he'd been placed in the tenuous position of having to deal with her status as a fugitive.

The DA from Meridia County wanted her immediate return to California, with the full intention of using the outstanding warrant for her arrest in abducting her son as leverage to force her to testify against her ex-husband. In retaliation, Jason charged her ex-husband with a barrage of offenses, ranging from assault on a police officer to the use of a deadly weapon to attempted murder, and refused to release him into the state of California's custody. The two men were now locked in a jurisdictional standoff.

Judge Hornblower cleared his throat and lowered the sheaf of papers to his desktop. "Seems to me that you boys in California are asking for the moon, but you're not willing to budge an inch in return. You want Mrs. Stuart to agree to be your witness. And yet you refuse to drop the charges against her."

"Your Honor, Mrs. Stuart knowingly and willfully broke the law. It is within our rights to carry out the warrant for her arrest. After all, she did violate a court order by taking her son out of state."

Judge Hornblower carefully removed his glasses. "You and I both know she was only protecting her son. No one in your neck of the woods would listen to her pleas for help until it was too late. She had no choice but to take matters into her own hands. I have no doubt that, once the circumstances are reviewed, all charges against Mrs. Stuart will eventually be dropped. You're just buying yourself some time, Mr. Evans."

The DA shrugged. "That's for a judge in California to decide."

"And it's for *me* to decide whether or not to turn Gerald Stuart over to you," Judge Hornblower said, casting a shrewd glance at the attorney. "Seems to me the state of

Missouri has a solid case against Mr. Stuart, unlike our brothers in California. Has your office considered what it might do when it loses its bargaining tool against Mrs. Stuart? Once the charges against her are dropped, there will be nothing to keep her in your fine state. You will lose your witness."

Evans seemed to shrink beneath the weight of the judge's gaze. In lieu of an answer, he fidgeted with his tie, his face flushing a rosy hue.

Releasing a disgusted breath, Judge Hornblower turned his attention to Maggie. His expression and voice softening, he said, "Mrs. Stuart, has anyone bothered to ask you if you want to testify against your ex-husband?"

"No, Your Honor," she said quietly.

"Well, I'm asking you now. How do you feel about standing up against your ex-husband in court?"

Maggie glanced at Jason and saw his encouraging nod. Swallowing hard over the lump of emotion in her throat, she said, "Your Honor, I'd be lying if I said I wasn't afraid." She took a deep breath. "But I'm tired of being scared. I'm tired of running away. I want to testify. I need to testify. Gerald has to pay for all the things he's done to me—and to the others."

Judge Hornblower studied her for a moment, then nodded, seeming satisfied with her answer. "Well, then, Mr. Evans, what do you have to say to that? Seems to me you already have a willing witness. There's no need to bully her into complying."

Evans sighed. "Yes, Your Honor."

"Let's not waste any more of our time. Drop the charges against Mrs. Stuart right now, and I'll be more than happy to release Gerald Stuart into your custody."

"Yes, sir," Evans said, his tone brisk, businesslike. He

cut a glance directly at Maggie. "We'll sit down and work out the details of Mrs. Stuart's testimony with her later."

"Good, then this hearing is over." Judge Hornblower stood. The others followed suit, scrambling to their feet. With brisk strides, he rounded the desk, stopping in front of Maggie. Taking her hand firmly in his, he said, "Mrs. Stuart, I want to wish you luck. This hasn't been an easy time for you. I hope things will be different from now on."

"Thank you," she said, feeling the tension ease from her muscles.

He released her hand and returned to his desk, barking out orders in his wake.

Maggie took this as a dismissal. As she walked numbly out of the judge's chambers, she couldn't believe it was finally over. Granted, she'd have to return to California to testify against Gerald. A task that no doubt would be difficult. But for the first time in almost two years, she could wake up in the morning without the pressure of constantly looking over her shoulder, of being on guard. Of waiting for someone to guess her secret. Of fearing that Kevin would be taken away from her.

And she owed it all to Jason.

Anxiously Maggie glanced around the halls of the courthouse, searching for him. But he wasn't there.

Not allowing her disappointment to show, she headed for the exit. Her step felt unnaturally light, as though she was floating. Her heart soared with the heady power of freedom; she was drunk on the realization that she could go anywhere, live anywhere and never have to hide again.

Her step faltered. She didn't *want* to go anywhere else. She wanted to stay in Wyndchester. She and Kevin were comfortable here. It was their home. She didn't want to leave, not now, not ever.

That is, if the people of Wyndchester approved. The

thought stopped her. She didn't know how they would react to having a former fugitive living in their midst.

Maggie sighed. She didn't know if Jason would want her to stay, either. She'd caused nothing but trouble for him since the day they'd met. She wouldn't blame him if he wanted her out of his life.

Her spirits drooping, Maggie stepped out of the courthouse, squinting against the brilliant sunlight. When her eyes adjusted, she blinked, once...twice, unable to believe what she was seeing.

On the steps of the courthouse, there stood a gathering of familiar faces. Jenny, whose wedding never did take place, with Stan Wilson at her side, sporting a black eye and a proud grin. Dot and Mel from the diner. The gray-haired regulars, the group of diehard customers who'd subjected her to countless hours of good-natured teasing. Maggie's breath caught when she spotted Bob Williams, her favorite customer, back on his feet after his recent heart attack. And there were others. Kevin, who had been with Jenny earlier, was now grinning from ear to ear, standing with his friends, his baseball team and his classmates. They were all there, waiting for her, smiling.

Maggie stopped, too stunned to move. An unnatural stillness filled the town square. All that could be heard was the chattering of a nearby squirrel and the pounding of her heart. The weight of all those gazes pressed down upon her, making it hard to breathe. She didn't know what to say, how to react.

"Congratulations, Maggie," Bob Williams called out, breaking the ice. "Welcome home."

Laughter followed his proclamation, quickly accompanied by a round of applause, with a few whoops of delight sprinkled in for good measure.

Tears of joy stung her eyes. Slowly Maggie made her

way down the steps. Fielding the handshakes and hugs from well-wishers, she felt overwhelmed by so much goodwill.

For the first time in her life, she truly felt she was part of a group, a community. Not just an onlooker, peering in from the outside. She'd never felt happier, more accepted, more at home.

Smiling widely, Kevin threw himself into her arms, hugging her tightly. Her life was almost perfect. Only one thing could make the moment complete.

Searching the crowd, she spotted Jason, watching from afar. Releasing Kevin, she strode across the courtyard, not stopping until she came face-to-face with Jason. For a long moment, she simply stared into his eyes. Then, before she lost her courage, she reached out and wrapped her arms around his neck.

Hesitantly Jason settled his hands on her waist and pulled her close. His chest rose and fell with his sigh of relief. Whispering in her ear, he said, "I thought you'd never forgive me."

She lifted her head to look at him, frowning. "Forgive you?"

He nodded. "If it wasn't for me checking into your background, your ex-husband would never have found you. None of this would have happened."

"If it wasn't for you, I'd still be on the run," she said, drawing in a shaky breath. "You've given me back my life. For that I'll always be grateful."

His growl of frustration vibrated in her ears. "I don't want your gratitude. I want your love."

"You already have it," Maggie whispered, brushing her lips against his.

Impatiently he took her mouth in a hungry kiss, ignoring the catcalls from the crowd around them.

Maggie melted into his embrace. Nothing else mattered—not Gerald, not the lost months of hiding, not the pain she'd suffered at not knowing what the future would bring. All that mattered was the here, the now. The feel of Jason's arms around her, holding her close, keeping her safe, knowing that Kevin would always be safe now, too.

Too soon he broke away and gazed into her eyes. "I love you, Maggie. I want you and Kevin to be part of my life forever. Marry me. Promise you won't ever leave me."

She smiled. "Are you sure you want to marry me? I come with an awful lot of baggage."

"It's nothing that we can't handle together," he said, his tone and expression much too somber.

"Then I will...I mean, I promise." She laughed, touching his cheek with her fingers, savoring the contrast of smooth skin against his midday beard. "I will marry you, Jason. And I promise to never leave you."

"Thank God for that," he said, pulling her close again. He sealed the promise with a kiss.

And Maggie knew her world was finally complete.

* * * * *

If you enjoyed what you just read,
then we've got an offer you can't resist!

Take 2 bestselling
love stories FREE!

Plus get a FREE surprise gift!

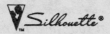

Coming in May 1999

BABY *Fever*

by
New York Times Bestselling Author

KASEY MICHAELS

When three sisters hear their biological
clocks ticking, they know it's
time for action.

But who will they get to father their babies?

**Find out how the road to motherhood
leads to love in this brand-new collection.**

Available at your favorite retail outlet.

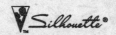

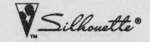

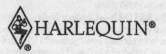

COMING NEXT MONTH

#931 THE LADY'S MAN—Linda Turner
Those Marrying McBrides!
When special agent Zeke McBride was sent to protect wolf biologist
Elizabeth Davis from death threats, his usual flirtatious ways came to a
complete halt. The lady's man was suddenly tongue-tied around the gorgeous
scientist. And when Zeke's duty came to an end, he knew the job might be
over, but a lifetime with Elizabeth was just beginning.

#932 A HERO FOR ALL SEASONS—Marie Ferrarella
ChildFinders, Inc.
Savannah King was desperate when she entered Sam Walters' detective
agency. An expert in finding missing children, Sam was an amateur when it
came to love. He knew Savannah had come to him for help, but suddenly he
found himself wanting more than just to get her daughter back—he wanted
to give her a lifetime of love.

#933 ONCE MORE A FAMILY—Paula Detmer Riggs
Social worker Ria Hardin was dedicated to helping everyone—except
herself. Then she received a call from ex-husband Captain Grady Hardin
and relived the day their son was kidnapped. She was determined to help
Grady solve his most important case—finding their lost little boy—and
reunite the family she missed…and recover the love she'd *never* forgotten.

#934 RODEO DAD—Carla Cassidy
Mustang, Montana
Marissa Sawyer and Johnny Crockett had spent one passionate month
together—before he was arrested for a crime he claimed he hadn't committed.
But now Johnny was free, and Marissa knew she had to help him clear his
name, uncover the truth about *their* nine-year-old son—*and* admit that they
belonged together.

#935 HIS TENDER TOUCH—Sharon Mignerey
As soon as Audrey Sussman got to the Puma's Lair Ranch, she had the
feeling she wasn't exactly welcome—except to ex-cop Grayson Murdoch.
While they tried hard to deny their attraction, both were caught up in a long-
buried mystery that threatened to destroy any chances at survival—and the
future they were desperate to share.

#936 FOR HIS EYES ONLY—Candace Irvin
Duty demanded that undercover agent Reese Garrick keep the truth of
his identity hidden from his sexy new "partner," U.S. Navy lieutenant
Jade Parker. But how long could the lone lawman conceal the dangerous
truth of his mission—and his secret, burning desire to make Jade his
partner…for life?